The Reluctant Detective Under Pressure

A Martin Hayden Mystery

by
Adrian Spalding

Contents

CHAPTER ONE	1
CHAPTER TWO	12
CHAPTER THREE	37
CHAPTER FOUR	56
CHAPTER FIVE	77
CHAPTER SIX	89
CHAPTER SEVEN	104
CHAPTER EIGHT	121
CHAPTER NINE	134
CHAPTER TEN	154
CHAPTER ELEVEN	179
CHAPTER TWELVE	190
CHAPTER THIRTEEN	203
CHAPTER FOURTEEN	213
CHAPTER FIFTEEN	221
CHAPTER SIXTEEN	237
CHAPTER SEVENTEEN	247
CHAPTER EIGHTEEN	268

CHAPTER ONE

"Martin should be here soon," Susan told a nervous-looking Ernie as she handed him a mug of what she would have described as hot milk. Ernie had insisted that he always took his tea with copious amounts of milk, and Susan needed to add four large splashes before he finally smiled in approval at the colour.

"He's been away for a weekend in the south of France. A place called Bore Doe, I think he said, never heard of it, meant to be a posh place. Some school friend of his was having his stag do at his vineyard. Can you believe it, Ernie? I bet they got really sozzled having a whole vineyard to get through."

Ernie simply nodded, then sipped his tea. Susan wondered why he looked so anxious; after all, they did know each other reasonably well.

A couple of weeks ago, as Susan and her boss, Martin, were preparing to move office, Ernie had asked if they could do him a favour. Martin had agreed immediately. As Ernie had told them it was not urgent, they decided that Ernie could pop round on his day off when they were settled into their new premises.

Ernie was still the caretaker, security guard, receptionist, and general handyman at the previous Victorian office building where Martin and Susan had worked. Hayden Investigations was now located in a modern glass-sided building close to Tower Bridge. It was a very compact office, allowing just enough room for Martin and Susan to work at their small desks. It did have the advantage of an

1

uninterrupted view of Tower Bridge, which compensated for the lack of office space. The real benefit of their new office was that it was rent-free. Such an arrangement enabled Martin to carry on with his investigation agency and not worry about having any clients. In fact, his objective was to have no clients whatsoever.

"Hmmm, tea's good," Ernie approved, "and it's good of you to help me. Nice view, better than the old office."

"Smaller though," Susan pointed out, "in fact, I'd say it was plain poky."

Ernie laughed nervously. "I won't say it's that bad. At least you have a lovely view of Tower Bridge and a bit of the tower. I look out over a busy road from my little flat in Peckham. It can be interesting sometimes, but always there's traffic noise that never seems to go away.

"Do you live alone?" Susan asked for the first time, although she had often wondered. Ernie had never mentioned a wife in their previous conversations.

"Yes, just me and the cat, her name is Money. She keeps me company and from what I have seen with my brothers, is a lot less trouble than a wife. Although I have to wait on her hand and foot, all I get in return is a warm lap while she sits with me watching TV. But I wouldn't do without her for the world."

"I bet you are a Coronation Street fan?" Somehow Susan imagined Ernie to be a bit of an old woman at home, happy to sit down with a mug of tea and watch the stories of the street. She was wrong.

"I'm not really a live TV type of person. I like the news. It's always best to keep up with what is going on around us.

I like comedy films, absolute fan of the Carry On films; I love everyone in them and have seen all of them many times, I can tell you. I think Sid James was such a funny man; he always makes me laugh, no matter how many times I watch his Carry On films. Never met him though, but I did meet his daughter once, Reina James. I bought a book of hers at one of those signing events. Told her how much I loved her dad. She did smile politely, but I imagine everyone says the same thing. 'The Old Joke' it was called. Never did get round to reading it; not my type of book, you understand. I think I just wanted to shake hands with one of Sid's relatives. You can have the book if you like; I'll never read it, I'm sure."

"Never say never, Ernie; best you keep it for now."

"If you change your mind, Susan, just ask. You do make a nice cup of tea."

Martin walked through the door. He looked at Ernie with surprise and said, "You're here already? Am I late?"

"No," Susan pointed out, "Ernie was an hour early. The buses were better than expected, weren't they, Ernie?"

Ernie nodded and now looked guilty, which was not the way Susan meant him to feel.

"Not to worry," Martin said as he slipped his coat off. He sat on the side of Susan's desk, as Susan and Ernie already occupied both chairs. "Right, Ernie, the last time we met, you wanted a favour, so fire away."

Susan could see that Ernie looked uncomfortable with being the centre of attention. His eyes dropped to the desk where he had placed his empty tea mug.

"It's my brother; I think he's being taken for a ride. Sorry, not a ride like on a bus, but I think some people are taking money from him. Not stealing or robbing; well, I suppose they are. What I mean is they are not mugging him but taking his money…"

"Ernie," Susan stopped him, hoping to help him focus his thoughts. "Start at the beginning, tell us a bit about your brother and then how you think the people are taking his money. Let's start with his name and what he does."

"My brother's called Terry. I'm his older brother, that's why I feel responsible for him. He's a researcher looking for alien life, you know, life on other planets and stuff like that. I was never good at school; Terry was the brainy one. They haven't found life on other planets yet; I don't think so anyway."

As Susan listened to Ernie describe his younger brother, she could see that Ernie was not the sharpest knife in the drawer. She had always liked chatting to him as he sat at the reception desk in the old office. He would always smile and even wished her luck when she arrived for her job interview with Martin. Ernie worked hard and was keen to help all the different offices in the tall building. She looked across at Martin, who was frowning. She imagined he was getting a little confused as Ernie talked of aliens, research, the small team that Terry worked with and the couple he suspected of taking advantage of, who Ernie described as his 'generous brother'.

"I think the couple who help him are up to something. I am sure they are getting Terry to pay for things he should not have to pay for," Ernie concluded.

"Why do you think they are up to something?" Martin asked. "You mentioned stealing earlier." Susan was surprised that Martin seemed to be keeping track of what, at times, were nervous ramblings from Ernie.

"Well, the detectives, they must have asked me for a reason," Ernie explained poorly.

"Wait!" Susan asked, "What detectives?"

"I don't think they are real police detectives, maybe private detectives, like yourselves. They knocked on my door and asked me a lot of questions about Terry."

"What sort of questions?" Susan asked, trying to delve into this revelation.

Ernie swapped his gaze between Susan and Martin, almost as if he was unsure who to talk to directly. In the end, he settled on Martin.

"They asked if Terry had ever given me anything to look after. I told them that I had once stored his CD collection when he got divorced, but I had given it back ages ago. Then there was the time I took a lot of his old shoes off him; he wanted me to take them to the charity shop." Ernie paused and looked thoughtful. "Then they asked if I knew the people Terry worked with. I told them I knew Ashley, as he and my brother had known each other for years, but I didn't know the couple he worked with. They kept asking me if I knew stuff about what he was doing at his work. I told them it's far too complicated for me to understand, although I do know there might be life on other planets."

"Did they actually say the couple were stealing from him?" Martin asked.

"Not in so many words, but I think that detectives normally go after criminals. I know Terry is a generous person, so I guess they might be taking his money somehow.

Could you have a word with him, ask him, maybe warn him about the couple."

"Why can't you ask him?"

"There was a family falling out a few years ago. We don't talk much, just the very occasional short telephone call. I send him Christmas and birthday cards, but he only sends me a birthday card. He wouldn't listen to me, but he might listen to you. It would really put my mind at rest. I'm happy to pay you, Mr Hayden; I have some savings put by. I might not speak much to Terry, but he is my younger brother. Now our parents are dead, I feel I should still try and look after him."

There was a short pause. Susan looked at Martin, who stood up and stretched his legs; the edge of the desk was not a comfortable place to sit.

"Give us his address; we will pop round and have a few words with him, see what he says. It is a favour, Ernie, so hang onto your savings. We'll let you know how we get on."

***

Once Ernie had left, Martin turned to Susan and handed her the address that Ernie had written on a scrap of paper. "Let's have a coffee first and then we can pop round and see Ernie's brother, get it all done and dusted. I imagine if there are detectives already poking around, as Ernie said, then we had better keep it all at arm's length and let them sort out any problems. No point getting embroiled in investigations, not the sort of thing I want to do."

After looking at the address, Susan commented, "Terry is not that far away from here, only at Greenwich. He must be part of the Greenwich University." She then asked, "How was the stag weekend, lots of posh blokes flat on their backs drunk?"

"Actually, it was a rather civilised affair. There were ten of us, most of whom I knew from my younger days, only three old boys from the school. Richard has this beautiful vineyard and it produces something like a hundred thousand bottles of wine every year. We spent the main stag night in a wine cellar working through wines over the last ten vintages, which is how long he has owned the place. I would say, compared to some of your past hen nights that you have told me about, we were all very refined. There was not a stripper in sight, male or female."

"And how was the flight? Not too bumpy, I hope; I know you hate that rough stuff."

Martin did not want to mention too much. The flight there was uneventful, but that was more than could be said for the return trip. Going through security at Bordeaux did not go exactly as he had planned and he wondered if he should say anything about it all to Susan.

For a start, he had felt awkward undressing in public. It was not so much he was shy or ashamed of his body; it was just standing there in an orderly queue waiting to get on a plane did not seem to be a good place to remove his clothes. Shoes, jacket, belt, wallet, watch, the contents of all his pockets, a mobile phone and a Kindle were all heaped into a grey, plastic tray, which was then dispatched on its journey through a metal contraption to be x-rayed.

Partially undressed, Martin stood in a short queue of similarly partly clothed individuals. All were waiting to go through what he described as the 'Doorway of Justice', all praying their beltless trousers would hold up. If the light remains green, you have passed the test and once fully dressed, you can be on your way. But if the light goes red, then you are delivered into the eager hands of waiting security guards.

To Martin, flying was not a pleasure because of the long, drawn-out process of getting on the plane. At each stage he avoided any form of eye contact with officials as well as holding back on any one-liner that could have seen him swiftly taken to one side and interrogated.

In his stockinged feet, Martin moved as instructed through the 'Doorway of Justice'. To his relief, the light stayed green. As he looked around for his grey tray of belongings, he noticed two female security staff looking at him with a frown. They had spotted something about him and did not seem happy. They gazed intently at his trousers. Martin was sure they were still in place, even without the aid of his leather belt, which was at that point still undergoing an x-ray procedure. The tall, blonde officer stepped forward, not taking her eyes off his trousers.

"Excuse me, monsieur, what is that lump in your jeans?" Her voice was warm and French as she pointed towards Martin's lower regions.

Martin now faced a dilemma of a magnitude he had not encountered in a while. His natural and favoured reaction was to smile then answer, 'It's my special friend who is pleased to see you and would welcome the opportunity to get to know you better'. Fortunately, he realised before he uttered those words that such a response would not benefit him in the least; in fact, there was a good chance that if he gave that reply, he would, at the very least, miss his flight.

The fundamental predicament lay in finding the right thing to say that would not spark a security alert, given that the lump in his trousers was an integral part of him and had every right to fly along with the rest of his body. To admit, rightly, that it was his penis would seem to be a bizarre thing to say out loud in such a crowded place. If he were allowed within whispering distance of one of the not unattractive female security officers and whispered in her ear, 'my penis,' then he had no way of gauging her reaction. Martin stood dumbstruck and mute as if he had just been teleported to a distant planet deep in the solar system. His silence turned out to be the best course of action. The security officer to his left stepped towards him and pointed towards the mysterious lump. Martin looked down, following the line of her finger and realised her focus was on his right-hand pocket.

He pulled a small packet from his pocket. "Tissues!" he said with an unusual degree of relief in his voice.

"Next time, everything goes into the tray," she pointed out with a smile on her face.

Martin beamed back; he felt like a naughty schoolboy who the teacher had reprimanded. He collected his belongings from the recently x-rayed grey tray, wanting to get dressed and onto the plane back to London as soon as possible.

"The flight was okay; you know how it is, lots of hanging around and numerous security checks, on the whole boring." He decided that was all he was going to tell Susan about the flight.

"Talking of bored, did you get to see much of Bore Doe?"

"Not really, I flew into Bordeaux, but Richard's place is about an hour's drive away. Bordeaux is just another big, boring, bustling town."

"All driving, like all the French do, on the wrong side of the road!" Susan quipped.

"Did you say, Bore Doe?" Martin emphasised the pause in the middle of the name of the town.

"Yes, that's where you said you went, Bore Doe."

"No, it is Bordeaux," Martin added a hint of a French accent to help Susan comprehend.

Susan looked at him; her face had a thoughtful, puzzled expression as she asked, "What, like the wine?"

"Exactly like the wine."

"Why would they call a town after a wine?"

"No, Susan, the town came first and the wine came second."

"That's a bit mad calling a wine after the place where it is made. It's not as if there is a place called Merlot, Shiraz, Chardonnay or Champagne. Beers might get names that way, London Pride and the like, but not wines?"

"This might come as a bit of a shock to you, Susan. Champagne is a region in France and the other three are the grapes from which the wine is made. Most wines are named after the town or region they come from; it saves fortunes on hiring expensive marketing executives to come up with some catchy name."

"Well, that might be the case for the people who make the stuff, but for me, it's the alcoholic content that counts." Susan laughed as she handed Martin a coffee.

CHAPTER TWO

"Surely this must be the place," Susan commented as Martin parked his car alongside a row of well-kept terraced houses. He also wasn't convinced it was the right place; he leaned over and looked at the address once more. Martin had expected to arrive at a university car park at best, at worst, a nondescript portacabin that housed a secretive research unit. He looked around at the residential doors and wondered if Ernie might have made a mistake. Susan sounded equally doubtful as she said, "Now we're here; we might as well knock on the door anyway."

A tall, slender man in his forties answered, giving them a distrustful look. He took off his rimless glasses, looked them up and down with a disapproving look, holding the door half-open or half-closed depending on your viewpoint.

"Terry Gray?" Martin asked.

"Who wants to know?" came the curt reply.

Susan took up the conversation, "Your brother Ernie asked if we could pop in and have a word with you. He is worried about a few things and we're his friends, so why would we refuse him?"

Terry hesitated for a moment before he asked, "Ernie asked, you say?"

Martin and Susan nodded. Both wondered just how long Terry had owned the faded 'space invaders' t-shirt he was wearing, as well as how long they would be standing at the door.

Terry looked directly at Martin and spoke with a harsh voice, "Do you have a wristwatch?"

Martin was not sure he had heard the question correctly, but even so, as he replied, he pulled back his sleeve to reveal his watch. "Yes, do you want to know the time?"

"Rolex, that's okay. What about you, miss?" He turned his gaze towards Susan.

"Never bother wearing one; it only tells me I'm late, so a total waste of money."

Terry hesitated once more as if he weighed up some kind of risk before he opened the door wider and invited them in. As they followed him, they heard, "Bloody Ernie, always playing the concerned big brother. Always been a pain," he muttered.

There was no hallway; they stepped straight into a square room crammed full of computers, electronics and colourful wires that wove their way around the room. The walls were filled with pictures, charts and posters, of what Martin could only describe as flying saucers. There were a few newspaper cuttings pinned on cork boards, once again relating to UFOs. There was also a plump man hunched over a computer monitor.

"Ashley," Terry spoke to the plump man who turned around to look at the visitors, revealing an unusually high forehead. "These are friends of Ernie's, here to help me," Terry now sounded sarcastic.

The small room was doubtlessly claustrophobic even for just two of them working in it, Martin thought, but now with Susan and himself, there was barely room to swing a cat without getting caught in the maze of wires.

Ashley stayed seated looking at the visitors while Terry regained, presumably what was, his usual chair, leaving

Martin and Susan standing as there were no other seats to offer them.

"So, how are you going to save me? Please make it quick; I have a schedule to keep."

"Just to be clear, you are Terry?" Martin sought confirmation.

"Posh bloke wants introductions. Yes, I'm Terry Gray, Ernie's brother. This is Ashley DeVooght, my friend and associate."

Martin introduced both himself and Susan before he asked, "Your research, is it part of the university here in Greenwich?"

"Christ, no! If we were, then the truth would never get out. Only in being independent can we uncover the truth. But you're not here to talk about my research, are you? Unless Ernie did not send you."

"Let me explain why we are here." Susan repeated everything Ernie had told them and his concern that a couple Terry was working with were somehow conning him out of money.

Martin could see both Terry and Ashley begin to relax as they listened to Susan. The initial hostility he had felt seemed to be fading. It was getting hot with all the electrical equipment, monitors, gauges and computers, plus four adults in the room. The only window, which had a heavy curtain drawn across it, seemed to be closed as he could feel no refreshing air coming from it. There was to his right, an open door that appeared to lead into a kitchen. He guessed that as he could not feel any air coming from that direction, the rear of the house must be equally shut up.

"Let me tell you something about my sweet brother, young lady; he worries about anything and everything. He worries about putting the rubbish out at the right time; he worries that his cat has indigestion. He worries what the lady at the supermarket checkout thinks of him when he buys seven single person ready meals. Ernie worries. When he's not worrying, he frets about not being worried.

"I suspect the investigator who called on Ernie was a debt collector looking for my other brother James, who is not well suited to holding onto either money or jobs. The couple you refer to, both Ashley and I, have known for a little over three years, and we trust them fully. Janice and Luke contribute a great deal to this project. Tell my brother when you see him that I am simply fine and dandy."

"Let me be clear on this." Martin wanted no misunderstandings, he might be doing a favour for Ernie, but he had no plans to get between non-communicating brothers. "You seem to be a shrewd man, not easily fooled, and as far as you are concerned, this couple, Luke and Janice, are trustworthy and just a part of the research you are doing."

"Precisely. As I said, Ernie is not the most, how shall I put this, able of the three brothers."

"What exactly is this project?" Martin asked, shifting from foot to foot to stop himself from fainting in the increasing heat. "Ernie said it was research to find life on other planets."

"Oh, we've already found alien life," Ashley answered proudly before continuing, "we are now keeping track of what they are doing."

Terry took over, "Before you ask, they are here on Earth, alongside us, planning and plotting."

Martin liked to think he had always reacted well to some of the more abstract conversations he had encountered during the many dinner parties he had attended over the years. Alien life on Earth was a new one for him, and as such, he was not too sure how he should react. He decided to try and sound cool with it, he failed.

"You are telling me that walking amongst us are aliens, creatures from another planet?"

"Why the surprise? Every sane scientist will say that life on other planets in other solar systems is inevitable. Yet at the first mention of UFOs and aliens visiting our planet, those same sane scientists say, 'that's poppycock'. A bit contradictory, I'd say."

"Let me get this right," Martin started, wanting to make sure he was not missing some vital point, "you are saying that aliens are here on earth, but they are just hanging around, keeping a low profile."

"I think you had better explain, Terry. I see by his watch, he is okay," Ashley pointed out.

"My watch?" Martin asked, sounding incredulous.

"Clearly, aliens are not bothered about posh watches," Susan joked, not thinking for a moment that she was making a valid point.

"Exactly, young lady, you clearly understand." Terry then began to explain, first flicking a switch on a fan close to him to move some cooler air around the room, much to Martin's relief.

"Everyone, nowadays, is rushing off to buy fitness tracking watches, which tell you all about your heart rate, how many calories you are burning, even how far you walk in a day and your sleep pattern. Aliens have hijacked these watches to carry out a global experiment, helping them better understand humans' health and ability and what purpose we could be used for on other planets. In time they want to treat us all as slaves. It's just a case of working out the most efficient way of utilising us all.

"The watches in effect observe us all, well those of us who have them, in the same way, you might link a rat up to monitors during a laboratory experiment. It's that simple. We are trying to track down who is behind this hideous experiment. Once we have sufficient evidence, we can inform the authorities, or at least those authorities that have not come under the influence of the aliens."

"Where does my watch come in?" Martin asked.

"Simple," Ashley responded, "a traditional clockwork movement watch made in Switzerland that the aliens cannot influence due to the mountainous region around the country. If Nepal made watches, they too would be safe. Anywhere else, there is the prospect that they could be adapted to provide valuable data to aliens. There are very few traditional clockwork watches made nowadays."

Martin began to question whether he might have fainted in the heat of the room and was having some weird dream, which would make a lot more sense than the conspiracy theory he was now hearing. Susan's response did little to quell his concerns.

"I always knew UFOs were real, but to think we are part of some massive experiment, that's mind-blowing."

"UFOs are real?" Martin questioned.

"Yes. Think about it, Martin; there is so much we do not know about, influences from across the universe. You get your stars each day; they are celestial. Plus, since the dawn of time, people have reported strange flying objects; some have crash-landed, like at Roswell in the USA."

"And don't forget the UK's Rendlesham Forest," Terry added.

"Exactly, to say there's no such thing as aliens is like denying there's oxygen in the air. But to think they are around us here, that's something else."

Martin held his hand up to stop the avalanche of wild theories coming out of Susan's mouth.

"Okay, let's beg to differ on aliens for now. We're here to ask Terry about the couple and Ernie's concerns and I think we have established that Terry has no worries. Therefore, can I suggest, having done what we set out to do, that we leave these kind gentlemen to their work and get back to our office?"

The drive back to Tower Bridge comprised of Susan telling Martin non-stop that aliens exist and that UFOs are seen regularly. She also pointed out that he should be more open to theories that went beyond the traditional realms of science. Martin remained unconvinced; it was bad enough having his daily stars read to him during their morning coffee.

"Do you think we should at least speak to the couple before we report back to Ernie?" Susan asked as Martin drove past Southwark Park.

"What good would it do, Susan? If they are fiddling him, which I doubt, then they are not going to admit it to us. I might not understand Terry's obsession with aliens, but I can see that Ernie might have read more into the situation than there was. If Terry is happy, then I am happy to tell Ernie nothing is wrong."

"I am still not convinced. Terry is one of those people who are so focused on what they are doing; they have little awareness of what's happening around them."

Martin liked Susan; he liked her a lot. The downside of being near to Susan was she did want to get involved with other people's problems.

His phone interrupted his thoughts. Both he and Susan looked at the car's Bluetooth display; his mother was calling. "Oh dear," Martin commented as he answered her handsfree. But it was not his mother's voice that echoed around the car.

"Martin, it's Geraldine, your mother's neighbour. I have just found your mother collapsed on the kitchen floor." Geraldine sounded breathless and there was an urgency in her voice. Before Martin could respond, she continued with her account. "I called an ambulance and they have taken her to St Mary's hospital."

"What happened? Did she have an accident?"

"No idea, Martin. I popped in to borrow some garlic and found her unconscious on the floor. I couldn't go with her in the ambulance as I was looking after my grandson. I told them I'd call you and let you know. Are you able to go?"

"Yes, Geraldine, I'm going straight there now. Thank you for getting her help. I'll call you later and let you know how she is."

***

A short, plump nurse directed Martin and Susan into a cramped room before explaining that his mother was comfortable and awake and currently being examined by a specialist. Her stock answer to all of Martin's many questions about his mother was: 'the doctor will have a word with you once he has finished the examination.'

At first, they both sat in silence, examining the magnolia painted room. As well as six metal-framed chairs, there was a tired-looking coffee table with dog-eared magazines strewn across it. The walls were covered with frayed posters and yellowed notices giving out health warnings and advice for diseases and illnesses that Martin had never heard of. Then there was the hospital perfume that hung in the air, an odour that sent shivers down Martin's spine, a unique atmosphere that he only associated with illness and death. He recalled the last time he was here in St Mary's hospital, collecting his father's belongings and that memory triggered another recollection.

"I guess this place brings back sad memories for you." Martin looked at the unusually quiet Susan, who was looking around the room at the posters.

"Yes, my mum was here, up in the intensive care unit, the last place I saw her breathing. But it's the same for you; your father died here after his heart attack."

"Sad memories indeed," Martin confirmed. Yet he could understand that with the passing of his father, he had had time to grieve naturally, whereas, for Susan, he knew it was the start of an ever-widening chasm within her family.

"Have you ever spoken to your father since your mother died?"

"Since he gave permission to have her life support switched off, you mean. Only several abusive words in the days that followed, but not one since the funeral. I haven't even sent him a birthday card; none of his children have."

"There must come a time when you begin to forgive; he is your father after all."

Susan did not respond at once. Martin could see her mulling over her thoughts and he suspected there was turmoil inside her. He knew that some families have differences of opinions, even arguments, but he could not understand that such a family rift could last forever.

"To be honest, Martin, there are times when I do wonder what my father is doing. Is he well? Has he remarried? Is he happy? Then there are the other times when I hate him with such a passion, I know I would resort to physical violence if I met him. I suppose that's the dilemma for me and my sisters. We see him as the monster who took away the mother we loved, yet he is still our father, who maybe we still…"

A tall man with a wild mop of grey hair on his head burst into the room. He had to duck slightly to miss the door frame. Slung around his neck was a stethoscope and attached to his trouser belt was an identity card which hung down alongside a plastic bottle of hand sanitiser.

"Mr Hayden, Doctor Yaakob, pleased to meet you." The tall doctor, with rolled-up shirtsleeves, thrust his large hand towards Martin and shook his hand firmly. His eyes turned towards Susan. "Mrs Hayden?"

"A close friend," Martin corrected. "How is my mother?"

"Well, thankfully, she was not unconscious for long. She regained consciousness in the ambulance, much to the horror of the medics who, I understand, were told in no uncertain terms that unless they took her home at once, she would press charges of kidnapping. Clearly, your mother has a sense of humour. Fortunately, they pressed on and delivered her into our loving care, and I have just given her a thorough check over. I'm not sure just what the exact problem is yet, but she has a bit of an irregular heartbeat. Consequently, the heart is where I am directing my resources. I plan to hang onto her, if you don't mind, to run some more tests, get a positive diagnosis and then we can deal with what we find." The doctor spoke rapidly, appearing not to need to breath between sentences. "You can pop in and see her now. Don't stay too long; I'd like to give her a little something to ensure she gets a good rest tonight. Then in a couple of days, I am sure you can have her back."

The doctor opened the door and called down the corridor, "Heather, be a dear and show Mr Hayden and his friend where Mrs Hayden is." He turned back to look at Martin and Susan, smiled and gave a brief goodbye before taking giant strides and going on his way.

"Why is she here?"

Even in a hospital bed, with a drip attached to one arm and the other arm wired up to some sort of monitor, Martin's mother's voice had a depth of authority to it. Susan wondered what it might take to knock the old lady out. The question had been intended for her, although she was not in the least worried. Susan knew all about Martin's mother, the way she tried to dominate everyone around her and the way she insisted on things being done her way. Susan clearly understood that she was no more than a little common girl who had no right to be anywhere near her son in his mother's eyes.

"Susan is my employee and my friend. She is here for me, not you."

'That's it; you tell the old girl', Susan thought and grinned to annoy the patient. Doctor Yak-Off, or whatever his name was, would not approve.

"Well, how are you feeling now? Any pain?"

"Martin, whatever the doctors have told you, they do not know me. I believe I had a noticeably short dizzy spell and toppled over. It was that stupid, fussing woman from next door who insisted that I go to the hospital. A total waste of time if you ask me."

"Mother, you were unconscious; you didn't come round until you were in the ambulance."

"How would you know? Were you around? No, you were at work, or what you like to think is work. Just a slight dizziness, and now I remain in the clutches of the National Health Service; heaven knows what will happen to me now.

They say a couple of days, but I trust none of these white-coated do-gooders."

Susan wanted to laugh; if nothing else, Mother was entertainment. Quintessential old English lady, Susan could imagine Martin's mother dictating orders to rows of smartly dressed servants in a large country house, all of them curtsying or bowing as she went past, which was exactly where she belonged, in the past.

"However, if I am going to be in here for two days as they are saying, I will need you to get some things for me. Martin, you will need a pen and paper. Do you perchance have such basic items on you?"

"No, but I can make a note on my phone."

"On your phone? What are you going to do, send a message to your answer machine?"

"No, Mother, it's an app that allows me to take notes. Just tell me what you want."

Martin's mother huffed before she began her instructions, "First, I need nightdresses, three. They are in the large chest of drawers in my bedroom, the middle drawer on the left-hand side. I want the one with the white roses on it, the one with the small check, finally, the lightweight one that is plain pink. Have you got that?"

Martin was busy tapping his phone screen; he nodded when he was ready to continue.

"You need to call Harriet Simms and Florence Welch; I have social appointments with them: Harriet tomorrow morning and Florence the day after. Let them know I am unable to make our rendezvous. Say that I will call them later in the week to rearrange. Don't tell them I'm in a hospital; tell them I am a little poorly and in bed at home."

"Isn't that lying?" Martin asked.

"I do not wish to let them know I am in a National Health Hospital or under the care of any doctor for that matter. You will find their telephone numbers in the flip-up index beside the phone. That is also where you will find the number of Gordon McFarlane, our accountant. He is retiring, and I planned to speak to him about the replacement he is recommending. Again, tell him I will contact him in the next day or so."

"I can talk to him," Martin offered, trying to be helpful.

"Don't be so stupid, Martin; you are good at dissipating money; accumulating is not your strong point; leave that to me."

Susan sat back; she was enjoying this tender moment of mother-son relationship; it was so reassuring to see Martin under the thumb of his mother. It renewed her faith in the dominance of women over men.

"When you come back later –"

Martin looked up, a surprised look on his face. Susan guessed that he was not expecting to visit again later; she knew he planned to go out tonight from an earlier conversation.

Mother ignored the look and continued, "I will need some proper medication. All they have here are synthetic chemicals that do more harm than good and I know exactly what is required to settle this fluttering heart of mine. I want you to bring in the following teas: Lavender, Black Haw and Valerian Root. They are in the medicine cabinet. All are clearly marked, so even you should be able to differentiate between them and get the right ones.

"Plus, I wish to have something to read in here to avoid any type of conversation with the other persons that are in this ward. You'll find the books I want in the bottom drawer of my left-hand bedside table."

Martin looked at her, then asked a sensible question, he thought, knowing she had a bedside cabinet on each side of her bed.

"Which left are we talking about? Left if you are standing at the end of the bed, or left laying down in the bed?"

"Oh, for goodness sake, Martin, didn't they teach you anything at school? Left-hand side when you are laying on the bed, which is the only way you determine the left and right side of any bed."

For the first time, she turned and looked at Susan and then asked, "Why are men so exasperating?" Susan felt for a moment a sincere sense of bonding with Martin's mother – it was short-lived. "How would you know? I guess you're not too fussy about the men you acquaint. Now Martin, here are the titles I want: The Alice Network by Kate Quinn and Casting Off by Elizabeth Jane Howard. Then on the top of my bedside cabinet you will find the book I am currently reading: Sleeping Malice. Have you got that?"

Martin nodded without looking up from his phone.

"When you get back, you will also need to clean up the kitchen. As I recall, I had a plate with angel cake in my hand when I came over dizzy, and I guess it will still be on the floor."

Next, Martin's mother pulled the rings from her fingers, wrapped them in a tissue and offered them to Martin. "Take these and put them in the top drawer of my right-hand bedside cabinet. You know the one, right-hand side if you are laying down. I want no valuables on me in this place; you can't trust anyone these days, and I am sure they do not vet patients before they come in."

"Maybe they should do what they do in America," Susan suggested, "do a credit check before admitting anyone into hospital." All she got in response was a stony face stare from Mother plus a stifled laugh from Martin.

"You need to be off now and get back to the house. I doubt that Geraldine has enough common sense in that wrinkled head of hers to have locked the door. I'll see you later with the essentials I have asked for."

***

Martin inched his car through the heavy rush hour traffic, making his way towards Susan's flat. He had assured her that he did not need to rush back to check his mother's front door, as he was confident that Geraldine was a lot more responsible than Mother gave her credit to be. He intended to do what he had planned, and that was to drop Susan off to show her a small sign of his gratitude for having gone to the hospital with him.

Susan watched Martin tapping the steering wheel impatiently as he waited for the traffic lights to change. "I do have one question?" Her voice was tentative.

"Only one, Susan, you are slipping. What's your question?"

"Does your mother only do things in threes? She wanted three nightgowns, three teas, three books and even for you to arrange three appointments. Tell me that was just some weird coincidence and not an obsession."

"I would call it a weird obsession. Yes, you're right; Mother only does things in groups of three. Shopping is a nightmare. If she wants a simple tin of baked beans, she will end up buying three different brands. It's just her thing."

"Has she always been like that?"

Martin continued talking as he finally pulled away from the lights before just managing to get to the other side of the junction and stopping to join yet another queue for the next set of traffic lights.

"You want an explanation, but I can only offer you what my father told me, for the simple reason if you ever mention it to Mother, she will vehemently deny her 'three addiction'. Father told me that when she was a young girl, she became obsessed with the story of Goldilocks and the Three Bears: Daddy bear, Mummy bear and Baby bear. But I don't need to tell you that, I'm sure you have heard the story. Anyway, somewhere in her young mind, she decided that if you bought three things, one of them must be 'just right'. Hence, she would go into a dress shop and come out with three outfits. Happily, she only married once and only had the one perfect son! Pretty much everything else is in threes."

"That's weird."

"Careful, it is contagious; have you never had a three-course meal?" he laughed.

"Don't be so bloody daft, Martin."

There was something else that had been bothering Susan ever since they had arrived at the hospital. She peered into the door mirror and looked at the car behind them. She had first noticed it as they walked towards Terry's house, a grey BMW with a man inside looking as if he had fallen asleep. It was not so much the car, or the man that she had noticed; it was the letters of the registration plate: SDA. Susan had a habit of making up phrases out of the letters. SDA, she had translated to 'Susan drinks alcohol', which summed up one of her habits, or more likely a hobby, she thought at times.

When they parked at the hospital, she thought she saw it again. She tried to commit to memory the remainder of the BMW's number plate. To the first part, NT, she applied the words, 'National Theatre'. She had no idea why she did that as she had never been to the National Theatre in her life. The numerical part, 19, was easy; that was how old she was when she lost her virginity.

Now, as she sat beside Martin, who was still crawling his way through the slow-moving traffic, she could see in the rear-view mirror a grey BMW with a man driving and the registration NT19SDA behind them.

"Martin, we're being followed," she concluded.

***

It was not until Martin arrived home that he believed what Susan had told him. At first, he had thought that as he was in a traffic jam, it was highly likely that a car would follow him through the traffic. He was also fully aware that

Susan was not the most observant person in the world. Yet, once he had dropped her off and the traffic lightened, he kept a watchful eye on his rear-view mirror. The grey BMW was always there. Sometimes it was right behind him, sometimes a few cars back. Susan was right; he was being followed. If the vehicle had been parked outside Terry's house, then it was in some way connected to him.

As Martin opened his locked front door – Geraldine had locked it – he noticed the grey BMW drive past slowly, no doubt observing where he lived before it drove off and out of sight. Ernie had mentioned a detective; maybe the driver of the BMW was the detective. It was a question that Martin put to one side as he had more important issues to contend with, Mother's instructions.

Sitting in the kitchen, he ticked off his mother's list of the essential items she required for a short stay in hospital. The books, the teas, the nightdresses, and he had already made the telephone calls. All boxes ticked; items packed neatly in a Waitrose bag. He looked at his watch; time to make a move back to the hospital.

He could not recall his mother ever being in a hospital before. Apart from having the odd flu bug, Martin always looked upon his mother as very fit for her age. Being alone in the house felt strange to him. She had not even gone away for a holiday since his father had died. Was that her way of mourning him without shedding any tears or seeking sympathy? Martin could not be sure. All he knew was that his mother was fallible, getting older, and there would come a moment in the future when he would be left alone in this house. Maybe this was a wake-up call for him, time to start thinking about his future. He realised he would want to share the rest of his life with someone and not live alone.

His mobile phone rang as he was about to lock the front door behind him and drive to the hospital. He pulled it from his pocket, expecting to hear his mother's voice with an additional request; instead, it was Terry.

"Martin, look, I wasn't completely honest with you earlier. I could use the help of a private detective as I do have a small problem I need help with."

"Okay," Martin replied as he got into his car. "Pop into my office in the morning, and we'll see if I can help. The address is..."

"You'll need to come to me again. Going out is difficult for me."

***

"Is that all he said?"

"Yes, Susan, apart from saying he could not talk about it on the telephone as others could listen in."

"I bet he means the aliens are listening to his conversation. Wow! Martin, this sounds so exciting."

Martin was unconvinced it was either aliens or exciting. All he knew for sure was that he was going to spend more time in a claustrophobic room with an immense amount of computer equipment and two weird men.

It was on the last point that Martin was wrong; today, it was just Terry in the room, which felt fresher as the heat was nowhere near as overwhelming. There were now a couple of foldable chairs that enabled all three of them to sit, albeit a little too close, but at least if he did faint, Martin thought he would not fall far.

Today, Terry appeared far more relaxed and happier to have them in the room; in fact, he seemed almost relieved they were there. Perhaps the couple were playing out some sort of fraud, Martin thought, and Terry did not want to admit it in front of his friend, Ashley. Martin's assumption was wrong; he seemed to be wrong quite often lately.

"Thank you both for coming today. I hoped I had not put you off yesterday, but you must understand that there are certain elements who would rather we were not undertaking the research that we are doing."

"The aliens?" Susan proposed. Terry nodded and continued.

"As you already know from our conversation yesterday, I believe that a race of beings from well beyond our galaxy is conducting a worldwide experiment on humans through the technology of smart wristwatches. All four of us here recognise that our research runs the risk of engaging the wrath of those beings as we try to prove and then make public their intentions.

"However, I believe the risk to us is now greater than I had first imagined and wanted to tell you privately of my fears. Within these walls, we have gathered and stored an enormous amount of evidence. Evidence that has enabled us to identify at least one alien who is masquerading as a human. That alien is here arranging for extra-terrestrial spacecraft to land and take away samples of humans."

Martin looked across at Susan, who was listening intently to Terry, taking it all in, without any sign of a question coming from her.

Terry continued, "Under the plasterwork of these walls, we have installed thick aluminium foil to deflect any attempts by the aliens to destroy our data using electrical pulses. That is the reason I rarely leave my home; I am here on almost permanent guard."

"You don't go out at all? Not even for food?" Susan now sounded convinced by the whole story.

"Not even for food. I rely on Waitrose for all my food; they deliver, you know."

Martin thought that at least he shops with a prestigious company, so he could not be that stupid.

"They deliver here each week and I meticulously check every item to ensure they haven't placed any sort of electrical device into my groceries."

Martin wondered if Waitrose had a section in their returns document for such eventualities as 'foreign electrical equipment found in the Camembert'. He had faith in Waitrose, so guessed they might well have. He did not believe Terry's spaceman story but continued to listen politely.

"I have not mentioned this to any of the others as I do not want to alarm them, but over the last few weeks, I have noticed the same car outside. It often follows Ashley when he leaves. The same happens when Luke and Janice leave; they are the couple Ernie is so pointlessly worried about. I can't be sure if the man in the BMW follows them home, but I suspect he does, trying to find out more about them to see if they could be targeted in any way. The same happened to you yesterday as you left; he followed you."

"Well, I can confirm that he did follow me all afternoon and only stopped when I got home last night," Martin admitted.

"You mean that yesterday we were followed by aliens!" Susan sounded a little too excited by the prospect.

"Don't be so stupid, Susan. He was just a bloke in a BMW; there is going to be a sensible earthbound explanation for all this."

"Susan is right, Martin. The aliens are gathering as much information as they can on my associates and me in order to, at some time in the future, take action to neutralise our research."

"How can we help?" Susan volunteered.

"I have tried to find out more about the car without success. As private investigators, I was hoping that the two of you might have contacts or ways of finding out who the registered owner is. That would help me to tie up some loose ends and make the connections between our main suspects."

"We can ask Colin. He's a friend of ours and an ex-police detective; I'm sure he can get into the police computer and find out who owns the car."

"Susan," Martin interrupted, "we can't ask Colin to do something as illegal as that; it would not be fair." He looked at Terry, "I'm sorry we don't have any way of finding out who owns the BMW."

"Don't be stupid, Martin; Colin would love to help, and he still has enough friends in the police to get a simple answer as to who owns a certain car. We'll do it for you,

Terry. Give us a couple of days, and we'll have an answer for you, I'm sure."

"Susan," Martin sounded exasperated, which indeed he was, as he felt things, including his sanity, were slipping away from him, "I don't think we should ask Colin. Can I suggest it is most likely the debt collector trying to find your other brother?"

"Martin, this is our chance to help save the world. You don't get chances like that every day, do you?"

Martin accepted that she was making a fair point, and it was more the fact that he was not convinced that finding the owner of a dull grey BMW would lead to saving the world from aliens, which he doubted existed in the first place.

However, he knew from bitter experience that Susan often would grab his hand tightly, jump in with both feet, and pull him in behind her when he was trying to avoid becoming involved in anything out of the ordinary. He knew he could continue to argue and point out the madness that she agreed with, but he also knew that it would be useless in the end. Ironically, a quote from 'The Hitchhiker's Guide to the Galaxy' reverberated in his head: 'resistance is futile'. Martin knew it to be true when reasoning with Susan, even though she was not a Vogon Guard.

Susan smiled at Martin and then turned back to Terry, "Leave it to us. We'll meet up with Colin in the morning and we'll have the registered owner for you in an instant. Then we can deal with these aliens."

As Martin walked back to his car with Susan, he wondered to himself, 'Am I the first private detective in the world ever to find himself searching for aliens?'

CHAPTER THREE

Scrutinising the cramped office, Colin did nothing to conceal the look of disapproval on his face. He was not in the least impressed by the new premises for Hayden Investigations. Not that it was his office, he only visited from time to time, so he did not need to be too concerned. At least it was clean and tidy; that was something. During his years as a police officer, he had worked in many neglected, untidy, messy rooms, crowded with people, filing cabinets and desks that had various initials and words carved into their wooden tops. He looked through the window at Tower Bridge and thought to himself, 'well, it could be a lot worse'.

"Is that a new dress you're wearing?" Susan asked.

"God no, it's years old! I decided last week that it was time for a nuclear style declutter of the wardrobe. Trust me, Suzie Baby, an hour into the process, I couldn't believe how many outfits I'd crammed into my wardrobe, which I am renaming the Tardis. Do you like it?" With his hand, Colin straightened out the imaginary creases in his dress.

"Not sure about the flower design, but I like the colour."

"Suzie Baby, I'm years older than you and a lot more mature, so if you liked it lots, I would be worried that it was a little too young for me. I was thinking it might be a bit on the small side for me, a bit like your new office. Where will you put the leather settee?"

"That's gone to a charity, so no more crashing out on it to sleep off last night's excessive drinking."

"Well, that's one large downside." Colin looked around the room once more.

The office comprised of one long wall followed by a short wall, in which the window and the view of Tower Bridge took up most of the width. Another blank wall went off at an obtuse angle and ended in the wall where the door stood. The room, Colin recalled from his schooldays, could be described as a trapezoid. However you might describe the office, it was still a small room.

"And you say Martin's getting it for free?"

"As near as, something about a peppercorn rent. It belongs to that restaurant guy with the habit of pulling up his trousers. I must have told you."

"Well, beggars can't be choosers, can they? I guess it means that Martin has even less incentive to find any sort of work with his family fortune available. Although I presume as you guys have asked me in for a coffee, you are after my help?"

"I'd thought it might be best if we wait for Martin to arrive and explain. He thinks I get too excited and will get stuff wrong, but this is an exciting case."

"Case? You have a case to investigate? Tell me more, Suzie Baby."

Susan needed little encouragement to gossip. "Well, not so much a case, more helping out with a question. You see, there is this guy who is being followed, and he's Ernie's brother Terry."

"I know Ernie, the old guy at the old office."

Susan nodded, then continued, "That's the one. Well, Ernie's brother thinks he is being followed and wants us to find the owner of a grey BMW; that's where you come in."

"So, we're not waiting for Martin to arrive before you ask me for a favour?

"Just make out you never heard. Anyway, as I said, this Terry is being followed by aliens, and he is trying to thwart their plans to conduct a vast experiment on the human race. How about that?"

Colin sat down, picked up his handbag and took out a vanity mirror. He held it in front of his face, blinked his eyes, then replaced it in his bag, speaking as he did so, "I was just checking that I was not asleep and having some sort of weird dream. You did say aliens and not Alans, didn't you? Because this Terry guy being followed by Alans is a lot more reasonable to accept than him being followed by aliens."

"No, I said aliens, as in creatures from outer space."

"Suzie Baby, stop for a moment and listen to yourself. You are describing the storyline of, most likely, numerous sci-fi films and not, I am sure, describing a potential case that you and Martin plan to get involved in."

"Martin's sceptical just like you."

"There's a surprise."

"But I say, do not discount anything until you see it proved or disproved. Plus, Terry seemed like a nice guy."

"You are sometimes too open-minded. What's the registration number of this car? I do hope it's a car and not a spaceship. The Metropolitan Police do not have a database of spacecraft, as far as I know."

"How did you know we want you to trace a car?"

"Suzie Baby, you are so sweet at times and mildly innocent. You want me for a favour; I am an ex-policeman, you mentioned Terry wants to find the owner of a grey BMW.

I made a little bit of deduction, like any good detective. You should try it sometime."

"Smart arse! Well, when Martin gets here, act surprised when he tells you all about it in his way." Susan's phone rang as she finished her sentence. "It's Martin," she said, looking at the screen.

"Oh my God...of course I will...well, let me know as soon as you know...Yes, I'll tell him, don't worry...Yes, see you when I see you." She disconnected the phone.

"Martin's mum has taken a turn for the worse. She has had a big heart attack, and they have called Martin in to see her. He sounds worried, well you would, wouldn't you?"

"Poor Martin, it doesn't sound good. Well, give me the registration number of the BMW and I'll see what I can do. You get off to the hospital."

"Hospital? Martin's going to see his mum; I don't think I'll be needed."

"Suzie Baby, he might not have asked you to go with him, but rest assured, Martin will want you beside him to hold his hand during what could be a very worrying time. Also, I know you care for him more than you would admit, so it will stop you from worrying at the end of a phone. Just give me the car details and get off to the hospital. It's at times like this we find out who our real friends are."

Susan scrabbled around and scribbled down all the details she had on the BMW. She grabbed her coat and made her way towards the door, stopped, turned back, and collected her handbag from under her desk. She made another attempt at going out of the door, stopped once more and turned back to look at the window, "I'll just close the window."

Colin grabbed her arm as she passed him. "Stop, Suzie Baby, just get to the hospital. I'll lock up here."

She kissed him on the forehead, "Thanks, Colin; love you."

***

Susan stepped into the same stale magnolia-painted waiting room she was in yesterday. Apart from Martin sitting with his head in his hands, there was no one else in the room. He looked up at Susan, his worried frown transformed into a smile.

"You need not have come. Yet I am glad you did," he confessed.

Martin stood up. He looked drained as he walked towards her. She opened her arms and embraced him fondly. She liked the feel of his body against hers; it was only the situation they were in that blemished it.

Martin spoke softly, his warm breath close to her ear. "They say it was a massive heart attack, which she has only just about survived. It was lucky she was here in the hospital when it happened. They say I may be able to see her but only for a few minutes. I am just waiting for the okay."

"She'll be fine, I'm sure. Being here in the hospital, she's in safe hands," Susan tried to sound optimistic.

Being with Martin in such emotional circumstances reminded Susan of when her mother died in this same hospital. She recalled the emptiness and the realisation that she could never ask for her mother's advice again. No more conversations about boys or fashions. No more warnings to be in before midnight. No more advice about curbing alcohol consumption. The protection that she had relied on from her mother had vanished forever.

Mothers, however infuriating, were still mothers. For all the words and deeds and moans that Martin made about his mother, Susan knew that he cared for her. If not, he would have left her years ago and found a place of his own. But she knew Martin could never do that as his mother always needed someone to instruct and boss around, and so he had stayed to make her life bearable. Now that life hung in the balance.

"Excuse me," a young nurse interrupted their embrace. "Mr Hayden, you can see your mother now, but only for a few moments. Just one visitor, please. She's awake but heavily sedated, so don't fret if she's not sure of you or her surroundings."

Martin sat beside his mother, whose limp, fragile body seemed to be at the centre of a mayhem of tubes and wires. He held her wrinkled hand, avoiding the cannula neatly plastered in place. Sluggishly she reacted to his touch, and her eyes opened. Seeing her son, she smiled, "Hello darling, thank you for coming to see me."

Her voice was slightly slurred and had a softness that Martin had never really heard before. The drugs were doing a good job, he thought. He hoped there would be a few tender minutes with her. Maybe even a conversation that would not involve her putting him down or giving out instructions. His hopes were short-lived.

"Martin dear," her voice strengthened slightly, "you now have to grow up and become a man." Her voice was still softer than usual; the drugs were still having some impact on her. "I am now at the end of my life, so you need to listen carefully."

"Mother, you're not going to die. The doctors are excellent, and they will have you out of here in no time, I am sure."

"Don't be so stupid, Martin." She now sounded more like the mother Martin had always known; she must have overcome the medication in her system. "They are National Health Doctors. Too many patients and not enough resources. I should have gone private. That is beside the point, Martin; just listen to your mother for a change."

Martin could not recall a time when he did not have to listen to his mother. He was starting to believe it would take more than a heart attack and a shed load of drugs to put her down. He quickly admitted to himself it was the wrong thought at the wrong time and felt mildly guilty, even in the knowledge that he was going to get a list of instructions.

"As I said, let us assume for one moment so as not to hurt your childish feelings, I do not get out of here alive. There are several things you will have to do on your own, so please pay attention. There are three essential things you need to do."

"Shall I make a list?" Martin could not help but make it sound sarcastic.

"If you must. Firstly, in my bedroom, a red folder is on the blue shelf entitled: 'Services'. In there, you will find a complete set of precise instructions as to how my funeral should be conducted. What hymns, what should be said about me, and what kind of wreaths and flowers I approve of. Plus, there is a list of guests who can attend my funeral."

"You have your funeral all worked out?" Martin was surprised to hear of such a plan; she had never mentioned it before.

"Why wouldn't I? Death is a simple fact of life. Let us return to the guest list; it is all up to date, but for Margaret Grassingham, make a note of that name. Do not invite her. She was simply dreadful to poor Dorothy at the bridge club last month, so she is no longer welcome to attend my demise. She would only gloat, and I am not having that."

"Am I on the list?" Martin genuinely asked, not putting it past his mother to ban him from her funeral, even though they were still holding hands.

"Stupid boy, of course, you are. Secondly, you will have to speak to my accountant and take his advice as to whom should look after the family affairs. Just accept whoever he recommends as he is well placed to know our needs, and it will make the transfer of my assets to you a lot easier if those dealing with it know the structure of our finances."

Martin was going to ask if that meant he would inherit the entire family fortune as he had always expected, although he would put nothing past his mother. He also wanted to ask if Margaret Grassingham was in line for any inheritance and, if so, should he delete her from that list. Sensibly he decided that it was best not to ask and waste precious time. There could be a nasty scene if the nurse brought his visit to an abrupt end before Mother had issued all three instructions.

"Finally, you need to get yourself married. There is no way that you will be able to run a household all on your own without everything going to rack and ruin. You need a wife. I would suggest Isabel Ashworth, a solid well-bred young lady. You met her last year at that strange Halloween party you attended. The Ashworths are a fine family, plenty of history, and the joining of our two families will no doubt produce some fine issue. Now have you got all that, Martin?"

As if on cue, the young nurse opened the door, stepped into the room and encouraged Martin to leave his mother to rest.

***

Standing by his car, Martin looked at Susan beside him. The rain had started to fall heavily on his head, and the wind was increasing. He was not sure of his emotions. Part of him was expecting another frantic call from the hospital sometime during the night to tell him his presence was once again needed.

"Susan, would you mind coming back to my place for the evening? I would rather not be alone, you do understand?"

Susan smiled and rubbed his arms as if she were trying to warm him. "Of course, I understand. It might be a very fraught few days until your mother is out of the woods. The company would be good for you."

Martin took his car keys out of his pocket and handed them to her, "I'll let you drive. I am having trouble concentrating on anything, let alone driving through London traffic."

***

Not since her test had Susan felt so nervous driving a car through congested London streets. Martin was always cautious not to be in any situation where someone else had to drive his car. To say he was possessive of it was an understatement. However, the honour of driving it for Susan was washed away by the fear that she might end up a little too close to another car and dent the bodywork. She felt a great sense of relief when Martin indicated that she needed to take the next left and find a parking space on the small side street off the King's Road where he lived.

The large terraced Victorian house had three steps leading up to the front door, on the left. Susan noticed that behind a wrought iron fence, the house also had a basement window a little below street level. The outside had been painted pink, making it stand out from the surrounding homes for all the wrong reasons.

She followed Martin into the hallway. There was a room to the right and a door directly ahead with stairs to its left, one set going up and another going down, the latter presumably leading to the basement. He led her into the long rectangular kitchen and pointed towards a seat at a large pine kitchen table.

"Grab a seat. Can I suggest a glass of wine to start?" Martin went to a cupboard, pulled out a bottle of wine, waved it towards Susan, and asked, "Red, okay?"

"Only if it's a bore doe!" She hoped that under the circumstances Martin would not react badly to her frivolous remark.

To her relief, he smiled, looked at the label, then explained to her, "I am afraid not. It is a Cahor, or as you would say, 'car whore' a dirty little wine that leads you astray."

"Sounds much like a wine I drank too much of once." Together they laughed.

Sip by sip, bit by bit, Susan asked and was told the chain of events for the day. From the time the hospital had called Martin to say that his mother had suffered a serious heart attack and was being resuscitated, advising him to come as quickly as possible. The way he had panicked leaving the house and driving to the hospital, hardly noticing traffic lights and other road users that he would typically be so careful of. He shared everything until the point when she had joined him at the hospital.

"I wondered if you could stay for the rest of the evening and maybe get ourselves a takeaway later."

"I'm at your disposal; nothing is more important than making sure you're okay. I just want to give Colin a ring as he was concerned. I'll tell him what's happened."

Martin offered Susan a polite tour of the house. The kitchen she had seen, so he now pointed through the French doors towards a small square paved garden lined with ornate pots, full of green shrubs with withered flowers. He then took her into the dining room at the front of the house. A large, polished mahogany table with twelve matching dining chairs dominated the room.

He took her up the first flight of stairs to a living room that overlooked the rear of the house. Here, he explained, Mother spends her evenings watching TV or reading. Susan picked up one of the many photo frames that lined a large sideboard.

"Is this you?"

Martin looked over her shoulder, "I was about seven when that was taken."

"What lake is that in the background? It looks a big one."

"Lake Garda, in Italy. When I was younger, my parents owned a small holiday home there; they both loved the area. We spent many summers there until my late teens, and then they sold it. After that, they had a small seaside home in Norfolk. I think Father preferred to be close to his business. I recall days during our Italian holidays when he would spend almost all day on the phone. Mother and I would just sit on the balcony and eat ice cream."

"Two weeks in Bognor sufficed for our family. All five of us crammed into a caravan. We had a laugh, though, especially when Mum and Dad got a little tipsy in the clubhouse. Ooh! Is this you all togged up for your passing out parade at university?"

"Graduation, hated the gown and everything. I spent three years there just for the chance to wear some fancy dress – odd tradition."

"When I left school, you had to wear a white blouse, and everyone wrote messages over it. I think I still have it somewhere."

After the numerous photographs that Susan asked Martin to explain to satisfy her curiosity, together they peered into

Mother's bedroom, which was on the same level as the living room, making it easier for his mother and her creaking knees, fewer stairs to walk up and down. Then they went up another flight to the top of the house and Martin's bedroom, with a large dormer window facing out onto the street and a grey marble effect en-suite. It was tidy and neat, just as Susan had expected. She saw it almost at once, a small book, standing on top of a low chest of drawers.

"My God, you do have it, 'Chicken Licken'. When you told me it was your favourite book, full of morals and stuff, I didn't believe you."

"Why would I lie about such a weird thing?"

"To endear yourself to me," Susan tried to make it sound like a joke, but she wanted to believe it was true. "So, how many young virgins have you tempted up to your lofty tower to seduce?"

"What you mean is how many I might have sneaked past my sleeping mother. Until I find a virgin happy to scale the side of a building to get up here, the number will remain at zero.

"Susan, I need to make a few telephone calls to aunts and uncles, keep them up to date with Mother's condition. If you want to hang around for a while, there's the TV or reading stuff downstairs. I should be no more than an hour or so, then we can order in a takeaway."

"No, Martin. While you make your calls, I will go off and buy some supplies. Tonight, I am cooking for you."

Martin hugged her, "Thanks, Susan, I'll look forward to that."

***

"I've never cooked on gas before; we always had electric," Susan put forward as a reasonable excuse for the over-cooked mince she served Martin. As well as being crunchy, some of it had a distinct charcoal flavour. Fortunately, the chilli sauce and rice made it look edible. "It's so much hotter and quicker than an electric hob."

"Well, it tastes good. Maybe we should rename it crispy chilli!" Martin laughed. "A sous chef Susan special, it could catch on."

"Or catch fire next time."

Thankfully, the smoke alarm alerted Susan that the mince she was browning had turned almost black while she was deadheading some of the plants in the garden. Susan did not have a garden where she lived, so the opportunity to tinker and tidy a garden was just too much of a temptation. It might not have been the best meal that Susan had ever cooked, but it was one of the most enjoyable. Martin did not seem to care about the food as they chatted effortlessly.

Once they had loaded the dishwasher and binned the burnt saucepan, they went upstairs to the living room with another bottle of wine and sat in front of the TV watching a comedy film on Netflix that had cropped up in an earlier conversation.

The conversation had begun over the dinner table with Martin asking Susan what her favourite film was.

"Ted2," Susan responded in an instant, "that bear is just so funny and witty, he had me in tears of laughter, just about unable to finish my popcorn."

"Ted2? But that's a kids' film, the one with the teddy bear, or is there another one?"

"Far from being a kids' film Martin, you have got to see it. You must have Netflix on that big telly of yours, we'll watch it tonight, and you can see for yourself that it's not a film for little girls and boys."

"We are talking about the same film?"

"Trust me, Martin, I'll give you an example. Ted and John are in a library full of sperm samples that fall over, spilling everything on John. Who says,' F! F! Oh, my God! It's in my eyes! You gotta f'in'' help me! Oh, my God! It's in my f'in' mouth!' Funny, but not kids' stuff."

"F'in'? You mean the F word?"

"Yeah."

"How come you didn't use it, there are no kids around, and I've heard those sorts of words before."

"Well, it doesn't seem right swearing in your house."

Martin topped up her glass of wine, emptying the bottle. As he collected and opened another from one of the kitchen cupboards, he pointed out, "My house is not sensitive; swearing is allowed if you feel the need."

"It just doesn't seem right using the whole proper F-word in your house in a posh part of London."

"Since when did you become all prim and proper?"

"You think me just a common girl who swears a lot."

"No, but you must admit you have used some colourful language in the past, and I just can't see the reason to stop just because you're in my house. Don't forget I work with you every day."

"It just doesn't seem right, and that's that. You'll hear the full word when we watch the film."

Ten minutes into the film, Martin could see it was nothing like he had imagined. He was just thankful that he had no young relations that he might have been tempted to take to the film.

They had planned that after the film, Susan would grab a taxi and make her way home. Neither of them made the end of the film. As the credits were rolling, both Martin and Susan were sound asleep, both emotionally exhausted.

***

"Have you missed me?" Martin enquired as he walked into the office where Susan and Colin were already seated. During the last two days, Martin had not set foot in the office. He had spent many hours at the hospital close to his mother, watching over her recovery and taking instructions as to what might or might not be needed when she was discharged. Defying expectations, she was now almost back to her old self, complaining about the excessive number of times nurses needed to check her vitals and pointing out that the food was enough to kill her if the doctors failed. It was evident to all she was getting better.

"Well, it's been quiet here without you," Susan commented as she hugged him. "Good to have you back."

"Have we beaten the aliens away from our door yet?" Martin asked, knowing full well that the presence of Colin in the office indicated that either the aliens were still fighting

Susan for control of the earth or, worse still, there was a new case for Hayden Investigations.

"Not so, I'm afraid," Colin said. "Suzie Baby is still fighting her interplanetary wars. My measly contribution has been to identify the pilot of their earth-bound spacecraft, better known as a BMW 5 series."

"Just get on with it, Colin; you can be so unexciting at times," Susan grumbled.

"The BMW in question, which followed both you and numerous other people, is a rented car, Hertz, as I am reliably informed. The thing is, you might recall, I am no longer a police officer, so even though they still let me wander around the office passing on gossip, which is fine, apparently searching a police database is frowned upon. I got my cute wrists slapped. Hence, unless we can convince a serving police officer that there's an alien driving around in a rented grey BMW, and he can twist the arm of the car hire firm to hand over the details of the renter, we have reached a dead end."

Martin smiled, thinking at least that was some good news. If they had nothing to offer Terry, then they could close the book on the aliens. Then tell Ernie his brother is all good and get back to social living.

"Sorry, Colin, it was never our intention to get you into trouble."

"Don't fret, Martin, it was not the first, or will it be the last time I get my wrists slapped by authority. Mind, I think Suzie Baby has another message for you. She is getting to be a right little Miss Secretary in her old age."

"Enough of the age thing," Susan pointed out. "One of your old school friends called while you were away. Some bloke called Grant Fisher; he wants a video call with you. He wouldn't say what he wanted. I guess knowing you and your schoolmates it will include a drunken evening with strippers."

"Grant Fisher?" Martin repeated. He knew the name alright. He knew Grant at boarding school; they were both in the same year. It was just that Grant had the most oversized ego in the school. Added to that, he was the biggest pain in the butt of any of the boys in Martin's year.

Schoolboy Grant's future plans had included owning a big multi-national company producing commodities that consumers would fight to the death over, thus making him very rich. An ambition that he rammed down the throats of the other boys non-stop. The fact that he wanted a video call did not surprise Martin in the least. Apart from using as much technology as he could, Grant was undoubtedly interested in seeing how Martin might have aged. Without a doubt, Grant would have had several Botox and facial treatments to keep the slightest sign of any wrinkle at bay.

"Did he say why he wanted to see and speak to me?"

"Nope, just arranged a video conference call, as he put it, to start at 10.35 tomorrow. He said that it would not last more than fifteen minutes as he had another conference call from his Hong Kong bank at 10.50. He sounds a right arsehole."

"You're not far wrong in that judgement. Well, I can't do it in the morning. I have my accountant calling around tomorrow at 11.30am at my place to sort out a replacement for him when he retires later this month."

"You could always take the call at home. I'm interested to know just what he wants. Oh, he also added that I, as your PA, should be in on the call. I'll set your laptop up for you, so it should be easy enough; just a couple of buttons need to be pressed. What does this Grant do?"

"I have no idea and care even less. Okay, if you can set my laptop up for me, I'll log in from home and you can log in from your place as well, no point in you coming in tomorrow as I will not be around much again. Although, what you could do is to pop around and see Ernie, tell him his brother is not being taken for a ride and then we can get back to normal."

Colin added, "Just because I have not been able to establish who the driver of the BMW is, does not mean that he will stop following Terry or his visitors. For what reason, we have no idea, but I doubt it will be charitable."

"Colin, that is not helpful in the least."

"But he's right, Martin, aliens or not, something is going on with Terry and co. being followed."

"Okay, we will put off talking to him until the two of you come up with some hair-brained plan. In the meantime, Susan, can you sort out my laptop for tomorrow's wonderful conference call, please?"

CHAPTER FOUR

It was 10.25, ten minutes before the call. Martin clicked the shortcut that Susan had created for him and waited for the video calling software to load. Within a few moments, he was looking at himself in a small square at the top right of his screen. He wanted a better background than the current kitchen cupboards if he was about to speak to Grant Fisher. Martin took his laptop into the dining room. He sat facing the window allowing the light to illuminate and flatter his face. It was time to position the computer on a small pile of books to ensure the camera was at eye level and create a far more favourable image. Then he adjusted some of the ornate silver tureens on the buffet behind him, guaranteeing they were clearly visible in the camera shot. Also in view was an elegantly framed painting that his mother bought years ago and always praised even though she knew Martin hated it. Far too classical for him, but it looked good in the background. One last adjustment of the webcam, and he was ready. No sign of Susan or Grant yet, so he waited.

To waste some time, Martin scrolled through the menu and the various settings, including multiple backgrounds, none of which bettered the silverware. Then he saw a range of face templates, which intrigued him. The link offered a selection of cartoon faces that could replace his features. Millions of pounds were spent on research, development, and infrastructure so that he could change his features into that of a cat. Martin thought that he did not make a bad-looking cat. Then there was a werewolf, although the hairy face did not suit him in the least. He felt that was confirmation he should never grow a beard. Then came Martin, Mr Potato Head. It reminded him of when he was a child, holding a large potato and sticking glasses, mouths and noses to create a variety of weird and exciting faces. He loved that toy and was amused to see his eyes behind the big round, black-framed glasses that characterised Mr Potato Head. His head was now distorted into a potato.

Another screen ballooned up in front of him; it was Susan. "Why are you a Mr Potato face?"

"Bored and playing with the programme. I think I look cool being a childhood toy."

"That might be so, but your mate Grant will be on soon, so let's have the regular Martin on the screen."

Martin pressed F7; nothing happened; he pushed it again just to be sure. Once more, nothing changed on the screen."

"Martin, come on, stop mucking around!" Susan spoke from the laptop.

"I'm not. Is it F7 or F8 to get back to my real face?"

"I don't know; try them both."

Martin tried all the F keys at the top of his keyboard. He managed to change the volume and brightness on his screen. He was still Mr Potato Head. Then he tried space bar, caps lock and shift, all to no avail.

"Susan, what button is it? Just tell me!" Martin sounded desperate.

"I don't know; I've never been that unhappy with my face that I felt the need to look like a potato. There must be a help menu some place. Come on; it's almost time."

Even under pressure, Martin still managed to find the help menu. It offered him a range of frequently asked questions. Evidently, no one before him had become stuck with a face they no longer wanted. He typed into the help search box, only to be distracted by a third screen popping up and to see the face of Grant Fisher staring out at him.

"Good morning all. I'm Grant Fisher, CEO of Pinkcast. I guess you must be Martin's PA; a lot more attractive than I ever imagined. And..." Grant stopped. Martin could see him move his face closer to the webcam. "Unusual. I was expecting Martin, not a cartoon potato."

This was not the impression that Martin had wanted to make on his annoying school friend. He tried to present some reasonable excuse for his appearance; unfortunately, he could not think of one. Thankfully, Susan was a lot quicker in her ability to concoct an explanation.

"I'm sorry, Mr Fisher, Mr Hayden could not make himself available for this morning's call. He was called away to Paris to meet with an important client. In his place, we have our Southeastern Regional Director."

Not only did Susan sound like a very efficient Personal Assistant, but even Martin almost believed what she was saying. Sensibly he let her continue.

"I guess you might be wondering why there is a cartoon image across the face of our Southeastern Regional Director?"

"That question had floated to the top of my mental agenda."

"Often our regional directors are actively involved in high level, sensitive investigations. Mr Hayden insists that they remain anonymous; he is a really caring employer. We will refer to the third person in our conference as Maris, as in

Maris Piper, but you can call him Maris. He has full authority to make decisions on behalf of Martin."

Doubtfully Grant spoke, "Well, Maris, it's good to see you or at least your disguise."

"Pleased to speak to you too, Grant," Martin replied, wondering how he had ever got himself into this predicament. Realising that currently hidden behind a potato and feeling a little hurt at being demoted to a regional director by Susan, he guessed he might not get a word in edgeways. He was right; Susan started with questions at once.

"Grant, your company Pinkcast, is that the same as the Pinkcast watch? The one that tracks your steps and stuff."

"That's the very one, Susan." He pulled back the sleeve of his double-cuffed striped shirt, revealing a bright pink watch with a corresponding strap. "As our slogans say: 'Your portal to a healthier life', or our new TV advert: 'Be in the pink with a Pinkcast'. It's the watch that not only tells you the time, but it also reveals your health strengths and health weaknesses, allowing you to improve your health and better understand your body..."

"Thanks for the advert, Grant. You wanted to speak to Martin about something," Martin, currently known as Maris, interrupted.

"How do you go about designing a watch that does, well, just so much?" Susan asked, ignoring Martin the potato.

"Plugging into the Pinkcast group mind, then overloading ourselves on big ideas. Do you have one, Susan? A watch that is, I am sure you are just brimming with exciting big ideas."

"No way I could afford one, although I bet it's on everyone's Christmas list."

"Well, you should ask Martin to give you a pay rise. He was always a meanie at school. Better still, I am sure I can arrange a special Pinkcast delivery. I am the boss, after all."

"Can we please get back to business," Martin once more tried to steer the conversation back to the reason for the call. A call he wanted to end as soon as possible.

"Sorry, Maris, no need to give me the roasting." He lamely laughed at his joke and then turned his mind to the reason for the video conference.

"The reason I wanted to speak to Martin, although Susan, you too relate to this matter, so I do not feel that I am talking behind Martin's back, is I have in my employ, ironically, some private detectives. If I'd known Martin ran a similar agency, I might well have asked him first. Still, I have a first-class private investigation company with a Terry Gray under surveillance. I know you have recently been in touch with him because I saw the name Hayden on the list of people who have contacted him."

"You're investigating Terry?" Susan asked.

"Yes, and I will tell you why. As I am sure you know, Terry is very much an expert in computing and manipulating technology. You also know that the Pinkcast watch is not only one of the most commercially successful fitness watches on the market, but it is also the envy of the industry. To put it plainly, Terry has broken into our computer system and stolen documents and information. Unmistakably, he's an industrial spy for one of our competitors. I am not sure which one, but we're following him intending to find out, or alternatively, retrieve the documents from him, which is my preferred option."

"You've got to be kidding," Susan exclaimed.

Martin also thought the allegation about Terry was off track. He seemed a total geek, not an industrial spy. Industrial spies, not that Martin knew any, he guessed would be a little more discreet and not hang around getting followed by BMWs.

"Why not go to the police?" Martin asked.

"If I involve the police, there is a danger that it will appear in the public domain, and I do not want that sort of publicity. I wish the whole matter to be dealt with discreetly, and that's why I want to enlist Martin's help. As he knows Terry, maybe he could convince him to return everything to us, and we can forget the whole matter.

"My detectives have told me that so far, he does not seem to have passed on the information. It could be he's planning to sell it to the highest bidder. If Martin is close to him, then there is the potential for some sort of wriggle room where both Pinkcast and Mr Gray can resolve the dilemma we find ourselves in. I was hoping Martin might be a mediator for me. Susan, do you think Martin would agree?"

"Of course, he will. I am sure he would be happy to help an old school friend."

"Susan, sorry, but are you sure that Martin would be happy to help out in this situation? He might not like to be considered a mediator."

"Of course, he will, Maris, you know how kind, considerate and always eager to help others Martin is."

"Sounds like he has changed since I knew him at school," Grant quipped as he looked at his watch. "I have another video call due shortly. Do you think Martin will agree?"

"I have full authority, and on his behalf, I will agree. We'll have a talk with Terry on your behalf and hope to make him see sense."

"Thanks, Susan, really kind of you. Bye Maris, bye Susan, I look forward to hearing from you. Oh, tell you what, it might help you if you visit our London distribution centre. Have a word with our manager there, Nigel Butler; he will be able to fill you in on the situation. And Susan, I'll arrange everything for you and ensure that your special gift is waiting for you on Nigel's desk. Ciao." Grant disappeared from the screen and the conversation.

"Susan, why did you agree to help the twat?"

"Well, I know I never went to school with him, but he seemed nice and reasonable, and if Terry is an industrial spy, well, that's like doing a real investigation. Also, how could I take anything you say seriously when you are in your Maris Piper outfit?"

"Very funny. I suppose the inducement of a high-tech state of the art expensive watch did not influence your decision."

"Maybe a little," Susan confessed.

***

The Pinkcast depot turned out to be no more than a dull, metallic warehouse located discreetly in a quiet corner of a south London industrial area. No passer-by would ever imagine that one of the latest, most fashionable watch companies would ever consider residing in such a nondescript building. The Pinkcast shop on the high street stood out from those around it with its very loud trademarked pink colour, gaudy lettering and loud music, all tempting people into the store to buy, what Martin considered to be, overpriced watches.

Susan did point out that even if Martin considered them to be expensive, they were still a lot cheaper than the Rolex on his wrist. Martin countered that his watch consisted of a precision Swiss movement fashioned by craftsmen with expertise passed down through generations of watchmakers. Susan laughed with derision. Then Martin added that Pinkcast watches were no more than a small computer affixed to your wrist that hands out the information you don't really need to know. A wristwatch tells you the time; that's all one needs. Susan laughed again, so Martin gave up.

The entrance to the depot was a plain grey door where a security guard greeted them. He required them first to register themselves as visitors into a big book. The guard then asked them to stand in front of a small camera to add a photograph of themselves to the paper visitor pass they were to be issued.

The next stage was to be accompanied by another security guard through a small waiting area. They then climbed a flight of stairs and went through two doors that required the guard to use his electronic pass before he finally deposited them in a large conference room with a wide window overlooking the trees that enclosed the industrial estate.

Before Susan had time to try out all the chairs around the room, two men walked in. The first was short, plump, and of an age that should have allowed him to retire years ago. An extremely high forehead dominated his face, emphasised by his baldness but for a thin strip of grey hair. He introduced himself as Hugh Murphy of Millwall Investigations.

The second man introduced himself as Nigel Butler, with the title of southeast area manager. Nigel was a lot younger, a similar age to that of Susan and Martin. He wore jeans, an open-necked double-cuffed shirt, and carried a Red 'n Black A4 book with a mobile phone in the same hand. He had a warm, inviting smile that allowed his brown eyes to twinkle. Susan considered him to be not bad looking.

The four of them made full use of the space in the room, with no one sitting close to anyone else. Nigel carefully placed his large notebook in front of him and took one final look at his phone before placing it on the black fabric-like tabletop. He then took from his jeans pocket a small two-way radio, reduced the volume and then set it alongside his book. Susan thought he used these items to symbolize the power he held in the company.

"How was your Paris trip, Mr Hayden?" Nigel asked.

"I never discuss other clients with clients; confidentiality is paramount in our industry," Martin replied, with a confidence that impressed Susan.

"Of course, sorry to have asked you. I assume your PA has brought you up to speed on the conversation our CEO Grant had with Maris?"

"Yes, Susan is a highly competent assistant. I understand you are going to give us some additional information."

Susan was going to comment on the compliment Martin had proffered to her. For the sake of appearances, she kept quiet but planned to refer to it later.

"Indeed I am." Nigel opened his notebook and flicked through the pages, regularly referring to his notes, until he found what he was looking for.

"About three months ago, we had a security infringement when someone hacked into our central server here and downloaded some confidential documents. Once it had come to light, we worked hard to block the gaps in our computer security, only to find that an unauthorised user again broke into it.

"We identified that several emails sent to me by Terry Gray contained a trojan virus, which enabled him to gain access to our server. Although we have tried many techniques, he still seems to get around any defence we put up. I would say he 'pops' into our server every ten days or so, has a look around, then departs, in a virtual way, of course.

"I am sure you understand that I can't be too specific about the documents he has stolen. Suffice to say they contain sensitive, commercial information, which would be of great value to our competitors. Our aim here at Pinkcast is to recover the documents and neutralise any damage they may do. I understand from Grant that you are connected socially to Terry and that it's possible you might be able to convince him to return everything that belongs to our company."

"What I do not understand is, if he has these industrial secrets, then why hasn't he sold them to someone if what you say is correct, he has had them for the last few months?" Martin asked the question that Susan was about to ask. To her mind, if you have something to sell, why not sell it. This time the older man entered the conversation.

"There could be a number of reasons. Firstly, Terry is simply waiting to sell them to the highest bidder. The second reason could be as simple as he has no idea what he has in his custody, which might explain why he is still eager to get into our servers. Alternatively, he might know what he has, but a third party is instructing him. If that is the scenario, then it could be that he does not yet have all the information he has been asked to gather."

"What were the emails about in the first place? The ones that you must have opened to release the virus?" Susan asked. Nigel answered this time.

"He was waffling on about aliens and our watches being some sort of conduit of communication for them. To be honest, I was amused. Myself and my staff took it as a bit of light entertainment at the hands of a, well, oddball, shall I say. Then he started sending more and more. Now I know his motives are a lot darker than I might have first imagined."

"Sounds very much like Terry. Can we see any of these emails?" Susan asked, thinking that Nigel was looking a little nervous.

Hugh answered with a lot more confidence in his voice than Nigel was showing.

"Sadly not. We felt the need to quarantine the emails and then have them digitally shredded; we all agreed that it was by far the safer choice. Terry is, I hate to say a computer genius when it comes to hacking them."

"And I guess you have not just knocked on his door and asked for them back?" Susan asked. Nigel looked at Hugh, who took the hint and answered.

"We have approached him; however, he did not respond, which is not surprising. We have also tried to crack his computer remotely without success. I guess if breaking and entering other people's computers is your job, your own computer will be completely secure."

"One last question," Martin stepped in, looking a little bored, Susan thought, whereas she was feeling a little on the excited side. It might turn out to be their first case of industrial espionage. God, she loved her job. "What evidence do you have that Terry is the culprit?"

Susan thought that Martin's use of the word culprit made Terry sound more like a naughty schoolboy rather than the highly trained, world-famous, industrial spy, which people were accusing him of being. Again, it was Hugh who answered.

"There is irrefutable evidence that Mr Terry Gray is the person responsible for this nasty business. Yet before you ask, Pinkcast has no plans to share the evidence that we hold at this stage, as it might well compromise future legal action."

Martin stood up, ready to leave; he had heard enough and wanted to get this thing over. "OK, we will pop in and see Terry, point out the error of his ways and see what he says.

I am not making any promises. It is not as though either of us is a close friend of his."

The other three also stood up. Nigel shook hands with Martin then Susan; as he did so, he smiled at her. "Grant has asked me to offer you a small gift. It will be given to you when you hand in your visitor pass to security."

Susan felt like an excited child as she and Martin followed Hugh back to the front door. She hoped her gift would be a Pinkcast watch; she imagined it would look so cool on her wrist and be the envy of all her friends. Even before she reached the security desk, she was in the process of planning which coordinated outfit she could wear with it.

***

"It is just a watch, Susan, with plenty of silly features which are a waste of money and you will never use," Martin pointed out as he drove the two of them out of the car park. Susan eagerly opened the bright pink box. With a look of wonderment on her face, she took out her new Pinkcast watch and laid it over her wrist.

"It was a gift, Martin, from the CEO of the company, no less. So even if I don't use any of the features, it still hasn't cost me a penny. Looks good, doesn't it?"

"Well, on the high street, it is overpriced and over-functioning," Martin continued to emphasize as he again drove towards Greenwich and Terry's house.

"You're just an old fuddy-duddy at times, Martin; listen to what you're missing out on." Susan opened the neatly folded instruction sheet, which listed the functions the watch boasted. "Your Pinkcast device offers solar charging on its big 1.4-inch display. The multisport GPS watch puts no limits on how far you can go. Its solar power-replenishing feature extends battery life, so you'll have more time to enjoy the watch's colour mapping, music streaming. A first-of-its-kind PinkPace feature helps keep your pacing strategy on track and provides gradient guidance as you run cross country. You have preloaded ski maps for more than 2,000 worldwide ski resorts..."

"When was the last time you went cross country running, Susan?"

"I have been thinking seriously about going running, lose a few pounds. I'll continue. Other highlights include enhanced wrist heart rate, smart notifications, pulse oxygen sensing, Google Pay contactless payments. Pinkcast is the ultimate watch for active lifestyles. Customisable power manager modes let you see and control how various settings impact battery life. There's even a new expedition mode that provides an ultra-low-powered GPS mode that will last for weeks, assuming 3 hours per day outside in 50,000 lux conditions..."

"Expedition mode, are you planning a trip along the Amazon River?"

"Never say never, Martin, that's my motto. You're just jealous I have a posh watch given to me by your school friend."

"Now, if one of its many features is an automatic breathalyser telling you when you have imbibed enough alcohol on your wild nights out with the girls, that would be useful."

"Ha-ha! I will treat that comment with the contempt it deserves."

"Well, can I suggest you put away your super-duper watch while we visit Terry, or else he might think you are an actual alien."

Martin squeezed his car between two large transit vans - parking spaces in Terry's road were at a premium. As they walked the short distance to Terry's house, they spied the grey BMW. Both waved and smiled at the driver before finally ringing the doorbell. The driver looked less than impressed.

Today it was a packed house at 'Terry's Terrestrial Terrace', as Susan had nicknamed it, a name both her and Martin found amusing. As well as Terry, who answered the door looking pleased to see them, there was Ashley, who looked less comfortable. Also present were the couple sitting alongside each other on two folding chairs close to the window. The woman, who introduced herself as Janice, was thin to the point of looking a lot like a skeleton cloaked in ashen skin. Her narrow, sharp nose was pierced, and she wore three silver studs in it. On the lower part of her bare arms were several tattoos, mostly of flowers and the word Luke, embellished by virtual ivy leaves.

The man next to her was also short, a lot more obese than his partner, which was not hard to be. He turned out to be the Luke mentioned on Janice's arm. Apart from a short-sleeved Hawaiian shirt, he wore baggy beach shorts and flip flops. He would have looked more at home on a tropical beach than here in a room full of computers and people.

Ashley completely ignored the arrival of more guests. He appeared fully engrossed with his laptop screen and what appeared to be several complex calculations.

Awkwardly, Martin and Susan had to stand close to the front door, the only available space left to them as they were the last to arrive.

"How did you get on with the grey BMW?" Terry asked as he returned to his seat and closed his laptop so they couldn't see what he was doing.

"We have indeed found out a little more about the BMW," Martin confirmed. Then he added, "Have you ever heard of a company called Pinkcast?" As he uttered the trade name, a hush appeared to envelop the room. The couple and Ashley all looked towards Terry for an answer.

"The healthy watch company, yes. I think you will find a lot of people know of the company given its broad advertising campaign. Why do you ask?"

"Well, the grey BMW is used by a private detective agency employed by Pinkcast, who think you might have hacked into their computers and made off with some secrets that they want back."

The reaction Martin got from the room was not what he had expected. Everyone, except for Susan, burst out laughing, then Janice added the comment, "I bet they want their secrets back."

"Hold on," Martin started, setting about calming the joviality in the room, "you have stolen industrial secrets from them?"

"Okay, let me explain, for the simple reason that I would imagine they have not told you the exact truth." Terry then looked at the couple as if he was looking for a secret signal that would allow him to explain at least part of the story. "As I mentioned previously, aliens have hijacked the ever-increasing number of health watches that people wear. Pinkcast, being one of the biggest players in the market, is a prime target for them. We have evidence that aliens are using Pinkcast watches to coordinate potential landing areas across the country. So yes, I have broken into their servers and have downloaded various documents that help us track the progress of the aliens."

"That's my role," Ashley chipped in. "Terry passes me various information and I try to decode and interpret it to enable us to identify possible landing areas. I pass the locations to Janice and Luke, who track the movements of the aliens already here. Apart from that basic information, I know nothing more of their work." They nodded and smiled proudly as Terry took up the story.

"You see, I am the only one with all the information. Ashley knows just what he needs to know and the same applies to Luke and Janice. They know little about what Ashley is doing and vice-a-versa. It makes for a secure organisation. Plus, that is the main reason why I rarely leave this house.

"It comes as no surprise to me that Pinkcast, and those within the company our extra-terrestrial friends have turned, want me to return valuable data to them, which is not going to happen."

Martin looked around the room at four people who looked as though they believed every word; even Susan looked convinced. Martin broached the 'elephant' that was definitely in the room, even if no one else could see it. "Are you expecting me to believe that you are battling spacemen who are about to take over the earth from the front room of a terraced house in Greenwich?"

"Ironic," Terry smiled, "but what better place for such a conflict than the home of modern astronomy. Few people would believe what we are doing here, so your reaction does not surprise me. But did people rush to believe every word Madame Curie was telling them about penicillin? Possibly not.

"Pinkcast wishes to discredit what we are doing here, and why wouldn't they? It just goes to show that we are getting remarkably close to their secret."

"They know you are still hacking into their computer network."

"I am sure they do; they don't have the skills to stop me."

"You mean aliens from some far-off galaxy are less intelligent than you?"

"I would never presume that, but if they started showing how far they are advanced, they would soon lose the element of surprise. I am sure the aliens could stop me, yet if they did, then employees at the company might start asking awkward questions of those aliens masquerading as Pinkcast employees."

Martin felt as if he had walked into a brick wall. How do you argue with someone whose ideas are so far removed from reality that they can produce an imaginary explanation for anything you might say to them? In his frustration, he just surrendered.

"Okay. I have been asked if you will hand back all the data you have taken from Pinkcast, and I suspect your answer will be no. I have also given you the answer about the car following you. Therefore, I would say my business here is finished and wish you luck with your fight."

***

As he drove past the BMW, Martin stuck two fingers up at the driver for some reason he was not sure of. All it succeeded in doing was relieving some of the frustration he was feeling and a comment from Susan, "You are a terrible loser."

"I am not a bad loser; I am just a realist who has chosen not to believe in little green men from a faraway planet taking over our earth."

He felt Susan look at him. "You're still a bad loser, but I accept that it's not compulsory to believe in UFOs and aliens from outer space. I would add, and this might surprise you, that although I believe in aliens from other planets, I do not fully believe in what Terry was telling us."

Martin crunched a gear, jerked away from the lights cursing a cyclist who was doing nothing untoward; such was his bad mood.

"You are saying that you believe in aliens, yet not Terry?"

"Exactly, Martin. We're being asked to choose between two possible facts. First, Terry being an industrial spy, or two, a saviour of the human race. Well, as far as I know, saviours of the human race are hardly ever well paid and most only get sainthood long after they are dead. On the other hand, industrial spies, I would imagine, are paid very well in this life. I would add to that, the house where Terry lives is in a very sought-after part of London, so it will not be cheap, even if he's just renting it. Also, all that equipment does not come cheap. There is no sign he has an actual job. His brother Ernie is not well off at all; his other brother, we hear, has debt collectors chasing him. No family fortune like some people I know. I would say everyone needs to pay the bills, and, in my book, Terry is paying his bills with a bit of industrial secret stealing."

"You are getting to be a bit of a sharp detective, Miss Morris."

"Please, can you drop me off at Bermondsey tube? I'm off to see my sister."

"What is that going to be? An evening of sisters slagging off men whilst consuming glasses of white wine?" Martin asked with a hint of humour as his mood lightened. He used humour even though he sensed that Susan's request was linked to something more serious. He was proved right.

"Not exactly," Susan answered with a subdued tone in her voice. "It was something you said to me while we were at the hospital: 'there must come a time when you begin to forgive', that's what you said about my father. Then when your mum almost died, I suppose I thought about it even more. I mean, my dad is not getting any younger; none of us are. As a result, I imagined what if he died? Would I even hear about it? What if he got ill, needed someone to care for him? I guess I started to feel a little guilty that I had cut off contact with him over what must have been a tough decision for him to make."

Susan sounded wistful as she spoke softly about her father. Martin could understand the melancholy thoughts; he, too, harboured a similar viewpoint about his ill and ageing mother.

"Seeking advice from your older sister then?"

"Well, I haven't told her yet exactly why I am popping around tonight. I'd just want to run the idea past her."

Martin wished Susan good luck as she exited the car and walked into the tube station, then he continued towards the office.

CHAPTER FIVE

When Martin walked into the office, he had three surprises. The first was the door was unlocked. Cautiously he opened it, unsure of what or who might be on the other side. To his relief, the second surprise was to see Colin sitting at a desk. When Colin heard the door open, he turned and smiled at Martin.

"I was beginning to think that I might have made a bad choice. I kind of gambled that you'd be back after your trip out. I'm glad you're here. No Suzie Baby?"

"No, she has gone to see her sister. Who is he?" 'He' was Martin's third surprise. A young man, dressed in a blue polo shirt and jeans, sitting opposite Colin.

"He is known as Dan to his friends, but to you, he is Detective Constable Daniel Green. He wants a quiet word with you. Don't worry Martin; you're not getting arrested just yet."

Even though Colin smiled as he spoke, Martin was unsure why a real police officer wanted to talk to him. Maybe it was guilt; perhaps it was just a natural reaction to being 'questioned' by the police. Whatever it was, Martin freely admitted, "Look, I know I swore at that cyclist. It was wrong of me, but I was in a bad mood and he was wobbling around a lot."

The facial expression of the police officer did not change; it remained harsh. Colin stood up, so Martin took his seat and waited.

"I have no plans to arrest you, but I am here to discuss a serious matter with you. It will be in your best interests to answer my questions truthfully, without holding anything back."

Martin felt his pulse rising, a few beads of nervous perspiration welling up on his forehead. Mentally he ran through everything he had done over the last few weeks, well, as much as he could remember, but he could not recall committing an actual crime.

"Today, you visited a Pinkcast facility. To be precise, their London distribution centre. Am I correct?"

"Yes."

"Could you tell me the reason for your visit there today?"

Warily, Martin, still fearing he must have unwittingly committed some sort of criminal act, explained the reason. He began with the video call from his school friend and the company's concern that someone had stolen industrial secrets from them, someone with whom Martin had recently been in contact. Hence the visit to the depot to get some more details about the alleged industrial spy.

"Are you being employed by Pinkcast to investigate the alleged spy?"

"No, it was just I had previously visited the person they suspect."

"You're being very cagey about the suspect being an industrial spy. Why did you contact him in the first place?"

Martin wondered if his caution was looking like an admission of guilt. He changed his approach to being a little more cavalier, explaining the favour was for a friend. Reluctantly he talked about Terry's fixation with UFOs and aliens. Martin thought he sounded completely mad talking about digital watches, flying saucers and aliens on earth, none of which garnered any reaction from the constable.

"Okay, thank you for the explanation. I'll leave you both in peace. Thanks, Colin." Without another word, the constable stood up and shook hands with Colin and Martin before leaving.

"What was that all about?" Martin asked as soon as Dan closed the door behind him.

"Your guess is as good as mine. I'll give you everything I know, but that is not a lot, I warn you."

Martin picked up a pencil and started tapping it against his hand in a nervous fashion while waiting for Colin to explain.

"I get this call from D.C. Green earlier, referring to my poking around in the database for a grey BMW and telling me I was a naughty boy for doing it. Something that had already been pointed out to me, I should add.

"He then says, do I know a Martin Hayden? Well, although I was tempted to deny such a thing, I judged it best, to be honest. I told him yes, I helped with some of your cases. Don't worry; I made Hayden Investigations sound very professional indeed. I'm such a good fibber. Anyway, he then asks, was the BMW owner request on behalf of you? Well, now I am thinking this could be awkward for you. Are they going to think about pressing charges? For your own good, I confessed it was you who had asked me."

"Thank you, Colin."

"No problem, it's what friends are for. Lucky for you, he did then tell me that he wasn't worried about the BMW.

What he did want to know, informally, was exactly why you were at Pinkcast today. Hence the visit. The rest, you know."

"Well, not exactly, Colin; he was not forthcoming as to the reason he wanted to ask why I was there. What do you think?"

Colin brushed his chin between his hands. Martin was unsure if he was thinking or simply concerned that his stubble was beginning to show through.

"Hard to say what their interest is. D.C. Green, I know, is attached to a specialist group targeting high-value crimes, which gives us a little clue as to what he is up to. The fact that you only went to the depot this morning and they are asking me about you by lunchtime tells me a little more. They clearly have the depot under strong surveillance. I would also think they are not fully sure who they should be keeping an eye on. They're watching the place for some reason and you walked across their sights. That's all I can tell you for sure."

That was not much help for Martin, whose mood began to darken once again.

It had all began with what should have been a simple favour for Ernie. Now Martin found himself caught between aliens, industrial spies, grey BMWs and becoming a person of interest in a police investigation. He thought this might be a good time to walk away and let everyone else sort things out. A simple phone call to Ernie, 'your brother is fine, not being taken for a ride', which should end it all here and now.

***

Having two older sisters, Susan always felt that she could never match them, however hard she tried. Part of that was because, as children, they could always do things better than her. They were riding bikes competently while Susan was still clinging onto her stabilisers. They were busy making up their faces while Susan was told she was too young to put on lipstick. They were at work and earning money, which they could spend as they wished, while Susan relied on family handouts, aka pocket money.

None of this was helped by the fact Susan was the one perceived to be lacking in intelligence. Although they all went to the same comprehensive school, her sisters were always in the 'A' stream. As Susan progressed through her school years, teachers were keen to point out she was not doing as well as her older sisters had in that year. Hence, Susan spent a lot of time smoking, kissing boys and doing the odd bit of shoplifting during her period of statutory education.

One thing the sisters did have in common was the making of poor choices when it came to boyfriends. Not one of them was astute in the art of picking partners. Although Susan might have had a few disreputable boyfriends, at least she had not yet married one, unlike her sisters.

Her eldest sister married first to a man, two years her senior, a qualified plumber, reasonably attractive. They had secured a mortgage and were buying a house together, which was considered a rare family achievement, coming from their council house in Tooting. Within the first year of their marriage, her sister proudly announced she was pregnant. Susan was going to be called Auntie Sue; she liked the sound of that. The baby was born, and everyone stood around the cot 'cooing', 'arring' and making up nonsensical words. Susan always thought that uttering strange words must scare the heebie-jeebies out of all babies.

Appearances can, however, be deceptive. The loving husband and father was not only doing plumbing, but he was also doing every female customer he could. In the end, it was not so much the unfaithful behaviour that upset her elder sister, more the fact he was offering exceptionally large discounts for his work in exchange for sex. All this resulted in weeks of arguments, followed by months of expensive divorce lawyers. Finally, the house was repossessed and the older sister ended up back in a council flat with a baby whose first words were 'cheating bastard'!

Whatever happens, older siblings are still those that younger siblings turn to for advice, even if their own experience does not generate a great deal of confidence.

The baby was now six years old, loved to see Auntie Sue, had grown out of her 'bastard' phase and was sound asleep in her bedroom as Susan opened a bottle of white wine and poured two large glasses.

"He had no right," Susan's sister said after hearing the reason for her younger sister's visit. "Mum was on life support and three of us wanted it kept going. Her children, each and every one, wanted her to have a chance. Whatever the doctors told us, we knew Mum far better than they did. She was always a fighter, never gave up. She would have pulled through, I'm sure. So what right did Dad have to tell them to turn off the machine and kill her."

It was a rationale that Susan had heard before and had once subscribed to. She was no longer sure the children had the moral right to overrule their father.

"He was married to her. He was losing as much, if not more, than we were going to lose. He was just following the doctor's advice. Isn't that something we always do? But it's not about turning off a machine," Susan continued, "isn't it about forgiveness? We all make bad choices. Maybe with hindsight, we would have acted differently. All I am saying is, the past is the past. He's still our father. How long can we punish him? How long can we punish ourselves? He'll die one day, and then what? Do we stamp on his grave shouting good riddance, or do we look down and regret that we never said, 'we love you, dad?' That's all parents want for all their sacrifices and hard work bringing us kids up, a bit of love in return, not exclusion from our lives and their grandchildren."

Susan watched as her sister refilled her wine glass, took a large mouthful and concluded, "You're still my baby sister, just not so much of a baby anymore. It's up to you. If you're unhappy not talking to Dad, then I am the last person who wants to see you unhappy."

Susan took that to be a nod of approval, but she was on her own.

***

"Why?" was all Susan asked.

Martin had asked Colin to join them in the office first thing and made sure that Susan was planning to be there as well and not shopping as she had suggested she might be.

Now he had their attention, Martin began, "As far as I can see, the couple do not appear to be stealing money or any such thing from Ernie's brother. Terry asked about a BMW driver, and we found out. Terry is not giving anything, secrets or otherwise, back. We have done Grant's bidding by asking. The police are now sniffing around, onto something. Is it time to walk away from this?"

Susan answered, "There is something going on here and, like it or not, we are being drawn into the centre of it. Why abandon it now?"

"She has a point, Martin," Colin contributed. "The police will no doubt do their investigation and if a crime has been committed, I am sure they will manage well enough without us. But it could be that we get embroiled in that enquiry and end up on the wrong side of the law if we are viewed as co-conspirators.

"Nice pink watch, by the way, Suzie Baby. Beware the man bringing gifts; you can never be sure what he is after." Colin laughed as he examined the new Pinkcast watch on her wrist.

"Well complicated to set up, loads of buttons and stuff. I think I could ask it to do my makeup and it would happily crack on with the lipstick."

Martin decided to finish his bacon bap while Colin and Susan began debating some new waterproof lipstick that Colin felt was over-priced and in a range of colours he considered too gaudy. Susan disagreed; she liked the one called 'Brazen Blue', the perfect lipstick for a gothic night out.

"I am sorry to interrupt you two and your fascinating discussion. However, please, can we get back to the aliens you seem to want to continue investigating?"

"Yes, we do," Susan explained, "because we said to Ernie, who was concerned that his brother might be in trouble, that we would help. At present, there are a lot of things that make not the slightest sense. That is why we should poke around a little more so that when we go back to Ernie, we can offer him some solid information as to what might be going on."

"Just to be clear," Martin sounded unsure, "you want to investigate further?"

Susan nodded firmly; she had resolved to carry on. Martin guessed that would be her answer.

"As I suspected, so last night I did some thinking and made some notes." He laid out a sheet of paper on the desk. On it, he had written a flow chart that contained the key elements of the last few days as he saw them. As he flattened the sheets of A4 that he had sellotaped together, he missed the expression of surprise and disbelief on both Susan and Colin's faces.

"Does your sudden eagerness to carry out an investigation happen to coincide with your wish to impress an old classmate?" Colin asked. Susan smiled and nodded in agreement.

"My motives are my concern." Martin then pressed on, "Okay then, let's get cracking. First, I agree with Susan's question yesterday concerning where Terry gets enough money to live and pay for all the research he purports to be doing? Unfortunately, I cannot see an easy way of levering information out of him. Ernie might not be the sharpest knife in the draw, but he did point out he was uncomfortable about the couple Janice and Luke. Now having seen them, I agree they look suspect."

"I'd go more with weird, but suspect works for now," Susan contributed as she leaned forward, looking at the flow chart.

"They could well be the weak link in all this, so we need to find out more about them. That way, we may be able to get more information about Terry and what is really going on at his house. Ernie talked about them going away and staying at posh hotels, all paid for by Terry. Maybe we could find out more about which hotels and what they do there. What do you two think?"

Susan grabbed her phone and spoke as she scrolled through the screens, "Funny you should say that, last night I was looking up their Facebook page. I noticed Janice was on it all the time we were at Terry's. Security is not their strong point. All their posts are visible, even though I am not their friend. Plus, they check-in, I would guess, everywhere they go. From that, I can see that every other week they are at a four-star hotel outside Ashford. If they stick to their routine, they will be there this weekend. We could arrive and see what they are up to, maybe even meet a few aliens?"

"Sounds like a good plan, Martin. Watch them from afar and see what they are doing exactly. I didn't meet them, but they do not sound like four-star people. Every other weekend? That is odd, as well as expensive, I would guess." Colin pointed out.

"As you've not met them yet, Colin, that is going to change. Susan and I cannot roll up there as they know us already, but they don't know you."

"Well, you know I'd be more than happy to spend a weekend away and observe a couple of weirdos. The downside is, Martin, you may have noticed, I do tend to stand out in a crowd, let alone a four-star hotel."

"He has a point, Martin," Susan indicated the obvious to Martin.

Martin had already thought about that problem. "Well, here is the clever bit Colin, you'll be in disguise. You'll arrive, suitcase in hand, dressed as a man. An everyday, regular, executive type of guy."

Colin leaned back in his chair. A disappointed look appeared on his face as he spoke, "I'm sorry, Martin, my most macho clothes consist of a pair of baggy jeans and a very butch-looking check shirt. Apart from my funeral suit, which I keep in case of, well, funerals obviously, they're the nearest thing I have to anything a man would wear."

"You have no other men's clothes except your funeral suit?" Martin sounded surprised. Last night he had planned that Colin, dressed casually as a man, could watch the couple and discover what they were up to. Who better to go than an ex-policeman? Martin had just assumed that he would still have some clothes that matched his true gender.

"Zilch at this present time. Yet," Colin paused as his mind seemed to wander. "Yet, if I am going on assignment, then I guess a disguise would be in order. It's about time the male part of my wardrobe caught up with my female side. I'll pop along later to Marks and Spencer, just the place for an old bloke like me who prefers elasticated trousers nowadays," Colin pointed out.

"Okay, we are all set. Colin, you go shopping while Susan does some work making you a hotel reservation. Now that is a role reversal if ever I heard one."

"Martin, if you spent last night planning your flowchart of clues, were you planning to carry on anyway?"

"Sometimes, Susan, you just have to accept the inevitable."

CHAPTER SIX

Even with an elastic waist, the trousers still felt uncomfortable. Putting his discomfort to one side, Colin walked confidently into the hotel foyer, pulling a small green suitcase on wheels behind him. A young female receptionist greeted him with an insincere large white smile. She wore a badge that let the world know that she, Hetty, was a customer assistant.

The 'Four Oaks Hotel' at one time had been a large country house owned by a farming family whose wealth overshadowed the small village which neighboured it and its grounds. Colin liked the dark oak panelling around the room, together with the carved bannisters on the wide staircase to the left of the reception desk. The walls were lined with large oil paintings of robust-looking men from past centuries. He liked old buildings full of character and history. Every room must have had countless stories it could share, if only they could talk. He detested the modern glass and steel monstrosities that had sprung up over the past few decades.

Without losing her broad smile, Hetty went through the opening times for the restaurant, breakfast hours, how to contact room service. She also touched on the other hotel services available: laundry, spa, towel loan for the swimming pool. The availability of the gym was limited, so she would advise him to book if he wanted to make use of the modern gym facilities. Colin thanked her, took his key, then followed her detailed directions to his room. Walking upstairs in trousers, he found restrictive; his leggings had far more stretch.

Colin had arrived at the hotel as early as he could to ensure that he was sitting in the reception reading a book while waiting for the couple to arrive. Although he had never met them, the description he had drawn out of Martin and Suzie Baby indicated that they should not be that hard to spot. A steady flow of customers walked up to Hetty's desk; all were treated to her smile and spiel. Colin was impressed that she recited her instructions word perfect each time. He wondered if there was an Academy Award system for hotel staff. If there was, he would happily recommend her for it.

After reading five chapters of his book, finally, the odd couple walked in. Hetty's greeting was a little less formal, which suggested she recognised the regulars. From the conversation that Colin overheard, they planned to have dinner at 7.30. They requested that tea and sandwiches be served in the reception area in thirty minutes, allowing them time to unpack. Colin waited, and twenty-five minutes later, Janice and Luke Quinn took a sofa just a few feet away from him while they waited for the arrival of their afternoon high tea.

It had been a few years since Colin had worked any sort of surveillance operation on his own. As a detective constable, many of his days had been spent following or watching, gathering evidence, proving connections. Sitting in the hotel, appearing to read a book, ignited a feeling he had not felt in years. He began to recall the techniques and the operations he had taken part in. He enjoyed his days catching criminals. He relished seeing innocent victims get justice. Today was not the same as those years, so Colin was unsure what to expect unless a real alien appeared and checked in with Hetty. As with most surveillance projects, not a lot happened. The couple finished their sandwiches and tea before leaving and walking upstairs, no doubt to their room.

He was ready for them later, having booked his table earlier. He found himself sitting three tables away from them as they settled down for their evening meal. He watched them choose food, chat, sip wine, laugh occasionally and saw Janice regularly examining her phone. They were on their dessert course. A chef was beside their table setting alight some flamboyant dish when Janice looked up and waved at another couple, who had just entered the restaurant. Both couples chatted and smiled together for a few moments before the second couple walked to their table in the corner of the restaurant. Colin watched the interaction. Having eaten as slowly as he could, he had only now finished his main dish of Chicken Kiev with fresh garden vegetables.

Although Janice and Luke obviously knew the other couple, they were not friendly enough to eat together. The new pair looked average. Colin could see nothing that stood out to him. Mid-thirties, possibly married as both wore wedding rings. However, they appeared to be dressed differently. The man was in a smart suit; the woman wore faded jeans and a purple blouse, with what appeared to be tiny sequins across the shoulders. Colin liked it and wondered where she might have bought it. Colin picked up his phone from the table as if he were checking a text. He took a photo of the new couple, checked it to see if they were some sort of alien illusion. They appeared on his phone to be normal human beings.

"No way!" The voice startled Colin. "D.C. Higgins, what's the old bill doing here?"

They were words that no covert police officer liked to hear, even if they were no longer active. Colin looked up to see who it was that had recognised him. It was the chef pushing his trolley back towards the kitchen, having just served the odd couple their Crêpes Suzette. The face was unfamiliar to Colin and his uncertainty must have shown.

"Ha, you don't remember me, do you, Mr Higgins?"

"No, yet I sense you are about to remind me."

"Danny Holloway, seven years for making a cash withdrawal from a Barclays ATM."

"Ah, now I remember. Although, as I recall, you used a JCB digger instead of your pin number to get the money?"

"Never was much good with figures, Mr Higgins. What you doing here?"

"More like what are you doing here dressed up as if you're doing a real job."

"It's all legit, Mr Higgins. I'm the head chef here, got three others working for me back out in the kitchen, nice little number."

"When did you learn to cook? I always thought of you as an Indian takeaway kind of guy."

"In Wandsworth, doing my time. I still laugh about what you told me, don't expect to go to a prison that matches your surname. Huh, that would have been handy, seven years in Holloway prison, it being a girl's prison an' all. No, did most of me time at Wandsworth, grabbing a cushy number volunteering for the kitchens; you know, a bit of extra grub and stuff. Turned out I was a little bit nifty with the old cooking lark. Took some qualifications and got meself a job here at the hotel. I now use me pin number to get my cash."

"Well, I'm glad to see you have got yourself a real job." He was genuinely pleased to see Danny away from the confines of a prison cell.

Previously, Danny was well known to all the officers at the Elephant and Castle police station. Not just for his regular appearances in court, but his wife was a bit of a celebrity with the young PCs at the time. No one could understand why she had settled down with Danny. She was tall, brunette and had at one time modelled clothes for a large mail-order company. Consequently, when it came to the time that someone needed to arrest him, there was no shortage of volunteers.

Not that arresting Danny was hard, far from it. When they had a warrant for Danny over some crime he had committed, the arresting officers would be welcomed through the door by him. He would offer them a cup of tea while he went about his routine of changing his clothes into his 'going-away' outfit and then saying a fond farewell to his wife and children. Walking out to the car with the arresting officers, he would joke that his wife had better remember to finish the decorating that he had started.

It would have been natural for Colin to ask about Danny's family, yet the assumption Danny held that Colin was still a police officer was something that he wanted to make use of.

"So, Mr Higgins, what you doing here, holiday, or is it work?"

"Can't say too much, Danny; you should know that. But tell me a little more about the couple you have just served with their dessert."

"Luke and Janice, you mean, but you must know that. Been up to no good, have they? Guessed as much, they're a strange couple, not what I would call four-star hotel people. Yet, every other weekend, they turn up here. No idea what they get up to. Spend some afternoons out and about, I'm told. Always pleasant to the staff here. Come on, Mr Higgins, just a little clue as to what they're up to, for old times' sake? Is it drugs?"

"You know I can't say a word, Danny. What about the other couple who passed by and they spoke to? The ones sitting in the corner over there," Colin nodded.

"Now there's a story, Mr Higgins. We call them the lovers. They arrive and leave separately but sign in as Mr & Mrs, which says it all, I reckon. We don't see them until the evening. Once they have had their restaurant meal, they are off back upstairs, and on goes the 'do not disturb' sign. They don't come out until tomorrow afternoon. They pay for the extended check-out time, don't you know? Only room service meals get in there to sustain them during what we all know is a lot of sexual activity. They're here every other weekend, too, same as Luke and Janice. They have got to know each other but don't appear to be friends. No wife swapping as far as I can see. To get Janice in a wife swap would be like getting a horse with three legs in the Derby. Never looked upon the lovers as being villains, Mr Higgins."

"Maybe they're not. We will have to wait and see. Luke and Janice, what do they do after their meal?"

"They're creatures of habit. They have a brandy at the table then walk into the bar and spend most of the night there before going back to their room about midnight."

"Given that information, what are the chances of me getting into their room while they are drinking at the bar?"

"Always happy to help the police, Mr Higgins. I can have a word with housekeeping. I'm sure they would be more than happy to help. I'll go and see what I can do."

"Thanks, Danny. I do appreciate your help and let me tell you, you are a good cook. That Chicken Kiev I had was absolutely delicious."

"Thanks, Mr Higgins, but to be honest, I buy them frozen from Iceland. A lot easier, and no one knows; it's all about the presentation," Danny smiled and continued on his way to the kitchen. Once shady, always shady, Colin thought.

***

The Pommelers Rest Public House in Tower Bridge Road resides alongside the famous bridge, welcoming visitors from around the world. As well as the tourists, local office workers pop in for a lunchtime drink. At any time of day, the pub is bustling with patrons talking in a variety of languages. As it was opposite their new office, it was becoming the place to frequent, when the claustrophobic office became too much for Martin and Susan. Today Colin joined them for lunch.

They listened as Colin recounted his weekend between mouthfuls of beer-battered cod and chips. He explained in chronological order the key moments of it.

"Did housekeeping really let you into their room?" Susan asked. Having already finished her bacon burger, she was eager to hear more.

"Not only did they let me into their room, but they also gave me a master key. I could have entered every room in the hotel and I can tell you I was desperate to look in as many as I could to see what people do in them. In the end, I decided it was a lot safer just to go into Janice and Luke's room; at least I knew that was going to be unoccupied, or so I thought until I walked in. At once, I realised I was not the only person in the room. There, sitting in front of the mirror, was a small purple alien with no reflection." Colin winked at Martin.

"My God!" Susan exclaimed. "Does that mean they're working for the aliens, like double agents?"

"No," Martin calmly pointed out, "I imagine they are aliens that take the form of humans and like four-star hotels."

Colin laughed loudly. "Suzie Baby, you're so gullible; that's why we love you so much."

"At times, I really hate the two of you." Susan frowned and folded her arms, annoyed with herself for falling for such a fake claim.

"Okay, that's enough, you two. Back to the room, Colin. I guess it was unoccupied. Did you find anything of interest?" Martin asked, the smile still on his face.

"The room was empty. It was a mess, I should point out. An open suitcase on the bed, no garments actually hung up, just strewn across the bed. It looked as if they had just changed their clothes and left the dirty ones on the floor. The habits of some people absolutely disgust me. I thought it best not to go into the bathroom. God knows what state that would have been in, an unflushed toilet, wouldn't surprise me."

"Ugh, Colin, can we stick to the clean bits?" Susan pleaded.

"Trust me, Suzie Baby, the room was lacking any form of cleanliness."

"Being unsanitary is not a crime," Martin pointed out. He wanted to bring the conversation back to its purpose, which was why the odd couple were visiting the hotel every other weekend. "Did you find anything of interest?" he asked eagerly.

"Well, yes, there was," Colin paused, adding a hint of drama to what he was about to reveal. "Affixed to the wall beside the mirror, which the alien was not looking into, was a map, an Ordnance Survey map of the area around the hotel, with three locations marked out to the southwest. They were numbered one, two and three. All three were within, I would say, a half a mile of each other, and each one appeared to be on a flat field."

"How do you know the fields would be flat from a map?" Susan asked.

Colin wanted to tell her the map was flat, so the fields must be; however, he decided that he had already made use of her naivety enough for one lunchtime.

"The contour lines showed them to be flat fields."

"Contour lines?" Susan asked.

"You should have spent less time behind the bike sheds with the boys and more time in class. Trust me; the fields are flat. Also, the three locations had a big circle around them, and someone had written 'possible landing sites'. Here, I took a photo."

Colin drew his phone out and showed them the photographs he had taken of the room. The three of them crowded around the small screen; he zoomed in on the relevant part of the map.

"Well, they must be the locations that Terry talked about. It's really happening," Susan pointed out. "The other couple they spoke to, could they be the aliens they're tracking, as Terry told us? This is out of this world, literally."

"Suzie Baby, I suspect that there must be an alternative explanation," Colin said as he swiped along the photos until he had the couple, nicknamed the lovers, sitting at their table.

"Do these look like aliens?" Colin asked.

Both Martin and Susan looked at the picture, then turned to each other. It was Susan who spoke first, "It's the manager from Pinkcast, Nigel."

"You know him?" Colin had not expected such a quick identification.

Martin explained that the man in the photograph was Nigel Butler, manager of the Pinkcast depot. "I am starting to think that Terry and his cohorts are into some sort of industrial espionage."

"Or Pinkcast is a front for an alien invasion," Susan added, hoping that the science fiction explanation was going to wash with Martin and Colin. It did not.

"I'm going to regret saying this," Martin admitted, "but we need to pay another visit to Pinkcast and have a quiet word with the manager. If he is having an affair, then Terry could be blackmailing him," Martin concluded.

***

They had waited for almost an hour outside Nigel Butler's office. There was going to be the chance that Nigel would not be available, but they had decided to take the risk. Upon their arrival, the security officer on the door recognised them from their previous visit and greeted them like old friends. With little formality, he handed them each a pre-made pass, which he proudly pointed out would get them through all the doors on the way to Nigel's office. He gave them some vague directions before sending Susan and Martin on their way, then quickly he was back to his game of Candy Crush.

The next obstacle was Nigel's secretary, a thin woman in her forties who spoke at a breakneck speed. Having made it perfectly clear to the two uninvited guests that Nigel does not see external personnel, as she put it, without an appointment. Martin casually let slip that he was working on behalf of Grant Fisher, who was very keen for Martin to speak to Nigel in person urgently. That nugget of information prompted her to reluctantly offer a compromise. They would just have to wait until he had finished the conference call talking to potential clients in the United States that he was currently engaged with.

Finally, Nigel emerged from his office with a wad of papers that he handed to his secretary. He added instructions that they needed forwarding to the company solicitors for scrutiny.

Nigel then turned his attention to his guests and apologised when he learned they had been waiting a while, stating that Americans talk far too much without saying anything. He ushered Susan and Martin into his office as though they were old friends while instructing his secretary to bring in refreshments. Martin thought she hid her look of displeasure well. Nigel closed his office door then quickly pointed out that he could give them just twenty minutes before he had to chair a meeting with the sales team. The office was modern, with lots of stainless steel, glass and some abstract paintings. The pink carpet matched the company branding.

The three of them sat around a small conference table that had been squeezed into a corner of the room.

"Do you have some more on Terry?" Nigel asked. He looked less confident without the company private investigator by his side. Before Martin could answer the secretary carried a tray of hot drinks for them, together with a plate of custard cream biscuits.

"We do have more, just not on Terry," Martin began. "Would I be right in thinking you stayed at the Four Oaks Hotel over the weekend?"

The colour drained away from Nigel's face leaving a pale whitewash behind. He did not answer immediately. He carefully placed his custard cream on his coffee cup saucer before answering the question he had not been expecting to hear.

"Have you been following me?"

"Not as such," Susan stepped in. "We were in the process of tracking the movements of Terry and his associates. It just so happens that your paths crossed at the Four Oaks."

"Is he having me followed then?" Nigel sounded anxious.

"Well, Susan and I do suspect that could be the case. The reason depends a lot on your viewpoint; is Terry an alien hunter or an industrial spy? I know you think the latter. Maybe if you could tell us the reason you were at the hotel, it might shed some light on the rationale Terry is keen to know about your leisure movements." Martin thought he sounded like a prig, an obnoxious one at that. It was just he had a good idea why Nigel might be at the hotel and wanted to indicate to him that he already knew the real reason.

Nigel rested his head in his hands, ruffling his hair as he did so. He looked to be a man in trouble. He stared at his reflection on the glass table for a few moments, then looked back at Martin.

"Okay, if Terry is following me, then I think it proves he is an industrial spy. He must be doing it to see what dirt he can pin on and use against me, perhaps forcing me into helping him in some way and compromising my position here."

"The question we had was why were you at the hotel with a woman?" Susan asked, already knowing the answer after Colin had shared the suspicions of the hotel staff.

"Fair enough. I think and hope my wife believes that every other weekend I must attend a company briefing as it is written into my employment contract. I need not tell you, as I can see you are both very experienced detectives, that I am having an extra-marital affair with a woman I plan to set up home with once I begin divorce proceedings. Somehow or other, Terry has uncovered that I am having an affair, and he's no doubt planning to make good use of that information in the future to blackmail me and gather more industrial secrets."

"How did you meet the other woman in your life?" Martin asked as he tried to put the abstract pieces of information together. Each time he added everything up in his mind, he came to the same conclusion, if Terry is an industrial spy and has his hands on valuable Pinkcast secrets, then why has he not gone off and sold them? Why does he appear to be still hanging around Pinkcast and its staff collecting personal information? He does not need to blackmail any member of the organisation. From Pinkcast's own admission, Terry can pop into their server whenever it suits him; such are his skills.

"Her name is Hazel. She worked here at one time; that was how we met and soon became lovers."

Martin smiled and nodded, convinced that aliens were not at the centre of all this. Equally, he was beginning to doubt that industrial espionage was the only subject of the strange goings-on.

Susan continued with the questions. "I presume she's planning to divorce her husband as well, so when are you going to go public, so to speak?"

"Well, Hazel is already divorced, but she has a number of legal bits and pieces still to sort out before we can set up home together. Hopefully not too long now." Nigel bit into his custard cream using his hand to catch the crumbs.

"Returning to Terry and the secrets he has stolen. Are they of any real use to your competitors?" Martin asked. There was something else that bothered him. The last time they visited Pinkcast, it was insisted that the private investigator employed by Pinkcast was present when they spoke to Nigel. If Nigel was such a trusted and high-ranking employee of Pinkcast, why did he need a minder?

Martin noticed a look of caution in Nigel's eyes as he thought about the question put to him.

"All commercial intellect is valuable; that's why companies protect their assets so closely."

"You can't give us even a hint of what Terry might have? Your minder is not around to hear you."

Once again, Nigel was clearly thinking about his answer. "If I told you, I'd lose my job. It's big, but I'm not the one who will tell you what it is. Maybe you should ask Terry; he might know."

Susan did not say it, yet Martin guessed what she was thinking; the big secret was aliens. Like a ball stuck between two warring tennis players, Martin realised that he needed to speak to Terry once more.

CHAPTER SEVEN

Martin had spent the entire morning in the office alone so far. Susan was visiting an optician. Recently, she found it increasingly difficult to read Martin's horoscope, which was no significant loss for Martin. Even though the prospect of wearing glasses did not suit Susan's vanity, reluctantly she made an appointment and was by now, Martin assumed, in a chair undergoing tests.

He was making good use of the quiet surroundings to research as much as he could about the way industrial spies operate. It did not take him long to see there were copious ways of gathering information, especially via computers and the internet. Something still bugged Martin; why plan to steal commercial secrets from Pinkcast and spend a lot of your time targeting that same company about UFOs and making yourself a very visible, obvious target? There was something else that was nagging at the back of Martin's mind, something that Nigel had said, 'maybe ask Terry, he might know.' Martin believed that if Terry did not know what he was stealing, then that would qualify him as an extremely poor industrial spy. There had to be something else going on here. Martin had shared his misgivings with Susan as they drove away from Pinkcast. Although she partly agreed, her theory still reflected and supported what Terry had told them; there were, in fact, aliens planning to invade the earth, a view that Martin could not subscribe to. He might humour Susan with her daily horoscope; people coming from the stars was another matter.

A voice he recognised called his name, disturbing his concentration. He turned to see the noticeable tall, blonde figure of Becky standing at the door.

"Susan told me that the office was small, but God, it's minuscule! Is there enough oxygen for you both in here?"

"No, we only work in here one at a time."

"That's very sensible, Martin; you can't be too careful. I'll keep the door open just to be safe." Becky had missed the humour in Martin's voice; she sometimes took words a little too literally.

"To what do I owe the pleasure of this visit?" He watched Becky standing in the doorway. He was convinced that she genuinely believed that she would be asphyxiated in an instant if she dared to step into the office.

"Susan was going to help me do my C.V. for a job. Now I have just remembered she is getting her eyes tested this morning, isn't she? She did say to come in the afternoon, silly me."

"Are you moving away from your bank job? You've been there a while now."

Becky remained in the doorway, holding onto the door handle while she looked around the office. She decided there was not much to see.

"Cuts in the banking industry, more business online, fewer people are going into banks. It's a changing world, Martin. I'm being made redundant at the end of the month with three months redundancy plus my holiday pay. So now I'm looking around."

"I know you are good at figures and the money stuff; it should not be too hard for you to find another job with one of the other banks."

"Is it alright if I sit down, Martin? These heels are killing my feet." Without waiting for an answer, she risked instant death from suffocation and sat down, ensuring the door remained open by placing her chair in the doorway. "Banks aren't like they used to be. They're not so much about customer accounts but selling mortgages, insurance, and the like. That's not for me, so Susan suggested that we sit down and have a brainstorming session, see what other jobs I could do. I was thinking of gambling."

"What! Putting money on horses and stuff?"

"No, silly, working for one of the big gambling companies. They employ these people – traders – who work out the odds and do other clever stuff with figures. They also watch out for unusual betting movements. I think that would suit me. You sit in this big office and watch loads of TV screens; it's pretty cool."

"How do you know all this?"

"I dated a bookie a couple of weeks ago. I've dumped him now; he told me he owned a chain of betting shops; like most men, he lied. To be fair, he was contributing to the upkeep of numerous betting shops, but that is not the same as owning them. He also spent his time losing money at the dogs, not my sort of guy. But he did tell me he once went to the offices of a large online bookies and told me what he saw. Do you think that would suit me, being a trader?"

"Well, Becky, you've helped us out a couple of times over financial stuff, plus you do have a detecting gene in you. It might be fun."

Becky opened her handbag, pulled out some sheets of paper, unfolded them and proudly handed one to Martin.

"This is the one I want to apply for, but I need to upload my C.V., which needs updating and Susan is good at that. You must know, you saw hers when she got the job here."

"I did, Becky, but a lot of it did turn out to be a little, how shall I say, embellished."

"I know Susan likes to use long words. What do you think?" She encouraged Martin to read the job description she had.

Martin read aloud the preferred skills and experience the post required.

"Proven analytical, numerical, problem-solving skills, with a wide-ranging sporting knowledge." Martin wondered about her knowledge of sports.

"Ability to multitask and manage multiple concurrent issues shifting focus and priority as needed." This one he knew she would struggle on, she veered off in the middle of a conversation on a regular basis.

"Keen eye for detail." Maybe her strong point, he had often heard her picking holes in the fashion sense of other women.

"Systematic approach to work and ability to manage your workload efficiently." He guessed this would be a failure.

The last skill, "Ability to communicate clearly and concisely," she could achieve. Not that Martin was going to point out her potential failings, he knew she had a great many skills. He did, however, want to point out a slight shortcoming with the job.

"It says here that the job is based in Sliema."

"Yeah, I might have to travel, but a job is a job, Martin. Not all of us have the luxury of being able to work around the corner from where we live."

"That may be so, Becky, but it does say Sliema, Malta. That's a bit of a commute."

"Malta, like the island?" She snatched the sheet back from Martin and squinted her eyes. "I thought Malta said Morden; maybe I need glasses."

"Maybe you should have joined Susan for an eye test this morning."

Becky screwed up the job details and threw them into a wastepaper basket beside Martin with a degree of accuracy that alarmed him. He wanted to suggest that she might consider becoming a basketball player, for no better reason than he wanted to see her in shorts and a tight t-shirt but decided against such a suggestion.

"Do you have any jobs I could do, Martin? I'd like to work for you. I know we get on well."

That he could not deny. They had spent two very boozy sessions in bars recently. She was good company, attractive and easy to make fun of. But working alongside her day in day out, Martin was not so sure. Yes, he needed someone to look after his accounts. Still, he wondered if Becky would be up to such a task, dealing with investments, capital, tax returns and all manner of financial instruments that he little understood himself.

"Not really, I'm sorry to say, you know we are just a small company with not a lot going on most of the time."

"That's a shame! Susan mentioned you were looking for an accountant. I'm good with figures and even a part-time job would help. She said you were going to see some old fart who was retiring that day you wore a kilt."

"Kilt, Becky? I'm not sure what you are talking about."

"Susan said you did a video dressed as a Maris Piper, so I pictured you in a kilt and playing the bagpipes."

"Ah, I see. No, a Maris Piper is a potato and the old fart you referred to is our family accountant who is retiring. He brought some younger, well only by a few years, replacement, who he suggested would be good to take over our family accounts, you know tax and stuff. I'd love to offer you a job, but I think you need to have many qualifications. Sorry, Becky."

"Not to worry. Tell Susan I'll call her later. No point sorting my CV unless I have a place to send it. Nice to see you again, Martin. Fancy a quick drink?"

Tempted though he was, he declined, knowing that a 'Becky quick drink' could last long into the night.

***

Throughout the journey to Greenwich, Martin listened to Susan recounting what had happened at her eye test in alarming detail.

The half-hour wait for the optician would not have been so bad had she not been sitting next to an old lady waiting to have her hearing checked. The result was Susan having to talk to her in a loud voice which she was sure most of the shop overheard. Then the creepy optician, who kept calling her Susannah, complimented her on her beautiful eyes and had a habit of dropping contraptions into her lap, which he was more than pleased to retrieve. Susan then resorted to - what she described as a class one defence tactic - mentioning, as casually as she could, that she hoped he would not be too long as she had an appointment at the sexually transmitted disease clinic shortly to try and establish just what her rash was. That succeeded in speeding up the examination without any further touchy-feely action.

As they pulled into Terry's road, Susan broached another subject. "Maybe you should consider giving Becky a job. You said yourself that she's good at figures and getting information about people's financial situation. What about being your accountant thingy that you are looking for? Didn't you say your bloke was going to retire?"

"I did say those things, and I do need a bloke, as you put it, to look after the family affairs, but Becky is a girl at a bank, not a qualified accountant."

"Well, at least you can trust her, which is more than can be said about some accountants I have heard of who have run off with their client's money. She was more than just a counter girl at the bank; she was in some sort of special division. She has always wanted to get into bank fraud, well, not the crime, I mean the department at the bank. You could do a lot worse, plus she is a fast learner."

Martin edged his car carefully into a parking space that was only just big enough for it. "I'm not sure, our retiring family accountant, I know, spent hours and hours on our family finances each year; that's why he was so expensive. I don't honestly think Becky would be up to the job." He switched off the engine. "Right, let's go and have another word with Terry."

The engine of Martin's car had not even cooled before he was starting it once again; such was the swiftness of their visit. Ashley had answered the door, scowled when he saw them and offered just a curt 'hello', before continuing to bite into the brown bread sandwich he was eating. Martin could not make out the filling; the only clue was a matching brown spread of some sort oozing out from the edges and running over his fingers. From time to time, during the short conversation and between bites, Ashley wiped his fingers on his already grubby t-shirt.

"We're here to see Terry," Susan informed the scruffy doorkeeper.

"That'll be a little problematic for you; he's not here."

"I thought he never left the house?" Martin pointed out. Now he had to wait for a reply as Ashley finished a mouthful of sandwich.

"He does go out occasionally, couldn't stay in the same house forever; that would be like a prison sentence." Ashley dislodged a lump of brown bread from between his teeth and continued as he wiped his hand on his t-shirt. "Sorry, you missed him."

"Any idea when he'll be back?" Martin asked, feeling a little queasy watching Ashley eat in a manner that he considered uncouth.

"No, he's an adult and can please himself. And even if I did, I would not tell either of you. Being friends of Pinkcast, just turning up out of the blue. Pinkcast with whom we are locked in intellectual combat. There is no reason to trust either of you, Terry might be a little soft to people's sob stories, but I'm not. Have a nice day." He closed the door, leaving Martin and Susan lost for words.

***

"What was that stuff he was eating?" Martin asked.

"It looks like poo; it is a nut spread, sweet, sticks to your teeth like glue," Susan informed Martin as the two of them sat on a bench overlooking the Thames in the shadow of the Cutty Sark eating their own purchased sandwiches. "It's strange that Terry was not there having told us he never leaves his house. Maybe he has been taken by the aliens."

"If he had, I guess Ashley would have disintegrated us with one of the ray guns he, no doubt, keeps under his pillow."

"Do you think so?"

Martin ignored her answer and continued to pick out the fatty bits from his BLT sandwich, which pleased the ever-increasing number of pigeons congregating at his feet. He mulled the last couple of days around his head. Taking out the alien angle, which Martin thought was just plain stupid, there was possible industrial espionage, a manager having an affair and for some reason the police were watching the Pinkcast depot. No doubt they recorded his and Susan's second visit to the depot and he wondered what they might make of that. Stealing secrets was at the top of Martin's list now and he wanted to see Terry again so he could ask more questions. It was just how to find him; Ashley was undoubtedly not going to help.

"What about Ernie? He might know where Terry is," Martin asked Susan as she brushed the breadcrumbs off her jeans, creating another surge of excitement amongst the pigeons.

"Maybe, I can ask him. I said I would pop round to his place sometime as I have some old cat stuff he said he would like for Money."

Martin frowned, "You're selling cat stuff?"

"No, silly, his cat is called Money. It's my sister's, her cat died and she has all these cat toys; well, it's more like a funny tree house thing which the cat climbs up and down, plus there is a place for them to sleep. Ernie said that his cat Money would love one of those. I can take it around and then ask a few questions about where his brother might be."

"Good plan, Susan; I like your train of thought."

"Another good plan is you taking on Becky as your money manager. She would be good. She's not just a counter girl; she's some sort of backroom analyst, dealing with lots of figures and stuff. As I said, she wanted to move into their fraud section, but they reckoned she would be a distraction to all the blokes there. Now I remember, financial analyst, that's her job title, whatever that might be."

"A financial analyst, are you sure?"

"Well, I have been known to get things wrong in the past, but I'm sure that was what she told me once. Us girls don't talk about work much unless it involves a good-looking bloke," Susan laughed.

***

Money walked around the apparatus with typical feline apprehension as he watched the newly erected scratching post with a built-in platform, dangling toys and a cosy looking box that looked to be an ideal place for a cat to sleep. It smelt of another cat! Money wondered if his food provider might be getting another feline; he did not like to share anything.

"I think he will get used to it. Money has always been a very nervous cat; that is his way. He never goes out, stays in the flat the whole time," Ernie tried to make an excuse. He had hoped that Money would jump straight up onto the platform, then snuggle down and have a snooze. Ernie wanted that to happen to please Susan, who, in his opinion, had been kind enough to come all the way over to Peckham and was now refusing anything by way of a thank you. He had, however, made her a cup of tea.

On the other hand, Susan did not care in the slightest if Money liked his new toy or not. She was just glad to get it out of her own home. Her sobbing sister had dumped every piece of cat paraphernalia on her for the simple reason she was devastated at the death of her cat. Susan had thrown most of it out, apart from the tins of cat food, which she placed in a food bank basket at the supermarket. It was fortunate that she had talked with Ernie and learnt that he had a cat as only the day before she had planned to smash the damn thing to pieces and push it into her rubbish bin before the next collection.

She sat alongside Ernie on a compact couch covered with a floral design fabric. It was the sort of design one of her ageing aunties might adore. Considering Ernie was a bachelor who lived on his own, the flat was spotless and the expected cat pee smell was not detectable in the slightest. Not only was the flat clean but it was highly organised. The wall to Susan's right was lined with shelves containing books that were carefully arranged in height order, the highest being on the left of the shelf and then gradually dropping in height until the last book on the right was a small Observer's Book of Butterflies. The shelf below contained numerous small music tape cassettes, each one neatly labelled, and she guessed they were stored in alphabetical order.

Finally, the bottom two shelves were filled with VHS tapes. The left-hand side included some pre-recorded films and TV series. The right-hand side contained more videos, no doubt recorded by Ernie, each one deftly marked. As she looked around the flat, everything was symmetric and tidy, with not a speck of dust to be seen.

Even the teacups, a teapot, milk jug and sugar bowl Ernie had laid out carefully on the rectangular coffee table in front of her. The Eternal Beau patterned crockery was something, once again, her auntie would have loved. Susan picked up a biscuit from the plate and examined it.

"A Lincoln biscuit; I haven't seen one of these in years."

Ernie carefully put his cup and saucer down. "I know, very much a favourite of mine, which, as you say, is ridiculously hard to get your hands on. When I was at Sidcup Hospital for my annual check-up, I discovered that the

Friends of Sidcup Hospital have a little shop there. I like to support those kind people, so I bought a cup of tea as I was early for my appointment. Low and behold, there on the shelf were packets of Lincoln biscuits. I occasionally just pop in there to purchase a packet."

Susan finished her biscuit before she congratulated him on discovering the increasingly rare biscuit that had been a favourite for her since childhood. "Martin and I have been trying to make contact with your brother Terry. We just have a couple of questions for him, but he has gone off somewhere. You wouldn't know where he might have gone, would you?"

Ernie's face changed; he looked a tad more nervous than he had earlier. "He hasn't done anything wrong again, has he? What with the other detective and now you and Martin all wanting to ask him questions? Mother would be so disappointed if she were alive," he added.

"No, nothing like that. We just want to confirm a couple of things," Susan reassured as she watched his face shift from nervous to melancholy.

"The problem has always been that we as a family have never been that close. As the older brother, I was always the one in charge when Mother was out working. I have never felt comfortable ordering people about, especially my two younger brothers, both of whom always had a stronger character than me.

"I would be the last person that Terry would talk to about his plans. He always did his own thing, regardless of anything I might say or advise. I have no idea where he might be. Our other brother, James, might be able to help you."

"There are three of you?"

"Yes, Mother had three boys. She did have a girl that would have been the youngest of us all, but sadly she died within a few days of being born. I think that drove a wedge between my mother and father. Father left us all soon after we had buried little Judith. I was the firstborn, James the middle son and Terry the youngest. James and Terry always seemed to gang up on me. I think they resented me being the older brother and always in charge of them. As the years went on, James and Terry were close for a while, but they're not so much now. I'm not sure how much communication they have with each other, but James might know where Terry has gone. It might even be that Terry has just gone away for a few days and will be back soon. Can your questions wait, or are they important?"

"We like to get things sorted out and make sure that couple aren't pulling the wool over Terry's eyes. Do you have a phone number for James, or where we could meet him?"

Ernie knew exactly where Susan might find James. He gave a work address for James, a workplace that Susan thought to be very unusual.

***

While Susan was delivering cat paraphernalia to Ernie, Martin had another essential task to carry out. He knew it was a wild idea and some would consider it to be utterly foolish, but he preferred to think of it as inspired. Sitting in the Hanging Grapes wine bar, just behind London Bridge station, he began the interview with a question which he hoped would make him sound knowledgeable to the potential candidate. That was the downside of talking to a specialist who you want to work for you; they would always know more than you about the subject of the question. They had to as the only reason you were going to pay them good money was to do something you had little time or knowledge of.

In the past, Martin had been surprised by the high fees that his mother paid each year to their accountant. Fees for dealing with their tax issues, together with ensuring investments were providing sufficient return, working out capital gains taxes and recording tax-deductible expenses, all the things that bored Martin. However, their old accountant appeared to be doing a good job. Not that Martin or his mother would know if the job he was doing was good or bad.

It might not have been the most professional place to carry out an interview. Still, Martin wanted to feel at least a little comfortable in the environment, even if he was going to ask questions to which he was not exactly sure what the responses should be.

"How would you go about ensuring our family investments were maximising potential return without attracting excessive tax liabilities?" Martin asked, having read a similar phrase on the internet while he was attempting to build a vocabulary that gave him at least a bit of gravitas.

He watched as Becky took a sip from her white wine, no doubt giving herself time to build a credible answer.

She then proceeded to speak for almost five minutes, some of which Martin understood, some he was not sure of and some sounded like a foreign language. When Becky finished, she smiled, sipped her wine again, and then asked, "Do you want to talk about modelling of equity, debt or M&A transactions? Well, maybe merger and acquisition transactions might not apply to your circumstances, but I can tell you about them if you wish?"

Martin nodded. As Becky continued, he made small notes of her words, hoping that he could then use them on his mother to make her see the good sense in employing Becky as their family accountant.

He was now convinced that Becky could do the job. When he learned from Susan that she worked as a financial analyst at the bank, he had begun to ponder the idea of employing her. He would be the first to admit that Becky was, to put it mildly, a little weird in general conversation. Becky, who thought a Maris Piper played in a Scottish band, well, she might well think like that. She liked to drink, often to excess and dressed nothing like their current accountant. Her weirdness carried forward in a different and better way when she began to talk figures, accounts, money and investments. Her focus changed and she became as sharp and direct as any professional. Figures and money were Becky's 'thing'. They were her special gift and she was a lot more fun than a boring old fart sitting in an office punching his fat fingers onto a calculator keyboard. It was just convincing his mother that might be the problem. Even

119

though she had delegated the task of finding a replacement to him, his choice might cause a few raised eyebrows.

CHAPTER EIGHT

"You don't have to come along with me. It's maybe not the best place to visit, what with your mother being ill in hospital," Susan offered, as Martin drove past a wobbly cyclist before turning left towards their destination. He looked towards her with a warm smile, then returned his gaze to the road as he spoke.

"I do appreciate your concern and it is sweet of you, but she is not dead yet. Avoiding crematoriums for the rest of my life is not going to be practical. I am sure a few ageing uncles will pop their clogs soon and my presence will be required, no doubt, with a robust mother. The only time I would like to avoid going to the crematorium is when I am the one in the box."

"I just thought...."

"James works at a crematorium, so we'll go and see him there. I just think it strange that Ernie did not give you his home address, or suggest that we meet him there."

"To be truthful, I don't think Ernie knew exactly where his brother currently lives. He first offered me one address, then withdrew it saying that he might have moved recently."

"And working in a waiting room?" Martin queried once again, just as he had ever since Susan had told him that, according to Ernie, his brother worked in the crematorium waiting room, which seemed an odd place to work. Maybe, Martin considered, James might be some sort of usher or even a professional mourner if there were such a thing.

It was apparent from the outside that the waiting room was no more than a painted portacabin that had been stuck to the side of the original 1930s building. It provided some sort of space where arriving funeral-goers did not get caught up with the mourners from the previous cremation.

The room was uncomfortably warm, with just a few plain wooden chairs around the edges of it. One corner had a bright shiny vending machine offering confectionery, snacks and soft drinks, should any mourner wish to avoid a noisy rumbling stomach during the quietest parts of the service.

As Martin and Susan stood by the door examining the people in the room, they looked in the hope that James would stand out against the ten or so mourners who were milling around in small groups. At the back of Martin's mind, he imagined that James would be wearing a hi-vis jacket. More and more, the hi-vis was becoming a sign of authority and leadership, the danger being the more people wearing one for work, the less likely they would seem to be powerful. There was not one hi-vis jacket to be seen or even a staff uniform of any sort amongst the group of adults softly talking, being polite to each other. Martin decided that instead of walking around asking for James, he would address them all; it was a small enough space.

"Excuse me," he started hoping to attract their attention. "Sorry to interrupt, we are looking for James; we just need a quick word." Martin waited for a reaction. He got one instantly.

Everyone turned towards him. All of them were scowling. One woman started to sob and buried her face in the shoulder of the man she was standing next to. Blocking the front of the vending machine was a plump man with a grey handlebar moustache; his cheeks took on a red hue.

"If this is your idea of a joke, young man, I would suggest that it is in extremely poor taste. Frankly, dressed the way you both are, you have no reason to be here. It might be better if you both leave and take your foul sense of humour with you."

Martin did accept that he was not dressed to attend a funeral but suggesting that asking about an employee was being in poor taste, he would take issue with. "It was a simple question; it just needs a simple answer."

With that, the grey handlebar moustache seemed to twitch uncontrollably and the face behind it redden still further. "We are here to say goodbye to James, my beloved brother."

"So that must make you Ernie's brother?" Susan unhelpfully added to the confusion in her mind as well as the others in the room.

It was then that a tall man in his early forties with a receding hairline stepped towards Martin and Susan, his arms outstretched as if he was planning to direct a herd of cows back to a field. "Don't worry, I'll sort this," he said.

"Thank you, Derek," said the red-faced moustached man.

Derek ushered Susan and Martin outside into the cool air and away from the portacabin.

"How were we to know that James was dead and that he had another brother?" Susan pleaded. "Honestly, Derek, we meant no harm in there."

The tall man with the receding hairline took a quick glance over his shoulder before standing closer to them.

"First of all, I am not Derek," he started, as he pulled a packet of cigarettes from his pocket and lit one, inhaling deeply and blowing the smoke up above his head.

"Who are you then?" Martin asked.

"I'm James, Ernie's brother."

"Not the dead James?"

"No, he's no doubt on his way here in a box and about to be burnt, and nowt to do with Ernie or me."

Martin interjected, "Hold on, you are not Derek, you are James, not the dead James, but Ernie's brother. But you know the dead James? And, you work here?"

"That will be a yes, yes, yes, no, no. As you know my brother, I think it will be a lot easier and quicker for me to explain just what I am doing here."

He beckoned them to walk further away from the portacabin as a door opened and a young man called out, "Everything okay, Derek?"

"No problem," James, aka Derek, called as they all continued to move away.

Then he continued, "Okay, first of all, if you know Ernie, then you will also know that he doesn't always grasp the whole situation. I told him I work here. He understands that better than the real reason I am here every day of the week.

"Currently, I am unemployed and have been for the last three years. I'm getting on in years, lacking any skill set that modern-day employers want, so I am resigning myself to spending the rest of my working life on universal credit, which just about keeps my head above water.

"To help make ends meet and reduce my food bill, I turn up here every day about nine-thirty, check the list of deceased, make a note of their names, and then mingle with the mourners as they arrive. I have a little chat, sit in the service with them, wipe the odd tear away, follow them out to look at the flowers and another little chat with the relatives. Before long, one or more of them will ask, 'Are you coming back to the house?' At that point, I highlight the sad fact that I have no transport. Everyone at a funeral likes to be kind, so it is not long before I am in someone's car being driven back to the house for the wake. Food, drink, warm house, company, and conversation are a very pleasant way to spend the day, certainly a lot better than daytime TV. If I am not invited back, I just hang around for the next group to turn up. I've done this for about two years now, and so far, not a day has gone by when I have not got a free meal out of it."

"That's bloody brilliant! Why didn't I think of that when I was unemployed?" Susan said, it was clear she was impressed with the ruse that James was working. "All you need is your bus fare home and job done. But how do you convince people that you knew the dead person?"

"No one knows everyone at a funeral, especially the big ones; those have the best meals to be had. I'm just a little vague, ask questions as I go around and soon I know enough about the deceased to be a plausible mourner. Anyway, now I've explained to you both why I am here, what is the purpose of your visit?"

Susan told him of their wish to locate Terry. She wondered if they would have to explain the real reason for their interest. She need not have worried as James was someone who liked to hear his own voice.

"Ernie was always the odd one out in our family. Being the oldest, he always had to look after Terry and me, and we were never the best of kids, little brats we were. We got away with murder when Mother was out working. Even if he tried to grass about our bad behaviour, we'd end up getting our own back putting spiders in his bed. He hated spiders, so you can imagine the screams when he got into bed. I think he still checks his sheets every night. We were terrors.

"As for Terry, he was always the gifted one, always reading and knowing stuff, putting all the other kids to shame. Of course, he was a teacher's pet, which made him a bit of an outsider at school. Mind, he did well for himself. Whereas Ernie and me were doing manual jobs, Terry went and got himself a job as an insurance actuary. Bloody well paid, he was and, to be fair, at the time, generous with his money. Helped Ernie and me out a few times, I can tell you."

As the three of them talked, they walked around the grounds, passing the incoming hearse with two shiny black limousines following. The other James had arrived. The living James continued to mix opinion and memories to paint a picture of the three boys as they grew into men before he focussed on Terry.

"I don't know the whole story; it was very much cloaked in secrecy. Plus, I only heard about it long after the event. It was some sort of scandal or disagreement, not sure which, but one day he just gave up the whole insurance thing, walked away and began his stupid endeavour of saving the planet from the aliens. God knows what happened to him. I asked him time and time again, yet he'd never share with me the real reason he left the insurance business. He was even less forthcoming about his decision to go chasing flying saucers. That high IQ of his got the better of his manners. Things then went downhill. His marriage fell apart; we spoke less and less. Now we only send birthday and Christmas cards, but as for acting like brothers, not anymore."

Susan felt a shiver as she watched the coffin being carried in. She compared the brothers not staying in touch with her situation with her father, wondering if the next time she saw her father would be when he was carried into a crematorium. She did not want that to happen. Family are still family. Sharing each other's lives is what family is all about, even if your siblings or parents are not your best friends.

"As for where Terry is now is anyone's guess. If he has just gone off and not told anyone, I would put my money on him visiting his ex-wife, who he has been stalking and interfering with ever since she left him. He moaned at the time about being hurt and victimised, but I didn't blame her. When she married him, he was earning good money and he was a decent husband. Then his flying saucer thing became an obsession and he was no longer the bloke she had married. No surprise that she found someone else. Have a word with her; she might have seen him recently. As I recall, it is her birthday around this time of year."

James lit another cigarette before writing down the address of Terry's ex-wife, which he then gave to Martin. He smiled and wished them luck in finding Terry.

"I'm sorry if our turning up has caused you to miss out on a free meal," Martin said as he tucked the address into his pocket.

"Don't worry, there is always another funeral to go to; that's all they do here." James laughed loudly as he walked back towards the portacabin. Martin and Susan watched him go.

"Well, that's reassuring. If you ever lose your fortune, Martin, you won't starve!" Susan pointed out.

"Why wait, I'm thinking of trying it anyway," Martin retorted.

"Let's go and see his ex-wife Hazel, see what she has to say about her ex-husband," Susan said as they walked back towards Martin's car.

"Shall we leave it till later; I am hospital visiting."

"Nah, I can go and see her. It might be better woman to woman. We can put you men down without fear of retribution. Drop me near a tube station and I'll find my way there."

***

The moment the door opened, Susan's jaw dropped in astonishment as she recognised the person standing in the doorway to be Nigel Butler's lover. Hazel Gray looked into Susan's eyes; they were of remarkably similar stature. For a moment, Susan was speechless, so it was Hazel who spoke first.

"Can I help you, or are you simply lost?" There was a tone of caution, almost fear in her voice, accentuated when Susan asked her if she was Hazel Gray. "Maybe, who wants to know?"

"I'm trying to contact your ex-husband, Terry."

"What's he done, knocked you up or something? You'll learn he's not a bloke you can trust. Just a friendly warning."

"No, I just want to ask him a few questions about a company called Pinkcast. Didn't you work there once?"

A look of defiance swept across Hazel's face, her eyes narrowed. It was clear to Susan that the woman in front of her was jumpy about answering questions. She invited Susan in, not wishing to share anything with her snooping neighbours that lived along the same walkway.

"Who are you exactly, the police? If he has got himself into trouble again, there's no way I am helping out."

"I'm not the police, but I do need to speak to Terry," Susan explained as she followed Hazel through a narrow hallway lined with boots and shoes, all female, Susan noted. Several coats were hanging from hooks on the wall, again all female. Hazel appeared to be living on her own. The hallway felt dark and oppressive with the walls painted purple.

In the living room, Hazel offered Susan a seat. The room was just as dull as the hallway; the same purple paint covered the walls, or at least those parts of them that you could see. The room was fully adorned with numerous spiritual symbols, hanging dream catchers, as well as paintings that appeared to be just blobs of different shades of purple together with a thin scattering of random colours. The walls were not the only cluttered part; the remainder of the room was equally chaotic with random cupboards of differing sizes, as well as a couple of low coffee tables and a heavily marked pine table which was squeezed into a corner beside a window. Random cardboard boxes of various sizes were dotted around the room; they appeared to have no significance or apparent use. Close to the tiled fireplace, which consisted of an unlit, yet made up ready, log fire, was a two-seater couch draped in a large embroidered purple throw.

Even the atmosphere in which Susan found herself was heavy and full of fumes: odours of incense, perfume and cannabis. Susan was pleased to sit on the sagging cushions of the couch, while Hazel settled herself on a mismatched pine chair and leant on the table as she lit some sort of cigarette.

"Why do you want to speak to Terry about Pinkcast? He's never worked there, but as you rightly say, I used to."

"Apparently, even though he does not work there, he's accessing their computers and stealing industrial secrets."

Hazel laughed loudly, exhaling a plume of smoke as she did. "Terry, nicking industrial secrets, you're having a laugh. He's a nutter obsessed with saving the earth from little green men. He's so far off this planet; he'd make a great Martian himself. Terry might be good with computers and statistics, but he has trouble living in the real world with the rest of us."

"Then what reason could he have to download files from Pinkcast?"

"You want to know what I think? I'll tell you. He's trying to screw me over like he always does. Ever since I walked out on him, he has done his best to make my life a misery. Stalking me, turning up when I'm on a date, he even wrecked my second marriage. I presume you know I am having an affair with the manager at the depot, Nigel?"

Susan nodded, knowing that was going to be the next subject she was planning to broach. Hazel was not being shy about coming forward, which surprised her. Never having introduced herself fully, she wondered if Hazel knew who exactly she was talking to.

"Well, I suspect he's trying to mess up my affair with Nigel, which I guess he will do in the end. That is just the way Terry is; if he can't have something, then no one can."

"Any idea where he might be? He's not at his house like he says he always is."

"He popped in yesterday, but I've no idea where he is now."

"Yesterday?"

"Yeah, it was my birthday. He always calls around and gives me a present. Same one each year, a brand spanking new mobile phone." Hazel picked up the phone and showed it off to Susan. "Latest model, flash, don't you think?"

"But if he hates you so much, why buy you a phone for your birthday?"

"Hopes to sway me. No chance, I'm just taking him for a ride. New phone each year, that's a touch, don't you think?"

Susan was not sure if she was hearing things right; maybe it was the oppressive fumes in the atmosphere. Hazel hates Terry but is happy to take presents off him. She wondered just how ethical Hazel might be.

"What made you marry him in the first place? He doesn't sound your type."

"Back then, we were both each other's type. He worked for an insurance company, big bucks for doing just about nothing. We had a house and were planning a family. I was naïve about the spiritual side of life. I worked in an office typing and filing stuff. Then he goes and gets himself fired — no money, no payment on the mortgage and soon, no house. We did survive for a while in a crappy flat. Then I decided that the grass was going to be greener on the other side, took up with a new bloke and dumped Terry. He has never forgiven me."

"Interesting. I'm surprised you seem happy to share so much about your personal life with someone you have just met; I could be anyone."

"But you're not; you said your name was Susan. When, like me, you delve into white magic, then you can tell at once what a person is like. Your name, Susan, in numerology that makes you an eighteen, that converts to a destiny number of nine. You're influenced by the qualities of the planet Mars. You're an aggressive person who does not fear taking risks, but also a courageous person with traits of humanity and kindness. You're always ready to help others when they need you. Would I be right in assuming you are a Leo?"

"Wow! I am, and that sounds a lot like me. You must tell me more about this numerology thing. Could I do it?"

Hazel Gray liked the mystic world. She tried to exist in a dimension of life ruled by stars, fate and supernatural factors, thus saving herself from taking the blame for any mistakes she made. The other thing she liked was talking about her beliefs in the paranormal. In Susan, she had found an enthusiastic and willing listener. They spoke for well over an hour, and Susan left enthused and uplifted. As she walked away from the maisonettes, she was not exactly sure if she had found out anything more of value about Terry.

She became even more concerned as she recalled her conversation with Hazel. One thing stood out now she was no longer in a place to follow it up. Hazel had said, 'if he has got himself into trouble again'. What did she mean by that? Had Terry been in trouble with the police? If that was the case, it was the first she had heard about it. She decided it probably wasn't relevant anyway.

CHAPTER NINE

"Susan, what are you talking about – I'm a seventeen? You are making no sense whatsoever."

"Just listen and you will learn. Your name, Martin, translates into a seventeen, which in turn makes your destiny number eight. This shows you are ruled by Saturn. It says here: 'you have born qualities to manage financial matters and politics. The person with the number eight might become a great businessman, leader or game-changer in finance or politics.' It's what you could be."

"Susan, that is the biggest load of rubbish I have heard from you in, at least, the last twenty-four hours."

"There's more."

"No, thank you."

"Your heart desire number is more like you; you're a number two in this department. I quote, 'you want everything should be easy going in any situation.' Sounds like you, go on admit it."

"Susan, that is not even proper English. Whoever wrote that drivel, I would guess English is not their first language. I dread to think what sort of personal data they grabbed from you. Can we just stick to my daily horoscope? I have at least learnt to tolerate that."

"You should be more open to things you don't fully understand or physically connect with. There are in this world lots of things we just do not understand or are even able to recognise, given the limitations of our physical bodies. Once we open our minds to the world beyond where we live, only then can we truly find spiritual harmony."

"Is that what Hazel told you, and how much did she charge you?"

"Well," Susan paused before admitting, "I just offered ten pounds as a thank you for doing a tarot card reading for me. Which I'll have you know was perfectly accurate. Now can we get on with some work?"

"Maybe you are right. I would not have paid her any money, making me far better at financial affairs than you, so maybe my number eight is accurate after all." Martin laughed with ridicule, as well as affection.

To change the subject, Susan swiftly began to enlighten Martin about the main points that she had picked up from visiting Hazel. As she spoke, she began to realise that she did not learn a great deal from Hazel about Terry. Given the length of time the two of them talked, there was very little spoken about Terry. All she and Martin could conclude was that Hazel was selfish and Terry vindictive. Weirdly both dabbled in the cosmic side of life, Hazel her spiritualism and Terry his aliens. Maybe they should have made a happy couple, Susan speculated, before she asked,

"How is your mother?"

"Much better, thanks. The doctor says that she is making a good recovery and he hopes to let her out in a couple of days. I think she will be glad to get out of that place. Hospitals and my mother do not make for a happy relationship."

"That'll be a fun day when she gets back home and hears what you've done."

Martin frowned. He watched as Susan stood up from her desk, took three strides and arrived at the window which she opened partly. She had a wry smile on her face.

"What are you talking about?" Martin asked.

"Your new accountant. I'd love to see your mother's face when she learns that Becky is in charge of the family fortune."

"How come you know already?"

She turned toward Martin, leaning against the window frame. "Girls communicate; boys fight. It's a basic law of nature, Martin, even some boys understand it. She told me last night. I'm only glad you took my advice, although selling it to your mother might be hard. Have you really employed her, so if your mother sacks her, you'll have to give her notice and stuff?"

"Mother told me to find someone; I have found someone. Obviously, Becky does not fit the stereotypical dull accountant in a suit, but I think she knows her stuff and can do a good job. Also, we will not be getting ripped off by an accountancy firm that charges VAT on everything and charges for every little letter, phone call or email. I'm sure Mother will see the practicality of it."

"You hope," as Susan spoke, her mobile phone rang. She looked at the caller display, smiled and told Martin before she answered it, "it's your mate, Grant Fisher."

***

"Grant, how are you...? Thanks for the watch; I'm wearing it as we speak ... Yes, he's here. I'll put him on,"

Susan handed her phone to Martin. She had a big grin on her face. "He wants a word with you."

Unenthusiastically, Martin took the phone from her, wiped some make-up from the screen and held it to his ear. He felt a sense of foreboding as he greeted Grant with as much interest as he could generate, which was not a great deal.

"Sorry to have missed you on the last call, but your man Maris and your very efficient P.A. Susan did a great job in your absence. Just the sort of people I could use in my organisation. But that's all beside the point. As I am sure you are a terribly busy man heading up your detective agency, the reason for my call is that my investigators have just told me that they have lost track of Terry. I ask you, all they had to do was follow a geek, who supposedly never leaves his home, and they lose him. Bloody hopeless, I would conclude. Let's be honest, Martin, executives like us, do not need hopeless people around. Hence, I have terminated their contract and they are no longer working for me. I am sure you can now guess the reason for my call."

Martin did not need to guess; he could see where the conversation was going and it was not a direction he was happy to go. He kept quiet and allowed Grant to carry on.

"Having referred to your website, I can see you manage a very impressive company with a wide range of resources at your disposal."

"Website?" Martin asked, looking towards Susan, who quickly looked down at her keyboard.

"Yes, well put together. Not too many bells and whistles, just straight to the point information. That's what I have always liked about you, Martin, getting to the point. And before you ask, here comes my point. I want your company to take over tracking and to trail Terry for me, reporting back and handling any negotiations that might be required between Pinkcast and Terry. If you could see to it that you took on my request personally and not hand it over to one of your field agents, I'd really welcome it, even if your day rate is a lot more than the rest of your staff. What do you say, Martin? Will you take on this assignment for me?"

Not so much take on, Martin thought, he would prefer to turn down the request altogether, return the phone to Susan, then ask her what she might know about a Martin Hayden website with a range of resources. Instead, he decided he would play it diplomatically.

"I would love to, Grant, but as you know, I already have an interest in Terry, primarily from his brother. Sadly, we too have lost him and I am not confident that we would be able to locate him, even with all of our resources." He looked at Susan as he emphasised the 'all of our resources' part.

"Well, to be honest, Martin, I am playing a bit of a game here. Once my private eyes lost Terry, it was the perfect excuse to sack them as I was already planning to support an old school friend. Circumstances changed rapidly and now I am in the fortunate position to know what Terry is up to and his location."

"Then what do you need me for, if you know where he is?"

"A little bit of company politics, if I am honest with you, Martin. Terry wants to do a deal for the return of the documents he has stolen from us. We pay him some cash and he hands back our secrets. Quid pro quo, you might say. The last thing I want is Pinkcast to be seen dealing directly with the guy, so I want you to act as a go-between, a sort of PR barrier between Pinkcast and the whole sorry affair."

"You want me to deal with Terry in order to get your secrets back in case anything goes wrong. I get the blame, and Pinkcast can wash their hands of it all and be seen to be as pure as the driven snow."

"Nothing will go wrong, Martin. We'll get you the cash he's requesting through some clever accounting; he'll get what he wants; you'll get a fat fee and the industry will be none the wiser. We can all get on with our lives. Say yes, Martin, it will mean a lot to me."

Martin wanted to say no, a simple to the point refusal. Yet, there was a part of him that did not want to turn it down and potentially be considered weak, not too bothered about things, happy to get on with his own life. Of course, that was Martin to a tee and he would be the first to admit that, but not to someone he had been to school with. How often had he attended school reunions, when old boys come from the far corners of the earth just to gloat and see who has made a success of their lives and who has failed. In his view, that could be just about the only reason to hold a school reunion for pupils who are never in contact with each other at any other time.

"Before I give you my answer, what secrets are we talking about?"

"Difficult one to answer fully; otherwise, the secret would no longer be a secret. But I understand you want to know. Okay, here's the story so far. Nigel, my manager that

I know you have met, decided to have a roll in the hay with one of the female employees at the depot. If that was not bad enough, Terry, her ex-husband, boyfriend or whatever, took a dislike to her getting laid and started a campaign of hate. Part of the said campaign was to steal Nigel's user file from the server. This file contains all his emails, calendars, timesheets and other stuff that computers feel is important to record. No doubt Terry was getting some dirt on the guy. In Nigel's user file, something more existed. There was a memo that should never have been stored there in the first place. A message that should have been in a separate independent secure server such was the sensitivity of its contents.

"When Nigel told me what had happened, I was not in the least bit happy, so sacked his bit on the side then launched an operation to retrieve everything from Terry, amongst which will be the memo."

"That makes Terry an aggrieved divorced husband and not an industrial spy."

"Not a bad overview, simple to the point. Even so, the memo could be dynamite in the hands of our competitors, so industrial spy still holds good."

"What is so important about this memo?"

"As I said, Martin, extremely sensitive commercial information that our competitors, no doubt, would be happy to kill for. Well, not exactly kill, but close. I am sure you will understand that I cannot tell you the contents but trust me, they are particularly important both to me personally and to Pinkcast."

"Okay, Grant, I'll do it."

"Fantastic, Martin, I knew I could rely on you. Send over an engagement contract for me. I'll have my lawyers have a quick look and we'll get cracking."

Three seconds ago, Martin had said yes; now, he was already regretting it. An engagement contract, he was not planning to marry Grant, just help him out.

"Let's not bother with any paperwork; I trust you'll not do the dirty on me," Martin said, knowing full well that Grant would tread over anyone to get what he wanted. Martin handed the disconnected phone back to Susan and explained that he had, for some reason, agreed to Grant's request.

For Susan, this sounded exciting. She visualised a midnight exchange of suitcases beside a deserted warehouse, with a low mist seeping across the only dim streetlamp that illuminated the damp quayside where they stood shivering in the cold. She would be wearing a Mackintosh with the collar turned up. It was just a shame neither of them smoked as that would have completed the movie scene in her mind.

Martin punctured the bubble of her dream when he asked her, "Do we have a website?"

Having already heard one mentioned during the telephone conversation, a denial was going to be pointless. Susan prepared to confess her sins without hesitation, "Yes, we do, as all good companies should have nowadays. A presence on the world wide web is essential to ensure a seamless customer experience."

"And how did I acquire such a marvellous asset?"

"I was bored one weekend, kicking around the house and just sort of browsing the internet, saw an advert for a free website and registered, then I played around before publishing a Martin Hayden Investigations website. Grant sounded as if he was impressed. I'll take it off if you don't like it."

"Once I've seen it, I'll let you know. But for now, I have to call Terry on what Grant has described as a secure line. It looks as though we'll get to see Terry again sooner than we planned."

***

Standing majestically on the banks of the River Medway, Rochester Castle had survived many turbulent centuries. Warring Kings, battling Barons, destructive Dukes all have crossed the stone thresholds of the tower, which has seen skirmishes, sieges, and death played out around its substantial foundations. Visitors now arrive from across the world to see one of the finest examples of a Norman castle to be found in either France or Britain. Parts of the building date back to 1086, when William the Conqueror's son, Rufus, asked the Bishop of Rochester to build a new stone castle in Rochester.

Martin was learning a lot more than he needed to about what he would have described as a pile of old stones. Politely and patiently, he listened as Terry droned on about the history of the castle.

When Terry had suggested meeting on the grassy area in front of Rochester Castle, Martin had not been enamoured by the suggestion. It sounded to him both far away and exposed to the elements, neither of which appealed. Now he was sitting on a cold, slightly damp park bench; he was even less inclined to continue the history lesson that it appeared Terry was indulging in.

"In a nutshell, you like the place. I, on the other hand, have never been that interested in history," an exasperated Martin said. "Can we get down to the business in hand?"

The business in hand was a straightforward swap. For Martin, little more than a simple acknowledgement was needed before the exchange happened, quickly followed by a swift goodbye. Two minutes duration at most, in his opinion. He looked at his watch, ten minutes and counting. Terry had only reached Henry the Eighth in the history of the Castle.

"Your impatience surprises me; I had you down as a traditionalist, a staunch supporter of history."

"Well, maybe you are partly right, in the same way as I am surprised that you seem to be in love with this old castle," Martin pointed out, shivering slightly. The frail sun only appeared occasionally from behind ever-increasingly gloomy clouds, trying to neutralise the chilling wind that was blowing off the river. "Being a techie and searching out aliens, I imagined that you would have no interest in what the invading Normans were up to."

"How wrong you are, Martin. History is my escape from the fast-moving world of technology. It's also a place to learn. Imagine telling those humans who first inhabited Rochester Castle about what the future held. Fancy trying to explain to them that one day there would be lights that could just be turned on and off, horseless transport, a weapon that can kill your adversaries from hundreds of miles away. That it would be possible to communicate across the world with countries that they had no idea even existed. They would not believe you. In the same way, people don't believe Unidentified Flying Objects are crisscrossing our atmosphere and that creatures from other planets have landed here. Most people only believe in what they can see and touch."

"However grand all that might sound, I am keen to give you the cash that Pinkcast has provided me with to recover its data." Martin had collected the cash from an anonymous courier who called at his office with ten thousand pounds in a fat envelope. No paper chain to say where it had come from, just the knowledge Martin had that he was to purchase the data from Terry.

What concerned him was that the last time he had a wad of cash in his pocket, he was stopped by the police, who at once suspected him of being a drug dealer. Back then, he could prove it had come from his bank account, but now there was no such evidence.

"I am surprised that you have ended up working for Pinkcast. When we first met, you said that you were seeing me on behalf of my brother. Were you lying, Martin?"

"No, back then, I was doing a simple favour for your brother, helping out as any friend would. It was your business dealings with Pinkcast, together with the fact that I just happen to have gone to school with the CEO, that sees me now acting as a go-between. I could cast the same accusation towards you, telling me you never leave the house, then you pop around to see your ex-wife to celebrate her birthday.

"I am going to get the USB stick in the next ten minutes, or are you going to rattle on about Henry the Eighth some more?"

"I like to share my passions with people. But if you insist, here," Terry offered him a small USB stick. "You have an envelope for me?"

Martin passed the envelope to Terry, who simply put it into his jacket pocket without counting it. "Thank you, Martin, and thank Grant for me the next time you see him."

"What was so valuable it was worth Pinkcast giving you a large sum of money to recover?"

"Interesting question, that one. If I knew, I'd tell you, but I don't, so I can't."

That was not the answer that Martin was expecting. He was asking only out of curiosity as he presumed, rightly or wrongly, that Terry, if he were prepared to share the secret, would muddle him with technical jargon that went way above his limited knowledge of information technology and smartwatches.

"You don't know?" Martin asked, believing he might have misheard Terry's answer.

"Not a clue, Martin. I'll share with you the circumstances. You might know, given that I understand you have been poking around in my life, that I am a bit of a control freak and I, how shall I say, like to ensure my ex-wife has an unhappy life without me. When I heard that she was having an affair with someone from Pinkcast, where she was working at the time, I thought about how I could gather information about her clandestine affair. A few emails to the man in question, Nigel, you might have met him, emails laced with some clever trojan programming, and within a few hours, I am in their server, downloading his computer account. All his emails, documents, various picture files, other documents and computer files, plus, importantly, his calendar.

"Now, with his calendar at my disposal, I can see when and where he plans to meet up with my ex. It turns out that they go away every other weekend. All I need to do is gather some concrete evidence and present it to Nigel's wife so I can teach him a lesson. What better way to gather such proof than to tell Luke and Janice they need to track a potential alien? I make up a farfetched story about Pinkcast being the enemy and within a few weeks, I have everything I need."

"But you do believe in aliens and stuff?"

"Of course, Martin. I have spent a good few years now documenting UFO sightings and unexplained events across the United Kingdom. I just invented a story about Pinkcast so that I could send Janice and Luke off to do my dirty work and ensure that Ashley didn't pry too deeply into what I was doing."

"Are you saying there is nothing of interest or value on this memory stick?"

"When you get back to the office, Martin, have a look for yourself. As soon as I became aware that Pinkcast were falling over themselves to get the data back, I, of course, had a good look through, but I couldn't work out just what they thought was so important that they were willing to pay me a fat wad of cash to get it back. I've got the cash, and they will have the data; everyone is happy, I guess."

Whichever way Martin considered what he had just heard and what he knew, nothing made any sense. Grant had directed a team of private investigators to trail Terry and recover the data. At every point, Martin had been told that Terry was an industrial spy stealing valuable secrets. If Terry were to be believed, then Grant and Pinkcast had wasted an awful lot of money.

"I have a couple of questions for you, Terry. First, there is something I cannot make sense of: if you hate your ex-wife so much, why give her a mobile telephone for her birthday each year?"

"Hate is such a strong word, Martin; I would say despise her. I'm not sure how much you have found out about my background, so if I am repeating what you already know, then please stop me in my tracks.

"We were happily married all the time. I had a good job, and Hazel was getting all the trappings of what that meant. As soon as I lost my job with an insurance company, it did not take her long to find another man who could keep her in the manner she aspired to. Hazel is a greedy bitch! That is why every year she has no difficulty in accepting from me the very latest mobile phone for her birthday."

"That does not answer my question. Why give Hazel a phone when you seem hell-bent on ensuring her life is a misery?"

"The reason the keep of Rochester Castle is so tall is that it enables those inside to see their surrounding countryside and where their enemies might be. The phone I give Hazel each year has a small device in it that allows me to track her every move."

"If that is not illegal, it should be."

"The phone is registered in my name; thus, I can do what I wish with my own phone. And your second question?"

"You said you never leave your house, yet here we are out in the open. What was that all about?"

"That story was more for Janice and her stupid partner. Ashley and I had them petrified that I was about to be abducted by aliens. A bit of a joke that got out of hand. We've told them that I leave the house on a few occasions, but only if I leave all my credit cards and my mobile phone behind. I might be hunting beings that you don't believe in, but that does not mean I can't have a sense of humour.

"Well, it's been nice doing business with you, Martin. Please give my regards to your able assistant over there and the older lady with her. Did they think I would abduct you and whisk you off to another planet?" Terry laughed, zipping his jacket as he stood up. "I am off for some quality time inside the castle. You are welcome to join me, but I think maybe you have had enough of the Normans today."

***

As Martin strode along the Dickensian streets of Rochester looking for a place for refreshments, he recounted what Terry had told him to Colin and Susan, leaving out most of the historical parts, which Martin judged not to be of any great interest to either of them.

They found a small black and white timber-framed tearoom sandwiched between Boots the Chemists and a shop selling rolls of dressmaking materials. The three of them sat down at a table close to a set of stairs rising to the first floor, where there was further seating for the hordes of tourists that trample the quaint streets during the height of summer. Those days were far away; today, the café was peaceful. Apart from the three recreational detectives, as Colin liked to describe themselves, there was a mother with her toddler daughter and four elderly ladies tucking into scones, jam and thick cream.

As Susan perused the menu, Colin gave Martin a knowing look, which Martin returned with a smile. Only then did they return to view the menu themselves. There was a moment of silence before Susan spoke, "It's all a bit tacky here: Scrooge Scones, Oliver Cheese Twists, Little Dorrit Cakes. Why they want to make the place sound like a Charles Dickens Museum, I have no idea. I just hope the cakes aren't that old."

Martin chuckled, and Colin gave out a loud belly laugh.

"What?" Susan asked, having no idea why the two men were laughing.

"Suzie Baby, you're so predictable at times. We wondered how long it would be before you made some crack about the place being a little too Dickensian. I thought you would have at least waited until you were eating. Martin, on the other hand, gambled that you would speak out whilst looking at the menu. Martin wins the bet and now I have to pay the bill. It was worth it," Colin added

"You two are so childish at times. What's so funny? You tell me, why a café out here in the sticks would decide to theme itself after Charles Dickens. Up by London Bridge would be a far better place."

"Mr Dickens spent a lot of time around these parts, creating many of his stories on the very cobbled streets that we have just walked along. He lived for a while in Higham, just up the road from here."

"Can I add," Martin asked, "I was reliably informed by Terry that Charles Dickens is said to haunt the castle moat on Christmas Eve?"

"Alright, so you are a pair of know-it-alls. Let's get on an' eat something; I am starving."

***

The motorcycle courier had arrived precisely on time. He took the small package containing the USB stick from Martin, wrote out a scruffy receipt, then replaced his helmet before leaving the office, on his way as instructed to give the pack personally to Grant.

"Well, that's that done," Susan concluded and Martin agreed. He was pleased that Susan had accepted that Luke and Janice were not taking Terry for a ride, and in fact, it was the exact reverse. Susan could again speak to Ernie, reassuring him that all was well with his estranged brother, telling him no one was defrauding, deceiving, or generally being nasty to Terry. They had further agreed that Terry's odd relationship with his ex-wife would not be mentioned in case it upset Ernie. He was, undoubtedly, a person with delicate emotions.

Martin was starting to relax; things looked as if they were going back to the quiet normality he liked in his life. He preferred rolling into the office when it suited him, having coffee and a chat with Susan, even if that did entail having his stars read to him each day, followed by a long, satisfying lunch with a friend. For Martin, that was how all days at the office should be spent.

There, at the back of his mind, was still the worry over his mother. She would be home within the next few days, not that she wanted any assistance from her son. The last time he had visited the hospital, she was sitting up in bed, phoning nursing agencies across the capital to secure the services of a suitably qualified nurse to look after her when she returned home. A nurse to help her recover fully and do the chores that she needed to be carried out to maintain the household in a suitable fashion. Tasks she was confident her incompetent son would never cope with. Not that it worried him much; in fact, the thought of a nurse working around the house rather intrigued him. A number of his fantasies included attention from a nurse, although he doubted that any nurse employed by his mother would be dressed in the same way as in his dreams.

His phone rang as Susan was preparing to leave to see Ernie. She waited until he answered the call.

"Martin, it's Grant. I got the USB stick but what I want is not on it. Tell me what this is all about?"

"No idea, Grant, you tell me. I gave Terry the money, he gave me the stick, and I sent it to you. What were you expecting to find on it?"

"As I have told you, a certain memorandum that I wanted back, but it wasn't there. Terry has screwed us over. I want you to go back and grab him by the throat and ask him exactly what he has done with the memorandum and ensure he gives it back or else he will have to pay the consequences."

"Whoa! Whoa! Grab him by the throat; what sort of person do you think I am? You know I never liked fighting at school. What makes you think I do now?"

"Terry is being a little shit. He knows exactly what he is doing. Everything was on that stick, but for the very thing, the only thing that made that USB stick valuable. If he thinks he can get anything else out of me, then he is foolishly mistaken."

"Grant, what is this memo that you are trying to get back about anyway?"

"I can't tell you, Martin; it's a secret, and I cannot disclose its contents to you, safe to say it was downloaded amongst Nigel's documents that Terry stole. I need it back, and that is what I have paid Terry for. Get on to it now, Martin, or else there will be dire consequences if you cannot recover the memorandum."

"Calm down, Grant, you are getting yourself in a state, and as I recall, when you did that at school, it was out with the asthma pump. Terry told me that he has returned everything he took from your computer server. He only wanted to gather dirt on his ex-wife's lover. He sounds a little spiteful, if I am being honest."

"Martin, I want that memorandum back. If you don't get it, then first, I will not be paying you and secondly, I will be suing you for the ten thousand pounds that you gave to Terry. The way you're talking, I suspect that you might well be in cahoots with him." Grant's voice was slow, firm and plainly threatening Martin.

"What is the memo about? If I know that, I will have a better chance of finding it, or getting it back. Are you sure it was taken by Terry?"

"Martin, either get it back from Terry or else I am taking you and your company to the cleaners, getting not only my money back, but I will also be filing for compensation. Now get on and do it." Grant did not wait for a reply; he just cut off the call, leaving Martin with a silent phone pressed against his ear.

"Looks like we're not finished yet," Martin angrily commented as he dialled Terry's number.

CHAPTER TEN

The River Thames glistened as it reflected the late afternoon light into Martin's eyes, causing him to squint. Next to him stood Terry leaning on the railings of the Thames River Walk; he had no such problem as he was wearing sunglasses, very dark ones that had a circular lens and a tortoise-shell frame.

Apart from Martin getting fed up with seeing more of Terry than he considered healthy, he was learning that Terry had an annoying habit of explaining his surroundings to anyone he was with. Today, Martin discovered that Walbrook Wharf, which they were standing close to, is the last working wharf in the Pool of London. It is no longer bringing goods in from around the world; instead, it is a waste transfer site transporting tons of waste from the office buildings of the City downstream to Belvedere, where it is incinerated to create energy.

Martin was not bothered in the least what happened to the waste of the numerous banks and offices. He was not exactly pleased that Terry, who at one time boasted about never leaving his house, insisted they meet away from that very house. At least Martin's own office was located not too far from the chosen rendezvous spot.

After Terry had given Martin an informative lecture about the wharf, the way the River Walbrook still flows under buildings and runs into the Thames at this spot, he then proceeded to bore Martin about the Romans. How they had set up a river landing almost on the same site, just a bit closer to Cannon Street railway station, as the Thames at the time was a lot wider than it is now.

"Our meetings are starting to get boring. Please, Terry, let's get to the point of why we are meeting, then we can both get on with our lives."

"I do sense that your interest in history, or indeed life around it, is severely limited. I always imagined a person with a public-school education would have a natural thirst for knowledge."

"No, I have a thirst for red wine and enjoying life. What the Romans did here does not either affect or concern me. What do you know about this memo that Grant is convinced you still have?"

There was an irritable tone in Martin's voice. Grant's call had annoyed him. Being threatened with legal action is never a conversation anyone wants to have. Then being told you need to have an almost clandestine meeting, oddly once again beside a river - what was it with Terry and rivers - just because he did not want Ashley to understand how vindictive he was to Hazel. In Martin's mind, Ashley could have been chucked out of Terry's house while they talked, and what was it about Ashley's feelings that he had to be protected from Terry's actions. Martin was not happy.

"I have no idea; I gave everything back to you. Although I find it strange that even you can't tell me what the memo is about or what it's entitled given that you have spoken to your friend at Pinkcast. I can add no more to what I have already told you."

"You know what, I do not think you are telling me the whole story. If you had some sort of tracking device in

Hazel's phone, why did you need to steal some calendar to track her and her lover?"

"A few months ago, I could no longer track her. I could not, I am sure you understand, ask her, 'why is your tracking device not working?' That would have been a dead giveaway, as I am sure even you can understand. Hence, I thought the easiest way was to hack Nigel's computer. I found out when I gave her latest birthday present that the silly cow broke the phone and had been using some borrowed phone, but that was why I had to break into the Pinkcast server."

"And no one had any idea what you had or had access to? What about Ashley?"

"Well, Ashley knew I had downloaded some documents, that was why I had to give a cover story of aliens at the Pinkcast factory, but he never got to see the actual stuff I'd downloaded. It was always kept on that one USB stick, which I gave back."

Martin watched a large boat glide under Southwark Bridge, emerging into the sunlight, full of tourists taking photographs of everything they passed. Despite what he now knew about the city rubbish tip, he was tempted to wave. He resisted as the boat disappeared under Cannon Street Bridge and onwards towards Tower Bridge, something worth photographing.

"Do you think this might be connected to Hazel getting sacked?" Martin asked.

Terry did not answer straight away; he was undoubtedly thinking. Martin wondered if he was preparing a suitable reason, or simply working out a way to implicate Hazel and further disrupt her life.

"It's a good point. As I understand it, it was a simple sacking for having an affair with another employee, which even I think sounds harsh. I have wondered if it was more. Was she stealing secrets and commercial intellect to sell on? Knowing her, I doubt it, but as I said, she's a greedy person. It's full of mystery. Take her weekends away with Nigel. As you know, Janice and Luke were on hand to provide photographic evidence of what she was up to. Especially useful indeed when I send some photographs off to his wife. There is a caveat however, on two occasions, she was dropped off at the hotel by a man I cannot identify; sadly, my spies failed to get the registration mark of the car he was driving."

"Could he be a cab driver? She must have needed some sort of transport to get to the hotel."

Terry took his phone from his pocket, scrolled through some screens before presenting it to Martin. It was difficult to see in the bright sunshine, but Martin could just make out what they were doing.

"As you can see, that is a deeply passionate kiss to give a taxi driver. I'll email you a copy; maybe it can help you. Perhaps she has the memo."

Martin was still sceptical. Not just today, but every time he had spoken to Terry, there was always a reason, always an answer. Every reply suited Terry. Why Martin was sceptical was not down to his suspicious nature because he did not have one. It was something that Susan had said soon after their first meeting with Terry: 'Where does his money come from?'

There were, Martin would concede, several very unusual occupations around these days. He had read about golf ball divers, paper towel sniffers, dog food tasters, even a professional sleeper. What he had never heard of was someone making money researching unidentified flying objects, unless there was some sort of large university grant involved. Terry, however, did not look like the university type, more the weird geeky type.

"I know you are always keen to drop your ex-wife into the mire. Could it be you are pointing the blame for the theft in her direction while you have this mysterious memo and plan to sell it to the highest bidder?"

"Yes, I'll admit I am keen to drop Hazel in it at every opportunity. No, I do not have this memo. Even if I did, and it had some value, I doubt it would be prudent to join the professional ranks of industrial espionage without some sort of knowledge of how it works. Blundering into that sector might well see me getting my kneecaps blown away."

"Then how do you manage financially without a real job?"

"I could ask you the very same question. Although I have carried out a little due diligence, more than I suspect you have done and I can see that you are living off the family fortune and not making anything from your detective agency."

"And you have just picked up ten thousand pounds for doing nothing. Oh, stop, you did do something: you stole some electronic documents to spite your ex. Maybe I should look deeper into your history."

"Please do," Terry taunted. "I'll send you the photo and you let me know what you find out." Without waiting for a response, he turned away from Martin and continued along the river path towards Southwark Bridge.

***

"Does this mean that aliens are off the table?" Susan asked. She liked the idea that they were getting involved with an alien invasion. Telling your grandchildren that you saved the earth and humanity would be cool. There were still several stages before she would be able to relate such a story to her grandchildren. Firstly, she needed to get married, followed by getting pregnant, then her children would need to have children, none of which seemed to be probable at present. She would then have to engage in warfare against the invading creatures and defeat them. She did not have a plan for that. However, now that there were going to be no aliens, she would not have much to tell any grandchildren that she might have.

"Suzie Baby, let's be honest, they were never on the table in the first place. Although looking at him, he could well be an alien." Colin leaned over Martin's shoulder, looking at the laptop screen and the photograph Terry had sent across showing the man with whom Hazel was having a passionate kiss.

There were three photographs to be studied. The first showed Hazel getting out of the passenger side of a car, which Martin recognised as a Nissan Qashqai. The second photograph was of the mystery man taking a suitcase from the back seat. His face was unclear; his most distinctive feature was an ear, which was deformed and almost flat against his head. Colin at once nicknamed him Van Gogh. He had thick dark eyebrows which joined in the middle, never a good sign, according to Susan. His nose was rounded, almost bulbous and appeared to be pockmarked, although they could not be sure as the photograph was not as sharp as it could have been. The third and final photograph was of the couple embracing and kissing passionately. He was a little taller than Hazel and also broader. One hand looked as if it had some sort of tattoo.

"I have no idea what she sees in him; he's just plain ugly," Susan concluded. "Then going into the hotel to meet another lover. I am beginning to dislike her. She's either very greedy or taking advantage of one of those men for her own ends."

"The more I think about it," Martin added, "the more I think that Hazel and Terry are well-suited, both vindictive people. However, we must do something, I am afraid; otherwise, I might find myself ten thousand pounds down. What do you think we should do, Colin?"

"Me? It's your detective agency." Colin sounded a little surprised to be asked, yet he took up the challenge without any protest. "But since you ask, we need to find out as much as we can about Terry. His background, where his money comes from, does he have any friends besides Ashley and the couple. You mentioned he was sacked from a job at an insurance company; maybe we need to find out the reason for that. Once we know about him, we also need to look at his ex-wife. It would not be the first time two people appear to hate each other, simply to pull the wool over other people's eyes and get what they want."

"His star sign would help," Susan added. "And maybe find out why he was in trouble with the police."

Without any sign of a prompt, together Colin and Martin repeated, "trouble with the police?"

"Didn't I mention that?" Susan sounded a little sheepish.

"No, Susan, you did not. What exactly are you referring to?" Martin asked.

"Well, you were ribbing me about getting my number destiny done, so I forgot. Anyway, when I spoke to Hazel, she said to me, 'Who are you exactly, the police? 'cause if he has got himself into trouble again, I am not helping out at all.' And before you ask, I didn't ask her about it."

"You must have been distracted by your destiny forecast," Martin said with a smile on his face.

"Well, if he has been in trouble with the police before, I might well be able to gather some useful information on him. I hate to tell you, Martin, Suzie Baby is right, it would help to know his star sign, it might give us a clue as to his date of birth," Colin laughed, then continued, "do you think Becky might still have enough sway at the bank to get Terry's financial background?"

"What do you think, Susan, does she?"

"How would I know? She's your accountant."

"I think Suzie Baby is a little jealous that Becky has unfettered access to your house."

"I have no idea why," Martin offered in rebuttal, "Susan and I have already slept together."

"What!" Colin's voice rose in surprise. "You never told me, neither of you. And yes, it is important that you tell me, I like to know who is sleeping with who amongst my friends."

"Calm down, Colin; Martin is exaggerating. Technically I did sleep round his place, sitting next to him on the settee. Both fully dressed, all night, both sound asleep, both of us knackered. I think Martin felt ill after I cooked for him."

"The chilli was good, slightly overcooked, but not harmful to humans," Martin's tone sounded warm and affectionate.

"Back to work then, you two celibates. Do we have a glimmer of a plan forming now?" Colin asked, clear there was no indiscretion he could tease them about for the foreseeable future. Just then, Martin's phone rang.

"It's the hospital," he said as he answered the call, there was a hint of trepidation in his voice.

"Oh no... when was this...? thank you, I'll go at once."

Both Colin and Susan looked concerned as they heard Martin speak. He sounded equally anxious.

"What's happened?" Susan asked, fearing that the news would not be good.

"Mother's been discharged from hospital and she is on her way home in a taxi. I told her I'd pick her up and bring her home; she is so single-minded at times."

"Well, that's good news, isn't it?" Susan was not sure just why not picking up his mother from the hospital was such a problem.

"No, it is not good news. Becky is at the house working through some files that I have there. If Mother finds her first, all hell will break loose. I have got to get back. I'll call Becky on the way. You two sort yourselves out doing whatever investigating you think is good," Martin was standing, slipping on his jacket as he was speaking.

"Shall I come with you?" Colin offered, trying to be helpful. "I am sure between us we can come up with some sort of viable excuse."

"Thanks, but having a man wearing a blonde wig and dressed as a woman in the house as well as Becky dressed the way she does, well, it could give Mother another heart attack. Thanks, I had better deal with this on my own."

Before either Colin or Susan could reply, Martin had rushed out of the door and was on his way home.

***

Standing in the hallway, Martin knew things were looking bad. Becky had not answered her phone even though he had called numerous times during his frenetic trip home. His mother's bags were lined neatly in the hallway. He began to run through possible scenarios that might play out over the course of the next few minutes, most of which included his mother shouting and declaring her son to be incompetent. No doubt she would bring up the fact that the cost of his education was a complete waste of money.

Martin consoled himself that he had appointed a new accountant, exactly as requested. His mother would probably shout that it was Becky's long legs and short skirt that swayed him, not her financial qualifications. She might have been partly right on that point, although he had no plans to admit it as such an admission might prove fatal to him.

His mother called, "Is that you, Martin? I am in the kitchen."

Tentatively he walked towards her voice. He trusted he would not find her holding a carving knife. His only consolation was that if she were holding a knife, he could run faster than her.

She was sitting at the kitchen table looking slightly frailer than before her spell in hospital. Her face seemed tired and drawn, which was not surprising given what she had recently been through. She put down her cup and held her arms out to Martin.

"Give your old mother a hug now she is home."

Martin bent over, hugging her as she remained seated. Had Becky left early and not seen Mother? That would be a result.

"You could have called me to collect you from the hospital and carry your bags. You shouldn't have come home on your own."

Martin settled down in the chair next to her, digging his hand into the biscuit barrel. His nerves had made him feel peckish.

"There was no need to trouble you, the cab driver was extremely accommodating and the nursing agency had a young lady here waiting for me when I arrived. Her name is Becky, sweet creature, so kind and helpful, plus she makes a wonderful cup of tea. She is upstairs sorting out the mountain of tablets I have to take, such a bore. I'm sure she'll make you tea when she comes down. The only downside is she is not dressed as I would expect a nurse to be. She doesn't look very medical, more fashionable. Still, I am sure the agency knows what they are doing. I am only resting and gaining my strength."

"Upstairs sorting out your tablets, you say."

"The doctors were insistent that I have boxes of tablets and things, although I do not agree with ingesting random substances. However, Nurse Becky clarified how beneficial they would be for me and in a couple of weeks, I can go back to my herbal teas. Let's call Becky down."

Before Mother could summon Becky to the kitchen, the doorbell rang. Quickly, Martin answered it to see a woman standing in front of him, slightly plump, hair tied back, dressed in a blue medical uniform and holding a neat slim bag.

"Ah, you must be Mother's nurse," Martin told her in a hushed voice. "Look, here's a tenner. Can you go and grab a coffee or something and come back in about half an hour, please? Just need to straighten a few things out with my mother." He smiled and offered her the banknote, closing the door before the nurse had any chance to comment.

"Who was that?" Mother asked when he returned to the kitchen.

"Jehovah's Witnesses, I sent them away."

"They are such a nuisance. Ah, here comes Becky now. Becky, could you be a darling and get my son Martin a cup of tea, please."

"Of course, Mrs Hayden, but I think Martin prefers coffee. Black, isn't it Martin?" Becky was unaware of the sudden chilliness in the air or the look that Mother was giving her son.

"Martin, do you know Becky?"

"Yes," Martin conceded, moving into damage limitation mode, an approach that he often used with his mother. The least he said, the less chance there was of him dropping himself in it. Although today he felt there was going to be no way of avoiding a confrontation.

"How exactly do you know Becky?"

"I met her through work," Martin admitted truthfully. He now needed to take control of the conversation, which meant an admission. Whatever the consequences, he was going to have to confess just what Becky was doing in the house.

"In fact, she now works for us, the Hayden family, not as a nurse, although as you said, she is a very caring person."

"Thank you, Martin," Becky said as she stirred his black coffee.

Martin tried to contact her telepathically, to tell her to keep quiet for the next few minutes. Becky speaking now without thinking could prove disastrous.

"Becky is our new accountant. As you instructed, I have found a highly qualified and suitable candidate to replace Mr McFarlane." There, Martin thought, it is done, no turning back. He waited for the reaction.

Mother turned towards Becky, who was handing Martin his coffee and therefore did not see the look of surprise that Mother was giving her until she turned and spoke to her.

"It was just fortunate that I was here going through some of the files when you arrived. I'd hate to think of you coming into an empty house after such a serious illness. You must have been very frightened. I can finish off the accounting a bit later if you want me to make you some lunch?"

Martin felt the situation was at a crossroads. Mother was going to throw Becky out and banish her from the house, then turn on him for not providing the stereotypical accountant that she was expecting to care for and nurture her bank accounts.

"Becky, if you are an accountant, as my son has pointed out, how come when I gave you my bag of medicines, you seemed to know precisely what they were and how they should be taken?"

"My grandpappy had heart trouble. I looked after him for about a year before he just dropped dead. Oh, that sounds bad! It wasn't my caring that killed him, or so the doctor said. His arteries were all furred up and he hated doctors with a passion. I had finally convinced him that he needed the operation, but he died before they could do it. Sad, really."

"Poor you," Mother commented in such a concerned way that it surprised Martin to hear her speak in what was a rare tone for her. "Where were your parents? Could they not help you?"

"They both divorced and left me with Grandpappy when I was six. They were never around after that."

"My poor dear, you have had such a sad life." Becky nodded that she had. "Has my son employed you full time to be our financial guru?" Mother continued, "Would you mind also helping with my recuperation while looking after our accounts?"

"Oh, I'd love to. It's always best to have a break from the figures once in a while; helps keep the brain active."

Mother beamed. "Well, Becky, welcome to the Hayden household. You are just the person I am looking for to help me in my old age, and also you have a young, agile mind for economics. None of us is getting any younger, are we? Martin, be a dear and take my suitcases to my bedroom while Becky tells me a little more about growing up without her parents, such a distressing story."

Bewildered, Martin trudged upstairs. He tried to make sense of what had just transpired in the kitchen. He hoped Mother would continue to be keen on Becky once the drugs had worn off.

***

As Susan walked past the majestic architecture of the BBC broadcasting house, she felt a sense of nostalgia. She turned right into Duchess Street with Colin beside her, then sensed a little tingle on the back of her neck. She had only worked with Martin at this office for a few months before they moved, but even so, it held a special place in her heart. However, today they were here to see Ernie.

They walked into the narrow reception that in the last century would have been the grand entrance hallway to what at the time was an exceptionally large, luxurious home to some wealthy Victorian family. Now divided into small modern office units, the carpet was as deep and soft as ever. Once occupied by Hayden Investigations, the door to the right now bore a new name.

"Susan and Colin, how lovely to see you both." Ernie stood up from his desk that was squeezed into one corner of the reception. He smiled broadly. "I can tell you I miss you working here and Martin too. You all brought a little ray of sunshine and humour into a building full of serious businessmen."

"Thank you, Ernie. Who's in our office now?" Susan asked, pointing towards the door.

"Three young men, running some sort of consulting business, not sure exactly what they do, it all sounds complicated. They're always going off with briefcases for meetings here, there and everywhere. They are nice young men but not as nice as you two."

"Thank you, Ernie," Susan responded. "Well, we thought we would pop in today and tell you personally that the couple you were so worried about, Janice and Luke, well, they're not taking your brother for a ride at all. We have talked to Terry and Ashley, then Colin even followed the couple, and we can assure you that there's nothing to worry about."

"I bet you think I am just an old fusspot getting all het up about them. But I was worried; people I think can take Terry for a ride sometimes, and he can be gullible. It's just me being the older brother; I get worried about the younger ones. Thank you for doing it. Do I owe you any money?"

"Not at all, Ernie; take it as a favour we did for a friend." Susan wondered how well Ernie knew his brother; describing him as gullible was not the way she would have depicted him.

"Well, thank you. I have seen how busy you people are doing lots of investigations; it's nice of you to help me out."

"Yes, Suzie Baby is always on the go," Colin smiled, trying not to sound too sarcastic. "She is currently on the trail of a strange man, Van Gogh. She's searching as many wine bars as she can, hoping to find him in one."

Ernie frowned, his face shaded with a tint of uncertainty. "He died many years ago, I thought."

"Ignore Colin," Susan instructed Ernie as if he were a young teenager and she, his mother. She liked the innocence in Ernie, who could hear a conversation yet not fully comprehend or grasp the meaning of the words or inflections. "He is not talking about the famous artist, just some odd man we are looking for with a funny ear."

A little ashamed by his misinterpretation, Ernie added to cover his discomfort, "I know a man like that. Funny ear, but he is not an artist; not sure what he does exactly. Met him at Hazel's wedding. A strange man with a mangled ear, only exchanged a few words."

"A man with a mangled ear at Hazel's wedding?" Susan pulled up a photo onto her mobile screen, not quite believing that Ernie would recognise the man in it, but just in case, she thought it might be worth showing him. "Is this the man you saw there?"

"That's him, calls himself Goffie. Oh, a bit like the artist, I never thought of it that way before, definitely Goffie. Grabbing a suitcase, is he trying to escape from you two?"

"You say you met him at Hazel's wedding, so I guess both Terry and Hazel must know him?" Colin asked.

Ernie gave Susan her phone back and turned towards Colin, his eyes examining the floral pattern on his blouse; it reminded him of the type of clothes his mother used to wear.

He still missed his mother even after all the years that had passed by since her death. "I'm not sure if Terry knows him; he wasn't there."

Colin glanced at Suzie Baby with a questioning look before asking Ernie another question, hoping to clarify what sounded like a misunderstanding. "Terry wasn't at his wedding?"

"Yes, he was at his wedding, that goes without saying, but he was not at James's wedding." There was a look of understanding now on Ernie's face. "I'm talking about my brother James and Hazel, their wedding. Terry didn't go to that one; well, he was pretty fed up, his wife divorcing him and all that trouble. But that was when I met Goffie when James and Hazel got married."

"We never knew that James married Hazel. Was he the other man that Terry talked about?"

"Yes, it was a very horrid time for our family. Terry had lost his job and couldn't get another. They lost their house, and then Terry started his flying saucer obsession. That was when Hazel took up with James before she divorced Terry, and then she married James. That was the final nail in the coffin for our family; none of us brothers speak much anymore and rarely keep in touch, as you know."

"Where can we find this Goffie person? Do you know his real name?" Colin asked, now having a better handle on the affairs of the family.

"I'm sorry, I don't recall his real name or know much about him. I didn't like him much. I thought he wasn't really the sort of friend that James should have. Hazel, I think, might know, as I recall when James ran off with another woman, she turned to Goffie for support with her second divorce. Although I would have thought doing it for the second time must have made it easier. Not that I'd know, never been married, let alone divorced."

***

"You know this is going to cost us a bloody fortune," Colin commented as the black London cab skewed its way around the Elephant and Castle roundabout weaving between the congested traffic. Having left Ernie at his desk, they had first strolled along Regent Street while piecing together the disjointed picture of the three brothers and the now understandable reasons why they kept each other at arm's length. Assuming that Martin would currently be pleading with his mother for Becky to remain in the family's employ, Colin decided that it might be good to speak to Janice and Luke. They would have a non-family viewpoint of Terry and might well have picked up some gossip or overheard a telephone conversation that might throw some more light on the person who was Terry.

However much it might seem like a family feud, Colin kept returning to the simple fact that the police were mounting some sort of covert operation around Pinkcast. That had to mean something. He called the ex-con at the hotel where he had spied on the couple and easily obtained their address. Now they were in a cab swiftly heading towards the residence of Janice and Luke.

"I've got Martin's credit card, so cost doesn't matter. Sit back and relax."

"It's alright for you to say, sitting there in jeans, this bloody skirt keeps riding up on the leather seats and I'm not about to flash my thighs at either you, or the taxi driver."

"No, and I doubt the driver wants to see them either."

"And Martin actually trusts you with his credit card; the man is getting soft in the head."

"I will have you know I am very trustworthy. Although there have been very tempting occasions whilst passing shops in Oxford Street. However, my honesty has shown through, as it should. It's not as though Martin is a horrible boss; in fact, the exact opposite, he's even giving a job to Becky."

"And you're not jealous of long-legged Becky floating around Martin's house, flashing her eyelashes at him?"

"No."

"Not even a tiny bit?" Colin teased, knowing full well that Suzie Baby had a glint of envy in her eyes.

After Susan had paid the cab fare, they stood on the corner of Risdon Street, close to the Rotherhithe tunnel. They both looked a little lost as they surveyed the four-storey blocks of flats that surrounded them. They walked for about ten minutes through the various blocks, dustbin areas, parked cars and playgrounds looking for Albion House. It was a smaller block of just four terraced homes sandwiched between two larger ones. There was a rank of disabled parking bays in front of it, hinting the residents of that block might not be in the best of health. They rang the doorbell of number two, and the thin frame of Janice opened the door. Recognising Susan, she invited them into the ground floor flat without hesitation.

They were shown into a living room where Luke, on his back, was lying on the floor reading a newspaper, which he held above him. Susan almost missed him. The whole room was a mess. Not a dirty mess, just a mess of clothes strewn over chairs, tall bookcases stuffed with journals, books, framed photographs, as well as boxes that were overflowing with wires. Most of the walls were covered with maps, all of which had notations and highlighted text across them. The only framed picture in the room was a large black and white photograph of an older man with heavy-framed glasses and a cynical smile.

"Who's the man?" Susan asked by means of starting a conversation. She assumed it was either Luke or Janice's father. She was wrong.

"Erich Honecker, General Secretary of the Socialist Unity Party of Germany."

Susan was thrown by the reply, mainly because she had never heard of Erich Honecker and had little idea what the General Secretary of the Socialist Unity Party of Germany did. He didn't even look German, she thought. Lamely she responded, "A union leader, is he one of your heroes?"

"No," Luke replied from behind the newspaper, still lying down. "Janice found it in a skip, where she finds most of our things, don't you, darling? Like that reclining Parker Knoll chair. Worked perfectly but for the family of mice that had already made their home in it."

"I cleaned it up and now it works fine. Susan, have a seat," she indicated a chair which Susan assumed was the Parker Knoll recliner in question.

"Don't worry," Luke called from behind his newspaper, "the mice have gone, although I still think it smells a bit funny."

"Ah, shut up, you moron. Susan, what can we do for you and your friend?"

"The posh geezer back?" Luke asked as he folded his newspaper and sat up to look at their guests. "Jesus, what the hell are you?" he asked, staring in horror at Colin.

"A perfect example of the freedom enjoyed by the Western world. A direct contrast to the suppression and fear in places once run by the Socialist Unity Party of Germany. If you're lost for words, you can just call me Colin and ignore how I am dressed. In return, I will call you Luke and overlook what you are wearing. By the way, Mr Honecker would not approve of your untidy dress sense either."

Janice stepped in to defuse what was quickly becoming a tense moment between the two men. "Quiet both of you." She turned to Susan, "What brings you to our place?"

Susan declined the recliner and launched straight into a simple question. "As you might recall, the last time we were at Terry's, we traced a BMW. We understand there might be another car involved, this one." A little bit too dramatically, Colin thought, Suzie Baby showed Janice a picture of Goffie beside the Qashqai. "I know you might have seen it a couple of times, but have you ever seen it without the woman getting out of it?"

"Never, just seen it with her getting out of it on two occasions."

"And you have no idea whatsoever as to who the woman might be?"

"None, only what Terry has told us, that she is coordinating an alien landing."

It was a clever ploy that Colin had suggested and Susan liked the idea of. Ask a few simple questions with easy answers getting the couple talking before starting along a line of questioning that hopefully would uncover more information about Terry. Susan concluded that such a technique would be approved of by her TV detective idol, Jim Rockford.

"Are you sure you know nothing more about her?" Susan asked again.

This time Luke answered, "What are you going on about? You know Terry only tells us snippets of information for security reasons, as we all need to be careful. We are dealing with a potential invasion of Earth."

"The thing is," Colin broke in, "there is something you should know which must never go beyond these walls." He paused dramatically, ignoring the questioning look Suzie Baby was giving him from the edge of his peripheral vision. "The woman in the photograph is a double agent; she is, like us, working on behalf of the government in order to thwart the alien plans. We are, however, concerned that Terry, through his investigations, will expose her for an agent or, worse still, encourage the aliens to bring their plans forward. We need to know how much you know about the woman, or at least what you have been told, every snippet, from Terry."

There was a suspenseful silence in the room. Luke looked up at Janice, Janice looked at Susan, Susan looked at Colin, Colin checked his red varnished nails; there was an annoying chip on his middle finger.

"If you're from the Government? Can you prove that?" Luke asked.

Colin looked down at him, then began to speak, hoping his gift for reading people's personalities had not waned since he had left the police force. "I can't prove it; people from our department carry no identification. Just to say, our records have shown that you as a couple have always delved into conspiracy theories and relentlessly searched out mysteries. You are no ordinary people; you believe that the unimaginable is possible. The government trusts you both. Therefore, we are sharing this highly classified information with you."

Susan was confused. She had not seen Colin have any alcohol today or pop any sort of pill, not that he was the sort of person who would take drugs, but at that minute in time, he was either having a very senior moment, or he had simply lost his marbles in the taxi.

"Well, if you put it like that," Luke stood up, placing his folded newspaper on a chair which had a broken short leg, "There is something funny about the two of them, isn't there, Janice? Ashley is a miserable little git, always moaning and groaning about this and that, always pushing Terry about what he has from Pinkcast. At times they can be at each other's throats. They are meant to be best friends, but I don't see it that way."

Janice chimed in, "What was it last week Terry said to him when they were having words? 'I took the fall for you; never forget that.' Could they be alien spies themselves?"

"A theory we are considering. Did they get in touch with you in the first instance?"

"Yes, and I thought it strange at the time, didn't I, Janice? We'd been subscribing to their website for about a year. If you must know, for a fifty-pound annual subscription, they provide regular updates on alien activity across the British Isles. Good little website with lots of information. Then one day, out of the blue, they message us and ask if we want to join them. It all makes sense now; they are the aliens."

Susan was sure even in her often-mixed-up world, none of this was making sense. Wisely, she decided to keep out of the conversation and just continue to listen.

"It's looking that way. No doubt they realised how well-informed both of you are about extra-terrestrial matters. How many subscribers do you think the website has?"

"Terry told us fifty-odd thousand. He picked us, just us, out of all those people. You're right. Luke, we are being used; we're not going back. I'm out of there."

"That would be foolish," Colin warned. "They must not suspect who we really are or that you now know so much. You must go back and act normally. Say little and listen lots. We'll be back in contact with you in due course."

"There's something else," Luke added, looking at Janice, "that time we arrived through the back door, after collecting those large maps from Stanfords in Covent Garden." Luke turned to Colin, now regarding him as a fellow alien fighter and not a man in a dress. "Ashley was on the phone as I entered the room. I heard him say, 'what more can I do, Hazel? I just don't know.' He sounded agitated, and as soon as he saw me, he ended the call abruptly."

CHAPTER ELEVEN

"I have never heard such a load of twaddle in my life. I thought Colin had gone off his head," Susan told Martin as she sat on his desk holding a small vanity mirror in front of her to aid the application of a recently purchased cerise-tinted lipstick.

"You're a fine one to talk with your horoscopes, numerology and UFO theories." Martin moved his coffee, which was in imminent danger of being forced off his desk by Susan's bottom.

"I'll have you know all that is real. Colin was telling porkies which is not like him. Well, I suppose he does bend the truth sometimes as we all do. Anyway, we now know where Terry makes his money. Fifty thousand subscribers at fifty quid a year, that's a whopping quarter of a million pounds. Don't you think that's amazing?"

"No, Susan, I think it is scary that fifty thousand people are paying fifty pounds a year to hear a load of tripe about flying saucers. What I do think is amazing is this bacon bap," he held the object up for Susan to look at as if it was a trophy, "the best bacon bap I have had for years. It's from that small café around the corner, no big brand, just a bloke and his family. They are Italian, whoever thought Italians could make decent bacon baps." Martin bit into it as Susan ignored his bliss and continued to inform him about the visit to Luke and Janice, as well as what Ernie had said about Goffie.

She sometimes wondered just why Martin was so sceptical about anything he could not touch or eat. Was it fear, or just unless he understood exactly what was in front of him, he pushed it to one side? With his mouth full, he nodded politely as Susan continued with her report, wiping crumbs from his lips with a paper napkin.

"Now Colin has gone off to see his mates at the police station to dig up what he can find on Terry. It's looking more like he does have some sort of record. I'm going to give Hazel a ring to find out just who Goffie is." She slipped off his desk and picked up her handbag, digging around for the slip of paper on which she had written Hazel's number. The only reason she had taken a note of it was in case she wanted another numerology reading.

"No mention of the missing secret memo that Terry and his cohorts are meant to be in possession of?" Martin asked.

"Nothing, no one knows about it. Someone is clearly lying. You're forgetting the most important question; how did Becky get on with Mother? Did she throw her out?"

"Not exactly, more embraced her like a long-lost daughter, a daughter who is better equipped to deal with life than her hopeless son."

"Oh, will she be around your house a lot now?" Susan asked, hoping the motive for her question was not too obvious to Martin.

"Well, the original plan was that she might pop in, say once a week, to discuss matters, take and give advice. That was how it worked with the other accountant. In the short term, however, Mother has adopted Becky as a type of nursing assistant to help her through the next couple of weeks as she gathers her strength. I think Becky is looking forward to being her carer for a while. Once you get to know her, she is a very caring person, do you not think?"

"She's okay."

Martin could not fail to notice the curt remark. "You're not jealous, are you?"

"Don't you start; Colin said the same thing, and no, I am not jealous of you and Becky. I know it's purely professional, just like the two of us."

"See, great minds think alike. Newsflash: the green-eyed monster hits Susan," Martin laughed. "You've nothing to be jealous of, you're still my favourite oddball woman, plus I'm still waiting for my daily dose of star signs. What is going to happen to all of us Pisces people today?"

Susan opened her laptop in preparation to deliver his daily horoscope, something he was not usually too bothered about. Today, maybe he was just asking for it to make her feel better. If he was, that was sweet, she thought. She also still had a question for him.

"I thought your mother didn't like us common girls being around her only son, or is Becky different?"

Martin moved himself, returning the favour and sitting on her desk. He looked down into her blue eyes. He liked looking into her eyes; they had kindness engrained into them.

"Look, Mother is old-fashioned, incredibly old-fashioned. All her life, she has lived a very protected existence. Money does that; it protects you from the real world. So yes, she does stereotype people very quickly into an extremely limited number of divisions. You and Becky come under the umbrella of common girls with low moral thresholds." He saw the look of anger in Susan's eyes, saw that the kindness had washed away. "I'm just telling you what you already know. Becky is being paid out of the family coffers, so Mother is being Mother. If Becky does the accounts and gets paid for that and she is happy to look after Mother while she is convalescing, then Mother is saving money, and in Mother's mind, the silly common girl is being taken for a ride and it serves her right. Mother would put that down to going to a regular school.

"Mother cannot understand that people like you and Becky are naturally kind and want to help others without looking for any monetary reward. Mother would have a difficult time understanding that concept.

"You are still the only one I want to work with every day. Becky is bearable in small doses. Now, what does my future hold for me?"

Timidly Susan recited what the day was going to hold for Martin. At the back of her mind, she felt reassured that Becky would not be able to muscle in on her hopes.

"Well, according to the stars, your day is 'going to be swamped by authoritarian figures pulling you in directions that you do not see yourself going. Your confidence and charm will see you through.' I suppose that is always true; your charm gets you through." Susan smiled up at Martin, who was still sitting on her desk, when she heard the door open. There stood a grim-faced Colin and alongside him a smartly dressed man in a very fashionable three-piece suit. The tall man had a full head of jet-black hair and an equally stern chiselled face. It was not the sharp cut of his suit or his rugged good looks that caught Susan's attention; it was the warrant card he was holding out in front of him for all to see.

***

Politely Colin introduced the police officer, "This is Detective Inspector Higgs-Boson and he would like a word with both of you about Terry." The tall police officer solemnly nodded to acknowledge both Martin and Susan. They needed no introduction as Colin had already explained the dynamics of the office.

"What like the Higgs boson particle?" Susan asked, much to the surprise of both Martin and Colin, who had assumed such a historic scientific event would have passed her by. The only physics they thought she would be interested in was that of pouring white wine into a glass; evidently they were wrong.

"No, Miss, nothing whatsoever to do with that discovery," his voice was dull. "My surname is a simple amalgam of my father's name, Higgs, and my mother's surname, Boson." The knockdown to Susan was plain to all.

Martin stepped into the void. "So, what is this word you want?"

"First of all, I want to make it perfectly clear to all of you that whatever I say over the next few minutes should not leave this room. If it does, I will deny everything and ensure your life after that becomes extremely uncomfortable. I trust I will have no need to resort to such actions."

The threat was clear to Martin and reminded him of the time he had stood before the authoritarian headmaster at his boarding school, after having paid another pupil to write out a precis of 'Animal Farm' for him. The punishment for that misdemeanour was a four-thousand-word summary of the works of George Orwell. Susan had a similar memory of standing in front of her headteacher, her wayward behaviour centred around selling cigarettes to younger pupils.

"I am conscious that the two of you are aware of an operation my team are carrying out at Pinkcast Ltd. I intend to share with you the reasons we have taken such an interest in Pinkcast Ltd."

Susan wanted to tell him to get on with it, cut out the waffle and get down to the basic, no doubt, exciting facts. Wisely, she remained silent.

"Over the last few months, there have been several burglaries carried out in daylight. The method used and the sort of victim has been consistent across all these crimes. The victims live alone, generally in a flat in a respectable area. The victims are in the main professional people working long hours during the day and therefore leaving their residential home empty for most of that time.

"The other item that links all of them is that they each own a Pinkcast watch, different models, same brand. We have coupled this information with the only other clue we have to the perpetrators, which is some CCTV footage from outside two of the flats showing a cleaning lady arriving during the suspected time of the burglaries. Our enquiries have confirmed that no occupiers of any of the flats in those blocks employ a cleaner. Thus, all our attention has focussed on who the cleaning lady might be.

"She spends about thirty minutes in the building before exiting with a large cleaning bag. We assume it contains the stolen property. Property which in general is hi-tech:

laptops, voice assistants, watches, jewellery and on odd occasions a few DVDs."

"And you think Pinkcast are at the centre of these crimes?" Susan asked, for no better reason than she was fed up with hearing the monotonous voice of the Detective Inspector.

"Not the company but two of the employees who have shown up on our radar: Nigel Butler and Hazel Gray. Hazel recently left Pinkcast. They have access to live data and information as to the whereabouts of any potential victim, along with the fact they are lovers. They are persons of interest to our investigation. Now I understand you have asked about a Terry Gray and any previous convictions he might have. I can now add more information for you.

"Terry Gray was convicted of fraud some years ago, and I understand that he is also the ex-husband of Hazel Gray. Terry Gray has now joined Nigel Butler and Hazel Gray as a person of interest."

Martin watched as Colin moved from foot to foot in an attempt to keep himself alert as the police officer droned on. Even he felt his eyes starting to glaze over, wishing the conclusion to this monologue would soon arrive, and thankfully, he did not have long to wait.

"I now have three prime suspects who I am convinced have entered into a conspiracy to commit burglaries and steal high-value goods. My plan is to collect proof in order to convict the three of them. This will involve covert observation and evidence gathering, which is where I have a problem."

The officer stopped speaking, fumbled around in his jacket pocket and withdrew a packet of extra strong mints, which he courteously offered around the room before popping one into his mouth. He sucked on the mint a few times before continuing.

"The Metropolitan Police force is no longer governed by police officers but accountants and politicians. We all have our budgets and when they run out, our investigation needs to be scaled down. In my current situation, I have no budget to observe the three suspects covertly. Even trimming my sights just to focus on Hazel, who is, no doubt, the one entering premises unlawfully, I do not have enough budget left. In the meantime, they can carry on with their clandestine activities regardless. This is where you come in, Mr Hayden."

Those last few words snapped Martin out of the torpid feeling that was beginning to overtake him.

"What do you mean exactly by where I come in?"

"I am requesting that you take over covert observation of Hazel Gray for the next few days, during which time I strongly suspect another burglary will take place and we will have in our hands critical evidence. If you can connect her to one of the burglaries and we have the evidence, then the observation can stop."

"Isn't that your job, following suspects?" Susan unhelpfully asked.

"Miss, the clue is in the name of your company, Hayden Investigations. You investigate; you pursue investigations for profit, whereas I carry out investigations on behalf of the Queen."

"All right," Susan's tone was a little confrontational. She missed Colin's eyebrows move in disapproval of the tack she was taking. "We will still be charging you and you have just said you have no budget."

"I would also add," Martin contributed, "I do not think that me working on behalf of the police is a good idea." What Martin wanted to say was that ever since he had agreed to do a simple favour for a casual friend, he appeared to be getting deeper and deeper into a complex situation. Plus, being at everyone's beck and call was a place he did not want to be. It had to stop now.

Ignoring Martin, the officer responded to Susan, "That is just the point, Miss, we will not be paying you. It is a simple favour that you will be doing for me."

"Why would we want to do you a favour?" Martin asked, preparing to refuse to help the police, which sounded a tad inappropriate, but the officer's request did not seem in the least bit right.

"It is better if the clarification for this request comes from Colin's lips and not mine."

Colin started, his voice unusually timid, "You do have a choice. But I was hoping you would consider it very carefully before you make any final decision. I was, shall I say, doing a little covert stuff myself, hogging one of the computer terminals at the police station and pulling up Terry's details, something we all wanted. I pressed the print button to get a copy of his slender criminal record. Sadly, if you are going to commit a crime, in my case, unauthorised access to the Police National Computer, it would be wiser not to do it in a police station under the eyes of DI Higgs-Boson, who just happened to be beside the printer when it churned out my request.

"The options we have before us are: one, Martin follows and records the movements of Hazel over the coming days; I would point out that is my preferred option. Or two, I am charged under the computer misuse act and get a criminal record for myself."

A sardonic smile broke across DI Higgs-Boson's face; he rarely smiled any other way. "I repeat, would you be prepared, as a favour, to help the police?"

***

Susan closed the door as soon as Colin left with the Detective Inspector. She turned towards Martin and started jumping up and down, clapping her hands.

"Helping the police, how cool is that going to be? We have reached the pinnacle of private investigators aiding real crime fighters. I am living the dream, you know." She looked at Martin; his face was glum; it certainly did not appear to reflect her enthusiasm.

"I would suggest it is more of a nightmare, Susan, a bloody nightmare."

Martin stood up, walked the three short steps to the window. He looked out across Tower Bridge that had just opened for a large sailing boat passing through it to reach the Pool of London. He spoke as he continued watching the bridge, "First off, you do realise we are being blackmailed by the police, which I am sure is some sort of crime. Then you need to consider that we will need to be furtive, concealing ourselves behind trees, ducking down beside rubbish bins, spending hours in a stuffy car watching a door that never opens, that is what they are asking of us. All of which is not how I imagined I might spend the next few days."

"I am starting to agree with your mother that your paid-for education was a waste of money."

"What has my education got to do with any of this?"

"Terry has a device on Hazel's phone which tracks her. I am thinking we can sit in a wine bar and then just ask Terry for the printout of where his ex-wife has been. I think Jim Rockford would have been proud of me."

"Susan," Martin turned to look at her, "did you not get what that weird detective said? Terry might well be in cahoots with Hazel and Nigel. He is not going to help us track his co-conspirator."

"Oh, come on, Martin, use some of that logic you are always telling me you have. He is only a suspect because we wanted to know a little more about him. Alright, he had a fraud conviction a while ago, but you have heard him, he hates Hazel and I don't think he is lying about that. I am sure he has nothing to do with these burglaries; why would he? He is making a small fortune from his website and the UFO stuff. And if he were involved, would he have shared so much information with us? I don't think so." She watched as Martin sat back down; undoubtedly, he was considering what she had said.

"Okay, Miss Marple, what is your plan of action?"

CHAPTER TWELVE

Martin negotiated the small roundabout on Blackheath. Thankfully he was going in the opposite direction to the rush hour traffic, making his journey more manageable. Why on earth city planners had missed southeast London from the underground network was an absolute mystery to him. Jumping on a tube to arrive at your destination was easy. There was no need to negotiate heavy commuter traffic or find a place to park your car when using the Underground. South London roads seemed to be coloured either with red route lines or double yellow lines, neither of which aided parking. If you did find a vacant parking spot, it often turned out that a resident's permit was required.

Fortunately for Martin, the address that he was travelling to had none of those frustrating restrictions. The smart residential line of maisonettes in Lee Green welcomed drivers and their cars. He parked effortlessly just a few doors down from number seventeen, turned off the motor and looked across at his passenger. Susan had slept through the entire journey and only now did she seem to be stirring, sensing the car had stopped.

"You look rough, no, not just rough, totally wrecked," Martin commented.

"Thank you, Martin, I feel it."

Martin was grateful that Susan had called Hazel yesterday to try and extract the real name of Goffie. The phone conversation had sounded tense as Hazel appeared not to be keen to share who exactly Goffie was. About being photographed passionately kissing a man, she could not say as she did not recall the kiss. It was only when Susan promised faithfully that they would not mention him to Terry that Hazel relented and gave up the full name and address, describing him as just a friend. If Susan had tried the call this morning, it would not have gone well. As she slumped into his car this morning, Susan's brief explanation for her condition was a night out with the girls, which Martin understood had only just ended.

"Well, hungover or not, let's go and knock on the door and speak to this Ray Hill, AKA Goffie. Do you believe Hazel when she says he is just a friend?"

"I don't care," Susan groaned, her voice husky, which Martin thought should sound a little sexy, but he still preferred her normal chirpy voice. As she went to open the car door, she stopped and exclaimed, "that's him!" Her voice lighter, she said, "Goffie is coming out of his house."

"Let's go and grab him before he gets too far," Martin suggested. Susan ignored him.

"No, wait." Susan pulled Martin's arm, stopping him from exiting the car. "Let's shadow him, see where he goes."

"Why?" Martin asked. For him, the man was there, so ask the questions, get the job done.

"It might help the case. Know a bit more about him."

"Really?"

"Don't be such a bore, Martin. Let's get out and follow him. I've done it before with Colin, dead easy. Plus, I recall you have Googled how to, so you know the basics. Out you get."

Walking behind Ray Hill, Susan's head was now clearing. The cool fresh air was helping her gather her senses, although her headache remained. They kept a steady pace, ensuring they were always about fifty yards behind their target. There was no doubt in either Martin or Susan's mind that it was Goffie they had seen in the photograph. The ear, the nose and the rounded face, this was Hazel's kissing friend from the hotel. He strode along Courtlands Road, crossed the busy Eltham Road and continued walking along Horn Park Lane.

"Do we know how far he is going?" Martin asked, already fed up with just walking behind someone with no idea as to where their destination might be.

"Don't be so stupid, Martin; if we knew where he was going, we wouldn't need to follow him, would we? I would have thought you could have worked that out for yourself, as you're the one without the hangover."

Ray Hill walked with a relaxed stride, hands in his pockets, looking ahead all the time, seemingly unaware of anyone following behind. Horn Park Lane was long and very straight, with neat, detached houses on either side. Martin could have seen himself living in this part of London, but for the lack of a tube service. He wondered if there were any plans to extend the district line this far south in the future.

"So why the binge drinking with the girls last night, celebration, or a commiseration?" Martin asked, walking alongside Susan. He was hoping to start a conversation to take his mind off aimless walking. It occurred to him that Ray might be going on an exceptionally long walk through the streets of London, maybe one that would take a few hours. Thankfully, judging by Ray's physical makeup,

Martin assumed he was not the type to take part in long walks.

"Celebrating Becky getting a job, the one you gave her. We're all pleased for her. She has her funny ways, but beneath it all, she has a heart of gold. From what she told us, your mother seems to have taken to her."

"Yes, so I heard last night. Mother was gushing about Becky, although I think it is more to do with the fact that Becky makes me look bad. I made dinner last night, which I think I just passed the test for. It was the lack of conversation at dinner Mother chastised me about. 'Becky is sweet, helpful and always happy to partake in conversation', apparently I am not chatty at the table. Tell me which son is chatty with their mother?"

"Most nice boys are. It's just you."

Martin decided to change the subject. "This is a long road. Are you sure he won't notice that we are following him?"

"Martin, stop worrying. Few people, so I have read, notice others around them. We could be almost on top of him and he still wouldn't think anything of it."

Susan was not going to admit it, but she was starting to feel a little 'icky. The lack of breakfast, the excessive amount of alcohol still in her veins and the exertion of walking along this long road were beginning to take their toll on her.

Horn Park Lane ended abruptly as it abutted the busy dual carriageway of the South Circular. Ray waited briefly at the edge of the pavement before traversing between the fast-moving traffic to the central island. Then he paused again before crossing at the first opportunity.

Martin was not as brave as Ray when it came to crossing busy roads. He dragged Susan towards the pedestrian lights just a few yards further on. Even though Susan protested that they could lose the tail, which sounded far too American for Martin, he insisted they play it safe. All the while watching Ray as he walked in the same direction and into Alwold Crescent, precisely opposite the crossing where Martin and Susan safely crossed in front of stationary traffic.

Martin had often heard the term 'on the other side of the tracks'. Alwold Crescent was definitely the other side of the carriageway and a world apart from Horn Park Lane. A council estate built in the fifties; it was now a mix of private homeowners and housing association tenants. A blend of interests that left some houses tired and shabby. Unkept gardens next to pristine landscaped front lawns. The contrast was obvious.

As the road snaked onwards, they saw Ray enter a house close to a wide-open grassed area, which Susan assumed represented the centre of the estate, where they now stood waiting, waiting for Ray to reappear.

"What is the plan now, Miss Marple?"

"Wait, what else?"

"Well, he could be in there for hours. It might be a good friend who invited him round to watch a film, have a meal, a few drinks. He might not come out again until tonight."

"If that is the case, I will need two things: food and a 'pee'. Not necessarily in that order."

"Sorry to tell you but all I have seen so far are residential houses, no shops or toilets. If it is a long wait, you had better cross your legs."

They both tried and failed to look inconspicuous on the grassed area, where there was not even a bench to sit down on. They waited in silence, wondering who might be the first to suggest that Ray would most likely return eventually, in which case, why not go back and sit waiting in Martin's warm car. Susan was on the verge of conceding when Ray emerged from the house, carrying a plain brown cardboard box of a similar size to a family-sized packet of corn flakes.

Ray did not appear to notice that he was again being tailed along Alwold Crescent, across the South Circular and all the way up Horn Park Lane, before finally reaching Courtlands Avenue and stepping into his house holding the box.

Martin considered the last forty minutes a total waste of time. Susan tried to point out that it might provide vital evidence into whatever was going on. She would have liked to debate the matter further with Martin, but her bladder needed emptying; consequently, she was eager to knock on Ray's door. She just hoped his toilet was clean.

"I've been expecting you. Hazel called last night and told me all about you. Best come in."

Politely he opened the door wide and showed the two of them in. Susan quickly asked if she could use the facilities. She could not recall Jim Rockford doing such a thing, but when nature calls, you must answer. He looked at her with mistrust, then he saw the desperation in her eyes and directed her to the first door on the left. She scuttled off as Martin followed Ray through an 'L'-shaped hallway into what could only be described as a multi-purpose room.

It was a large rectangular room with a substantial window spanning the shorter right-hand wall flooding the room with light. A breakfast bar with the kitchen beyond where beechwood wall cupboards flanked a smaller window was to the left. The two long walls of the room had no windows but some unusual features. In the middle of the room was a long fabric sofa strewn with newspapers, which Ray moved to allow Martin to sit down. To Martin's right, along the entire length of the wall was a workbench, totally covered in part-assembled, or part dis-assembled laptops, depending on your point of view. There were a few flat-screen monitors, various wires, cables and computer components, as well as a range of tools, some hanging from a rack on the wall. Illuminating the bench was an Anglepoise lamp extending from the wall.

The other side of the room was similarly bizarre in that it had, what appeared to Martin, to be a very long empty fish tank for about three-quarters of the wall, with a large television completing the last quarter to reach the window at the adjoining wall. Martin also noticed an odd odour that he could not quite identify.

Once Susan had made herself comfortable, she sat alongside Martin. Ray had pulled over a stool from the workbench, allowing him to be higher than the two of them, thus making Susan feel a little uneasy.

"Hazel called me last night to warn me that I was going to get a visit from a couple of Private Detectives working for Terry. I gather he's still trying to ensure that any sort of happiness eludes Hazel." His voice was soft and a contrast to his face's hard, rough features, which Susan had described as being plain ugly. "Now you are both here; what can I do for you?" he asked, fiddling with a small terminal screwdriver he had picked up from the workbench.

Martin began, "Simple question. What is your relationship with Hazel? Are you lovers?"

"Simple question maybe, far from appropriate, but I am happy to answer. I have nothing to hide from you or Terry. The more I can upset him, the better I will feel. We never started out to be very close. I was friends with James, Terry's brother, but you must know that. I attended his wedding to Hazel. That was maybe only the second time I had met her. After the wedding, we kept in touch. Well, I was at that time friends with James and therefore came into regular contact with Hazel.

"As you know, James went off the rails and started an affair with another woman. Ugly bitch, but nevertheless, he was besotted with her and divorced Hazel. I told her the problem with marrying brothers in a sequence is that the apple never falls far from the tree. Although the older brother, Ernie, does seem a little different. Anyway, I stood by her during the divorce, much to the annoyance of James, who thought of me as some sort of traitor. I saw him as untrustworthy. Again, a trait that Terry exhibits.

"Now, before you start jumping to conclusions, we never started our relationship until well after the divorce and even now, it is somewhat unconventional. I think modern parlance is 'friends with benefits'. You must have seen her purple place; it would drive me mad. In the same way, my workshop first, home second attitude drives her mad. We could never live together unless we are in a bed and you cannot spend your whole life in bed, although I read that John Lennon tried it once."

"What about Nigel, her other boyfriend? You must be jealous of him," Martin reasoned.

"Our relationship is not exclusive. Hazel is free to see other men just as I am free to see other women. One day I hope that she finds true happiness and settles down. Talking to her, I doubt Nigel is that special one. She might not have told you, but the fact that she is now the 'other woman' makes her feel very uncomfortable. I suspect that Nigel will not be on the scene too much longer. The last thing Hazel wants is to be the cause of a divorce."

"Yet she still spends weekends away with him?" Martin was not sure just what sort of weird relationship Ray was describing.

"Yes, and some days during the week as well. It's to do with star signs and all that baloney. She's waiting for some sort of celestial alignment before she tells him it is over. Hazel is sweet, just a little bizarre."

Martin felt a slight connection to Ray; their disbelief in horoscopes was something they both had in common. Even though Martin had taken a liking to Ray, there was still something that was nagging him. "You seem to have a strong opinion of Terry; have you actually ever met him?"

"No, never seen him in person or even spoken to the man. My judgment is based purely on second-hand information that I have obtained from people around me, like Hazel and James. Some might say I am being unfair; I would say I do not really care what other people say."

"So you met James before he took up with Hazel? Yet you've never met either of his brothers socially."

"As I said, I've never met Terry. I have met Ernie; he was at Hazel and James's wedding. For obvious reasons, Terry was not there. If you are going to push me about where I first came into contact with James, please do not jump to any conclusions about me. I just want to be honest with you both as you are doing some sort of investigation and I am sure you will find out anyway.

"I shared a cell with James in Belmarsh prison. He was doing three months for stolen property; I was doing six for having a little too much cannabis on me. I would point out that I have changed my ways and being in prison gave me the time to learn a new trade, hence the workshop. Repairing computers is a lucrative pastime. I would buy my own place, but banks do not view ex-cons as being prime candidates for business loans."

"James was in prison as well?"

"Yes, I did say that the two brothers were alike in many ways. I am sure you know that Terry also spent, I think, about nine months in prison for fraud. He skimmed off some cash from the customer accounts, don't you know? As I said, the apple never falls far from the tree. I bet their old man was a bit of a rum character too.

"Well, now you know all about me, will you be passing all these interesting facts to Terry? Satisfy his warped curiosity?"

"He did ask us and now we know it would not be right to conceal just who you are from him. You don't mind?"

"Why would I? There is nothing to hide."

"I have a question," Susan spoke, "the box, there on the floor, I might be hearing things, but is there some sort of noise coming from it?" She pointed to the box that they had seen Ray collect earlier.

"That will be my mice getting a little fed up with being stuck in a box."

"You keep pet mice?" Having put Ray in the ugly but all right sort of bloke box, Susan was surprised that he was a pet lover, let alone one of little furry mice. "Is that their home?" She indicated towards what was some sort of empty, large, glass fish tank that almost dominated the room.

"I would suggest it depends on your point of view. Yes, I will be putting them in there later, but I don't see them making their home in there. They are feeder mice."

"What are feeder mice?"

"The clue is in the name. I feed them to the actual animal which inhabits that terrarium. That's another clue." Ray smiled warmly and he revelled in talking about his unusual pet.

Susan looked at what was to her a big glass box with some soil in it, together with a selection of what looked like bark and a lamp at one end. She felt a little scared to ask just what might be living in there that lived on a steady diet of mice. From her safe distance, Susan examined the rectangular home. She could not see any sort of creature in it, big or small. It appeared empty. Ray stood, walked over to it and moved part of the top from the terrarium. Then, with both hands, he delved into it.

A smile broke across Martin's face as he guessed what Ray might be pulling out. He wondered how Susan might react; he did not have to wait long. Ray carefully lifted a snake out and turned towards Susan.

"Meet my special friend, Sandie. Sandie, say hello to the nice lady."

Two things happened; Susan screamed then tried to back away. The sofa precluded any sort of escape.

"Don't tell me it's a poisonous one, and don't bring it any nearer." Susan was alarmed more than scared. She had never been so close to a snake before. The only ones she knew about were those in horror and adventure films, which in the main tended to be dangerous to the hero and were swiftly killed to allow the story to progress. Even though this brown snake was maybe only about two feet in length, it wrapped itself around Ray's hand and wrist. Susan had no intention of getting to know it better.

"Sandie is not poisonous. She is a Kenyan Sand Boa, who is, on the whole, very friendly and sees us humans, being so big, as a fight, she knows she is not going to win. Sandie will not hurt you. Although your reaction is not unusual, many people have an aversion to snakes. Hazel is as bad; she refuses to sit in this room because Sandie is in the corner sleeping peacefully."

"May I?" Martin stood up and moved towards Ray and Sandie. Soon it was his hand and wrist that Sandie twisted around, appearing to be pleased there was another man interested in her. He smiled and stroked the body. "She has lovely markings, so pretty. Have you had her long?"

Ray gave a short history of how he had acquired Sandie and how his interest in what he described as 'loveable serpents' had begun many years ago. He was now a strong advocate that they made perfect pets. Susan did not look convinced in the slightest.

She asked Martin, "How come you have such a soft spot for snakes? I wouldn't have believed it of you. I thought cats were your thing."

"You are right; a cat would be my first choice," Martin nodded. "I grew fond of snakes when I dated, only for a short while, a stripper who used one in her act, bloody great thing that was. Yet so calm and friendly, the snake that is, she was a lot more temperamental, or in the end, more mental than temper."

CHAPTER THIRTEEN

Her hunger had not yet abated, and her stomach still rumbled, complaining about the lack of sustenance. Susan was feeling better, though, now that the alcohol had diminished to the point of almost not existing in her bloodstream. She sat thinking as Martin drove back towards their office. She half-listened to him talking about Ray, who looked a tough sort of geezer, yet appeared to be a kind, pet-loving guy who just lived an odd life at home with his computers and pet snake.

Last night talking with her girls, as she liked to describe them, which included Becky, Susan had come to a decision. They had all agreed it was for the best. She called her father. The conversation was short, polite and he sounded pleased to hear from his youngest daughter. Tonight, she was going to see him in person. Without the alcohol in her body, nerves began to well up in her stomach, which did nothing to help the pangs of hunger. What would she say? Would it become tense and awkward? Would she regret making that call last night? She needed a prop to lean on.

"Martin, what are you doing tonight?"

"Nothing much; why do you ask?"

He listened as she explained who she was visiting and why she wanted someone beside her for support to give her a little more confidence.

"Are you sure you want me by your side? I'm not family, nor have I met your father before? Would one of your girlfriends not be a better choice? Or your current boyfriend, perhaps?"

"No boyfriend at the moment, but I would prefer a man beside me. I think it would feel better for me, you know. A strong man ready to step in if things get heated."

"Aah, you want a bodyguard. Well, I am flattered that you think of me in such terms. How can I refuse such an invitation?"

***

It was not a big surprise to Martin that when he called Terry to tell him the identity of the mystery man kissing Hazel, he did not know him. It just confirmed that the brothers did not converse about their lives in the slightest. Terry was, however, appreciative of Martin taking the time to investigate and complimented him on his detecting skills, which Martin thought was ironic.

"I need to ask a favour of you now," Martin began, "I know that you have a tracking device on Hazel's phone. Can you share that data with me, starting from when you gave her the new phone and perhaps for the next couple of days too? Just where she goes and when. I daresay you have the information on some complicated spreadsheet."

There was a short silence on the phone before Terry asked, "Why do you want that information?"

The question was what Martin had assumed would be asked, so he had already prepared a viable answer to cover the real reason. "I think she might be connected to that missing memo I am trying to locate."

It seemed the reason was one that Terry could imagine being true. "Sounds like the sort of thing she would do, especially as they sacked her. She would have taken what she could; vindictive bitch she can be."

Martin thought that was rich coming from Terry, who spent most of his waking hours devising plans to derail Hazel's life.

"You're right; I do keep an excel spreadsheet starting from her birthday; I'll send it to you in a couple of days."

***

He looked a lot older than Susan recalled. It was not just the deep-set brown eyes that were now under-scored with dark curves of sleeplessness, nor were those extra flashes of grey that peppered his thinning hair the reason. Maybe it was his rounded face, dry, almost flaking in parts, his skin looked stained with a pale hue, and there were lines of anxiety etched into his forehead. Yet his smile refused to be aged by either worry or battered by the emotional trauma he had endured. That ever-recognisable smile belonged to Susan's father, who, as soon as he opened the door to her, she hugged tightly. He returned the embrace, clearly relieved that his youngest daughter was once again in his arms.

The one-bedroomed flat where her father now resided met her expectations of the way he had always lived. Everything was neat and tidy. One sizeable reclining chair in the middle of the room was ideal for watching the wide-screen television that was affixed to the wall. To accommodate his guests, he had commandeered two chairs from the dining room table, which was placed against the Juliette window. On that table stood a half-assembled model of a Flying Fortress. That, in turn, was surrounded by the paraphernalia of an ardent model maker, a hobby Susan knew he had followed all his adult life. She could only imagine how disappointed he might have been producing three daughters, none of whom had any interest in second world war aeroplanes.

Susan was given the reclining chair with Martin and her father sitting on the dining room chairs, their backs to the television. The conversation started awkwardly and politely, slowly relaxing until it was as if they had just not seen each other recently. Susan talked about her new job with Martin, telling her father they were sort of detectives. They were, she reassured her father, as safe as houses. She said to him that she still drove the same old Ford Fiesta. Her father expressed surprise that the fan belt was still hanging on after all this time. He was convinced it should have been replaced the last time he had looked under the bonnet of the ageing car. Turning to Martin, he pointed out that the fan belt had the odd chunk of rubber missing and was cracked all over, advising Susan she should replace it. He guessed it was just like her not to get round to those sorts of things. To which Susan added, 'if it isn't broke, why fix it?' Martin nodded politely, having no idea where the fan belt in a car might be, and fully agreeing with Susan's point of view.

Then it was catching up on her father's activities since she had last seen him three years earlier. He still worked at the same engineering firm where he had spent the last twenty-four years refurbishing armatures. Once again,

Martin had heard the word yet was unsure why or how you might renovate one. It was only as he picked up clues from the conversation that he assumed that the armatures her father rebuilt were parts of a car, the words dynamo and vintage were mentioned as he half-listened.

"Are you sure I can't get you a brew?" her father asked, adjusting his gaze between Susan and Martin.

"No, thank you, Mr Morris, Susan and I are going out a little later. She is treating me to dinner."

"Call me Dickie; everyone does."

Martin listened patiently as the conversation moved onto the welfare of his other two daughters and his grandchildren. Susan updated him, all the time thinking of the elephant in the room and how to approach the subject which had split them apart in the first place. She need not have worried; Dickie was happy to broach that sensitive subject.

"I am glad to see you, Susan. I have missed you and your sisters over the last three years. I'm blaming no one," he pointed out firmly. "I know emotions at the time were running high. I understand how terrified you all must have been, seeing that your mother was seriously injured with broken bones and head injuries after the lorry knocked her off her cycle. When the doctors told me that they could not be sure if she would ever recover consciousness, and even if she did, there was no telling how far she could recover. They doubted she would be able to move and her mind could be just a shadow of what it had been before. They suggested it could be kinder to let her slip away peacefully. I don't know why I'm telling you all this; you knew at the time and you had all the same information as me. I understand that all of you wanted to fight. Just like your mother, you are all fighters, not wanting to give in until the last battlement has fallen. It was the hardest choice I have ever had to make in my entire life.

"It might surprise you, but parents often have private conversations that only they share. Death sometimes comes up in those conversations. Who might go first? How to care for the other? How to keep our dignity whilst fighting a serious illness? We just assumed such choices would be much later in our lives. Deep in my heart, I know that your mother would not have wanted to be a vegetable relying on others to do everything for her, feeding, washing, and emptying pee bags. Her family having to give up so much just to keep her alive, possibly in a state which would prevent her from communicating with us at all. I knew she would not have wanted that.

"It was not easy to let the only person you have ever loved slip into the arms of death. I miss her every day and still have restless nights, wondering if I made the right choice. I understand why you were all so angry at me. I am not asking for your forgiveness, just your love."

Martin saw the tears welling up in Susan's eyes as she lunged forward and embraced her father. He checked his pocket for a packet of tissues, as they were going to be needed.

By way of changing the subject, Dickie, still hugging his daughter, smiled at Martin and asked him, "How do you put up with this mad daughter of mine? Has she told you how much trouble she was when she was little?"

"Dad, don't give away all my secrets."

"Have you told him about the way you like tomatoes? Sliced in half, then a liberal squirt of tomato sauce all over them. Martin, we tried to dissuade her, but she was insistent, 'what else do you do with tomato sauce?'"

"Dad, I was only six at the time and I have grown out of it. I now just pour it over my chips." They all laughed. Martin continued the 'let's poke fun' at Susan theme with his mistrust of the horoscopes that she quoted daily. Susan felt relieved; it was so much like old times. Her dad was still her dad; it was just he was now alone and lonely, something she planned to change. Having broken the ice with her father, she aimed to visit him weekly.

***

"I was hoping for something a little more exotic for my treat than a chicken and chip shop," Martin pointed out as the waiter placed a plate of chicken, sweetcorn and chips in front of him.

Susan grabbed a sauce bottle then liberally sprinkled it over her chicken breast as she replied, "Nando's is not a simple chicken shop; it's a restaurant that specialises in spicy chicken dishes. Wait till you taste that Peri-peri chicken. I thought as you took me to that nice restaurant, The Papillon, the butterfly in French, I'd take you to a place where they serve chicken butterfly".

"That is a very tenuous link, Susan, but I'll accept the reasoning behind it. Is that why your meal was free, promoting this place and bringing in new customers?"

"No, it was my loyalty card. I've picked up enough points for a free meal. I bet your posh Papillion restaurant doesn't do a loyalty scheme."

"That is a good point. I'll mention it to them the next time I am there."

As they ate, Susan talked about her time as a young girl playing with her sisters. She shared memories of her mother, occasions where she chastised her daughter for wearing too much make-up or clothes that did not fully cover her vital parts. Susan acknowledged that her parents were the people who shaped her and made her the person she is today, however good or bad that might be.

Once they had finished their meal, they turned their attention to the other diners around them, ridiculing people's odd habits. The woman who had at least ten corn on the cobs filling her plate and nothing else. Their theory for such a food choice bounced between a dietary condition which only allowed her to eat corn, 'Turkey syndrome', as Susan called it, to being ultra-vegetarian, or possibly misreading the menu as she was not wearing any glasses. Martin tried the pun that it would be 'a-maiz-ing' if she finished her plate, which took a long moment for Susan to understand fully.

As Susan came to the end of her 'Gooey Caramel Cheesecake' and Martin finished his coffee, she asked a question that she had been pondering for some time.

"Now you have asked Terry to share the details he has about Hazel's movements over the coming days, do you think there is a chance he is in cahoots with her and will give us a pile of lies as to what she gets up to?"

"I thought you felt he was not likely to help his ex-wife in the pursuit of criminal profit."

"A girl can have second thoughts, can't she?"

"Of course. But to be honest, I don't care as long as I have some sort of log of her movements, accurate or not, to give to that pain in the arse inspector so that Colin is free and we can all return to normal."

"Isn't that being dishonest? Even more so as you've been asked to do it by a policeman."

"How come you have gone all legal and above board? I'm sure the police are not meant to delegate their work out to members of the public. He's doing it on the side; serves him right."

"Yes, but if Terry does make Hazel look as pure as the driven snow and she is still doing these burglaries, what about the next victims, the robberies you could have stopped? You'll be inflicting misery on all those people needlessly."

"Susan, has the free meal you have just consumed turned you into an angel?"

"No, but you have to admit I do have a point."

Martin thought, 'yes, you do'. It was one of the better arguments from Susan, which he was finding a little difficult to counter.

"Okay, tell you what, Susan, tomorrow you can call the inspector and get a list of previous burglaries, dates and times, and we will see if we can prove where she was on at least one of those occasions. Then we can get back to relaxing and seeing friends for lunches."

"But for getting sued by your school mate," Susan reminded Martin.

"Something will work out."

As if on cue, his phone rang. He looked at the screen to see just a number, no name, which usually meant a sales call, wrong number, or even possibly a rich, attractive millionairess he hoped. However, it was none of these. He answered the call and spoke for under a minute before putting the phone down and looking at Susan, puzzled.

"That was Nigel. He wants to pop into our office in the morning. He says he has something for us."

CHAPTER FOURTEEN

"It's a lot smaller than I imagined," Nigel said, standing in the office doorway, unsure if there was enough space for him to sit down anywhere. "You're a bit like a Russian Doll." A description that Martin thought was odd. "I got to this building and thought nice place, must be a big detective agency, just like you implied, then I saw you were only on the third floor. Again I thought, well, not as big as the whole building but a whole floor, not a bad-sized company. Then found out that there were other businesses on the same floor. OK, it's a detective agency, how much office space do they need? Then I find you both in this cupboard, again not what I expected."

Susan retorted, "Are you an estate agent now?"

"Just saying, being an international detective agency, I was expecting something a little bigger."

"That's because you don't understand the private investigator industry," Susan pointed out, getting annoyed that anyone was putting down Hayden Investigations. "This is not our main office; this is where we meet some clients. Obviously, for security reasons, we can't have members of the public walking into our main office and seeing our field agents, potentially seeing sensitive information on screens. This is merely a sterile meeting room."

'Sterile?' Martin thought; he hoped Nigel would not look on the floor and see the crumbs from the Danish pastry Susan had consumed earlier. Not only that, but cleaning was not included in this special arrangement with the landlord, and both Martin and Susan had not yet got around to giving it a good clean-up.

"Point taken. I see now I'd never make a good private investigator. Anyway, thanks for seeing me at short notice."

"You said on the phone you had something for us." Martin wanted to bring the conversation back to business.

"Hazel has told me that you know all about what we are up to, so to speak."

Martin was not sure what anyone was up to, let alone Hazel and Nigel. Yes, he knew they were having an affair, which according to Ray, was ending soon. Apart from that, Martin was blissfully ignorant of any other personal associations. He had a bad feeling that he was going to find out soon, and it was not going to be good news.

Nigel continued, "You also know that Terry is a very jealous ex-husband, to the point of being very vindictive towards her." Martin nodded; he had forgotten he also knew that maybe it was time to start taking notes. "Well, I never knew how far he would go until our IT security bods found there had been a breach. Someone had hacked into one of our servers, stealing my office documents, works schedule and my private calendar. They traced it down to a virus in an email I had been sent by Terry Gray. The IT bods didn't seem that worried about the whole thing, put it down to some sort of prank."

"That's not what you expect of IT security guys," Susan said, echoing what Martin was thinking.

"All our IT guys are lazy gits; they swan around in designer jeans and jackets doing sod all." The tone of jealousy was unmistakable. "But I knew the name, and I knew exactly why he wanted my personal calendar. He planned to get evidence on me and tell my wife, which I think is really cruel."

Martin wanted to point out that deceiving his wife was also cruel. He was sorely tempted, just for fun, to point out that Hazel was about to dump him but thought better of it.

"Now he had access to what happened in the past, entries which were pretty obvious, 'Haz her place', 'Weekend Haz', 'Long lunch Haz', it would not take a great mind to work it all out. Plus, our IT department gave me a firm guarantee that he would not break in again, which I know he did, collecting more evidence. I needed it all back and to stop him somehow. I came up with a plan. Please can we keep this next part to ourselves? I told Grant, your schoolmate, that a certain memo had been stolen in the security breach, a memo I knew he would want to get back at all costs, and as you know, he does."

"Let me guess," Martin interrupted, "that memo was never amongst the stuff that Terry swiped off your computer. By the way, I just went to school with Grant, and I do not count him amongst my friends."

"That's right. Terry never had it, so you see why it is difficult for him to give it back. I have a solution."

Nigel pulled a small USB stick from his pocket and placed it on the desk in front of Martin.

"The memo is on there, protected with my password to prevent you from viewing it. You can give it back to Grant and make him a happy man, and then we can all go back to the way we were."

Susan picked up the stick and examined it as if she was trying to read the memo telepathically, something which Martin would not have put past her achieving. She handed it to him; he had no idea what she wanted him to do with it. Susan then gave him an odd fifties private eye look. She turned to Nigel, who seemed to tremble under her gaze. Martin wondered if he should look around for some sort of spotlight to shine in his face.

"And where do we say we found this?"

"Tell him Terry gave it to you after you put pressure on him. Say what you like, just give it back to Grant, and everyone will be happy."

"You want us, Hayden Investigations, to lie? We have a reputation to keep and lying is something we do not do. What's wrong with telling him what you did?"

"Because he has been looking for an excuse to fire me ever since he found out about Hazel and me. He made threats, so I sacked her to get him off my back."

"You sacked Hazel?" Susan sounded and was astonished. "What sort of bloke sacks the woman he is sleeping with? Bet she wasn't too pleased."

"It was a sticky patch, but I think we are through it now. Things are looking good."

Martin and Susan looked at each other, both thinking, 'shall we tell him?' Maybe there was something in this telepathy lark, Martin thought. He turned to Nigel.

"I am sure we can come up with a solution where Grant is happy. Perhaps the next time you see Hazel, you should start sorting out a date when you are going to finally leave your wife and move in with her before Terry decides to force your hand."

"I will soon, I promise. There are just a few things I need to sort out. It is difficult to work out the best moment to leave the wife. I did at one time..."

Martin stopped Nigel; there was no way he wanted to listen to the sorrows of a philandering husband. "Do what you have to. We'll get this memo to its rightful owner."

As soon as Nigel had left, Susan was badgering Martin to plug the USB stick into his computer to see what the memo contained. Even though Martin pointed out to Susan that they had been told it was password-protected, she would not take no for an answer. Dutifully Martin plugged it in, only to be shown a screen that was waiting patiently for an expected correct password to be entered.

Never one to be easily beaten, Susan tried several possible passwords that Nigel might use. Martin looked on as she eagerly typed. 'HazelNigel', incorrect password was the reply, which came as no surprise to him. 'NigelHazel' drew the same response from the computer. 'NigHazlove', 'PurpleHaze', 'Pinkpurplehaze', 'Nigelb', all drew a blank. Martin was impressed by how Susan worked through a vast number of possible passwords, none of which worked. For now, she had to admit defeat.

***

"The email is on its way, so he said."

Susan sat in front of her laptop, staring at the screen, waiting for the email to magically appear; nothing stirred.

"I've been thinking," Susan sounded a little hazy as she spoke while staring at the screen (Martin knew the phrase was a warning of some madcap idea about to follow) "that we should have proper email addresses. You know, Susan at Martin Hayden Investigations dot com, like a real business. It would make us look truly professional and it's what every company has nowadays. I can't remember the last time I licked a stamp to send a letter. What do you think, a good idea?"

Martin laid his newspaper carefully on the desk before he looked across at her. Well, looking across sounded as if he was in some grand office, when in fact, Nigel had been almost right in saying it was more of an elongated cupboard. He could, if he wanted to, reach out and touch Susan on the shoulder.

"Let's examine the argument you have just put forward. By the way, stamps are now lick-less, and you just have to stick them on. We are not a real business, and I could not honestly describe us as professional unless being a headless chicken and running around is some sort of profession. Plus, I would not think we would fit into the division of being 'like every company'. At least in the old days before emails, all the junk that came through the post were things like Reader's Digest offers and money off coupons. Now all that ever seems to arrive in my inbox are messages from despatch services saying my new smartphone is waiting to be despatched, or some foreign general wants me to launder a few million dollars through my bank account. Besides, I thought you were a supporter of the theory; if it ain't broke, don't fix it."

"Yes, but I am also a supporter of the if it ain't broke, don't fix it but do replace it with a better model."

"I presume this has something to do with our website?"

"I just think we ought to present a more professional style to the world. My Gmail account is not the best place for work emails. Ah, at last, the email has arrived with the list of addresses we wanted."

Susan had called Detective Inspector Higgs-Boson earlier asking him for a list of the homes that had already been burgled. At first, he was a little hesitant as it was, after all, a police matter. Susan countered that she was now working with the police and so was entitled to have the list to compare it to the data they already had. In the end, he relented and asked for her email address, which he had expected to be a company one, not her personal Gmail account. Susan assured him it was all part of their security measures. Finally, he relented.

They had no real idea why they had asked for the list in the first place, and now that they had it, they were not sure what to do with it. Susan decided to look at the times she was with Hazel or had called; neither coincided with a burglary. That only proved Hazel could be the intruder. Next Susan suggested putting pins in a map to see if there was any sort of pattern. Despite Martin putting down such an idea as a waste of time, Susan remained convinced that it always worked on TV. While she was searching around the office for anything that resembled a pin, Martin saw a link.

"Look at this, Saturday afternoon. A second-floor flat was robbed of an Apple Mac, three TAG watches, two DVDs and a selection of smart plugs. Look at the date, Susan. That was when Hazel was under the watchful eye of Colin at that hotel."

Susan peered over his shoulder – he was wearing his Boss aftershave today, which she liked –he was also totally correct; it was the same day.

"So she can't be the cleaning lady who is robbing the flats. Assuming it was a cleaning lady, there were no CCTV images at that one. Still, we can assume that there is another woman in the frame doing the deeds. What about Nigel's wife?"

"What about her?"

"She could be the cleaning lady thief. That sounds cool, 'The Case of the Cleaning Lady Thief', or should she be a thiefess?"

"No, I don't think the academics who decide on words could ever imagine a woman ever doing any wrong."

"Very funny. Nigel must have someone helping him, and he's a bit of a ladies' man, so Hazel might not be his only bit on the side. Think about it, if that was the case, he gives his other lover the details, she commits the crime and he has the cast-iron alibi of being with Hazel."

"Let's not get carried away. We can just give this to the police and let them sort things out. Plus, if we then collect some more information from Terry, we can hand that over to them as well. That way, we wouldn't have to trail around behind Hazel to get Colin out of trouble, which is the only reason I am doing this."

CHAPTER FIFTEEN

They had arrived unannounced, much to Terry's annoyance. However, he invited them in, where they joined Ashley, who was busy bashing hard on the letters of his keyboard. Ashley barely looked up as Martin and Susan sat down on a pair of very rickety plastic chairs.

"I thought you might have at least called first so we could arrange to meet up somewhere," Terry pointed out. His tone was sharp, reflecting his irritation that the pair were here in his house. Knowing exactly what they were going to ask for, he considered trying to deflect the conversation, but as ever, Susan liked to get straight to the point.

"We've come to collect the information you have collected about Hazel's movements." As soon as she spoke the words, she felt an ominous change in the atmosphere in the room. Terry frowned at her. Ashley stopped typing and swung around on his worn typist chair and looked directly at Terry with a menace in his eyes.

"Hazel's movements? What are you talking about?" He waited for Terry to answer. Once again, Susan got in first.

"Her movements over the last few days, where she has been, the time she has been there."

"Why, what's it to you where she goes?"

"We need to find a memo that she might have some connection to." Susan tried to make her words sound convincing even though she knew full well she was lying.

"Are you tracking Hazel?" There was a firmness to Ashley's voice, which he directed towards Terry.

"What is it to you if I am? She's my ex-wife, and I like to know what she is up to. Don't tell me you never stalked an ex. Oh, sorry, I forgot, you've never had an ex for the simple reason that you have never had a real woman in your life."

Martin was shocked by the venom in Terry's voice towards a friend. He was also surprised that within minutes of arriving, the two of them appeared to be working towards some sort of argument that would do credit to any old married couple. Susan sat back in her wobbly chair and decided to watch the show that was about to unfold.

"If I did have an ex-wife, I would let her get on with her life and do exactly what she wants, without blocking every chance of happiness that she might have. Don't forget it was you who ruined the marriage in the first place."

"You know that is a total lie. She ran off with my brother because she could not hack a life without me earning megabucks and keeping up with her excessive spending. I never saw at first that she was a scheming bitch who loved only one person, herself. And before you start on me being a jailbird, do you recall it was me who took the blame for you?"

There was at this point a pause in the ever-increasing volume of their voices. Ashley looked timidly at Martin and Susan, reflecting that they had just been granted access to a long-held secret. He decided that if secrets were coming out, then this was as good a time as any. He now spoke to the two visitors explaining his side of the quarrel that had developed.

"Terry's right; he did do time for fraud. Someone was skimming a very small percentage off client accounts, building a nice little nest egg. Even if I was the one pressing some of the buttons and amending some of the programming, it was Terry who thought up the idea and convinced me to join him. So I don't feel guilty in the least or indebted to him for keeping my head down and him taking all the blame. He was, after all, the leader, something he always likes to be, bossing people around."

"I took the blame because your sister asked me to. I did it for her, the woman I loved at the time and I have regretted doing it ever since."

"Another woman?" Susan commented absently, trying to keep in touch with the developing number of accusations being thrown around.

"No, Hazel is Ashley's sister. She pleaded and begged me not to implicate her dear sweet brother. I was a bloody fool to do as she told me. I did my time inside while he stayed out and spent the cash."

"Hazel's your sister?" Susan sort to clarify, turning to look at Ashley, she did not wait for an answer. "You never mentioned it before."

"Why should I? It has little to do with interfering do-gooders."

"But the two of you are still friends? Why?" was the question that now bugged Susan. She had assumed that Terry and Ashley were friends with a common interest in flying saucers. She had not imagined their lives had been so intertwined.

Ashley and Terry looked at each other as if they were asking themselves, 'why are we friends?' yet they knew a common interest bound them. It was Terry who offered an explanation.

"I hate to admit it, but Ashley is a computer genius at programming, hardware, collating information, you name it, he can do it. He also shares my passion for making contact with those civilisations from other universes which are visiting our planet. I need his skills in the same way as he needs my skills, which are about financing our venture, the website, marketing what we do, investigating the practical side of things. We are a good team. It is just such a shame our history is chequered."

"Even so," Ashley added, "you are tracking Hazel for no good reason. Was she the one you sent Luke and Janice after?"

Terry nodded to confirm.

"That's why you drew in those gullible idiots to do your dirty work. You are a prize bastard at times. Just to be clear, you have data that shows exactly where Hazel has been over the past few months. A sort of Terry version of Google?"

"Yes. I suppose you want me to stop now."

"You're a grown man, do what you want. I'm her brother, I will tell her and you can do what you like." At that, he turned back to his computer and retreated into his world, once again tapping the keys with an added intensity built out of anger.

"Anyway," Martin said, relieved that the raised voices had stopped, "the information about Hazel, do you have it?"

***

Martin drove away from Greenwich with Susan sitting beside him, reading through the long list of entries Terry had made on a printed sheet. Martin braked sharply as the driver in front suddenly decided that a right turn was in order. "What is it with drivers who wear a hat while driving? Maybe it's a sign they should not drive, no fashion sense, no driving sense?"

"It is a known medical fact, I'll have you know, that drivers who wear hats do actually overheat their brains, thus disrupting the neural pathways and leading to confusion and bad judgment."

"Is that true?" Martin asked.

"No, of course not, silly. Like I would know what neural pathways are, but it sounded good. My stars said whatever I say should be convincing. Clearly, I appeared to know what I was talking about."

"There is a certain logic to what you said. I'm sure there is some scientist somewhere doing that sort of research. What does the list look like?"

"A lot of numbers and street names, times and dates, what else would you expect? I think the police will be happy with this. What do you reckon about Terry and his mate Ashley? They sounded like a gay couple having a fight about who is the better looking."

Martin did not fully agree with Susan, although he had found it odd that Terry and Ashley were working so closely together despite their apparent animosity. It did begin to explain why Terry liked to meet away from the house, thus preventing Ashley from overhearing conversations about what he was really up to. This led Martin back to wondering just what was in the memo? Indeed, it must be something so contentious it was forcing Pinkcast to spend a lot of money to get it back. He was as curious as Susan; he just did not want to admit it to her.

Still, as far as Martin was concerned, he now had the memo back and planned to return it to Grant. First, there was the handing over of evidence to the police, which technically Martin had collected, although not by following Hazel. Once the police had the information in their hands and Colin was no longer under threat of criminal charges, Martin would be free once again. Free in plenty of time for his next stag night to be held in Nottinghamshire this time. Friday night drinking with the wedding on the Saturday, that could be a challenge, a challenge he was looking forward to. All he needed was a companion to take with him. The invitation clearly stated Martin and guest, which at the time he was expecting to be Jenny, now his ex-girlfriend. He began to run through some of his other suitable female friends.

"Higgs-Boson has sent a text. He wants to meet up in 'Icy Cone'," Susan interrupted Martin's thoughts as she tapped out a reply, "not far from the police station. Sounds fun."

"What is Icy Cone?"

"Martin, I at times wonder if you are a resident of this planet. Icy Cone is one of the best ice cream parlours around, with an amazing range of flavours. I had a birthday bash there once. It's one of the advantages of being born in August; ice cream can be on the menu. Do you like ice cream?"

"It's all right, but that is beside the point. What is a police officer doing arranging a meeting in an ice cream parlour? I thought they did all their deals and meet-ups in smoky bars and pubs. You know, drinking whisky in the morning and stuff."

"You've read too many American thrillers. It's a new age, Martin. All those professions are now following a healthier lifestyle. Police, journalists, stockbrokers, all have dropped the alcohol and gone for the sparkling water."

"Is that one of your oddball theories?"

"No, I read it in the paper. I'll pop the address in the sat-nav. Then you do as the nice lady tells you, while I consider what I want as a treat."

***

The black-painted frontage of Icy Cone was sandwiched between a Heart Foundation charity shop and a Polish supermarket just off the New Kent Road. The only break in the single block of colour was the name Icy Cone that was spelt out in gaudy multi-coloured lamps. The lights would not have been out of place if they were on a tall Christmas tree as they flashed on and off in no particular order. The overall impression was of a cacophony of colour. At night, the name was only fully visible for about three seconds in every minute. Countless members of staff had tried to understand the controls for the shimmering lights. All had failed miserably to comprehend the written instructions, which appeared to have lost a lot in translation. They were waiting for a Chinese customer who might speak Cantonese to offer a better translation in exchange for a giant sundae.

Detective Higgs-Boson, looking as smart as ever, was already sitting on a red PVC chair in the centre of the parlour at one of the dark plastic tables. As Martin walked in behind Susan, it reminded him of some dark American diner from a fifties film he had once seen. He dreaded what the coffee might taste like.

"Hot 'n' Cold Chocolate Fudge Volcano for me, please." Susan smiled at the waitress standing beside the table, entering her order onto a small tablet.

"Banana Berry Split, with two extra scoops of mango," Higgs-Boson said as he carefully and neatly laid the menu back onto the table.

"Black coffee, please." It was all that Martin wanted, something that Susan was not happy to let happen.

"You can't come to an ice cream café and order just a black coffee. There's plenty to choose from, have another look, Martin, don't be an old fogey." She waved the menu in front of him.

"I am not really in the mood for an ice cream."

"These are not ice creams," Higgs-Boson pointed out as he brushed an imaginary speck of dust from his lapel. "An ice cream, to be clear, is what you get from an ice cream van or some tacky shop at the seaside. A dollop of half-frozen white creamy substance, loosely described as ice cream, is deposited into a stale wafer cone and that is what you are offered in both cases. You then walk along the street trying to multi-task, eating and avoiding other pedestrians. That is an ice cream.

"The offerings here are works of culinary delight, gelato creations that tease the palate, comfort the eyes and ignite a warmth within one's body. Try one, Martin, can I suggest, for a beginner like yourself, a simple choice. Based on your predilection for coffee, I would try a Coffee Arabica Gelato, which shows how real ice cream should taste; just two simple scoops to start you on your journey. In time you will be sampling the more complex flavours within a sundae and hopefully seeing the light."

The Detective's summary of ice cream only made the waitress more impatient. She curtly asked, "Does sir want the Coffee Arabica Gelato or not?"

Martin nodded that he did and then asked the inspector, "Isn't it a bit unusual to hold business meetings in an ice cream café?"

"Parlour," the detective corrected Martin. "You can hold them where you like. I prefer ice cream parlours for the simple reason that I am an addict to ice cream, the flavours, the syrups, the fruits. Sadly, my wife maintains that she's allergic to the stuff and refuses to have any in the house. I, therefore, purchased a freezer for my garage, which is the only place I am allowed to eat ice cream on my premises. Hence I must take every opportunity to indulge when I can. Now, talking of business, what do you have for me?"

In two parts, Susan presented their evidence, putting Hazel somewhere else during one robbery and then offering the most recent locations she had attended, all neatly listed in an Excel sheet that Terry had given them. Higgs-Boson started examining the data. He paused when his Banana Berry Split arrived to savour the flavours and question Martin on how he was finding the two simple scoops of Gelato. However much Martin tried, he could not summon up the enthusiasm displayed by both the police detective and Susan.

Once finished, Higgs-Boson returned to the sheets of data. He looked disappointed and began to explain in his slow, yet precise way, which Susan was sure would have sent her to sleep if she had not been watching Martin scraping the last of his coffee ice cream. She sensed he might be a little hooked. Higgs-Boson agreed that on the face of it, Hazel looked unlikely to be the cleaning lady, a theory that had formed the major plank of his investigation. He still refused to discount her and Nigel from his lines of inquiry. Together they would have enough background information to carry out the crimes; of that, he was convinced. The only thing this opened his mind to was that there might well be another woman involved in the conspiracy. Politely he thanked both Martin and Susan for their help, adding that Colin's misdemeanour had flagged up another possible co-conspirator in Terry, especially as he was Hazel's first husband.

"What do you think?" Higgs-Boson asked.

It was a simple question that sparked Susan into a frenzy of excitement. She loved being asked by a real police officer for her opinion of a suspect in a criminal inquiry. The emotion caused her to flip her empty sundae glass off the table onto the floor, where it smashed into tiny pieces. After the weary waitress had cleared up the mess, Susan, now a little calmer, answered the detective. Higgs-Boson listened with interest as Susan gradually revealed her main suspect, followed by her reasoning. At the back of her mind, she felt she was acting out the end scene in an Agatha Christie mystery.

***

"I'm pleased to report to you that I am no longer under the threat of being carted off to a police cell. D.I. Higgs-Boson, bless his little cotton socks, has got what he wants thanks to my two diligent private detectives." Colin spoke as, by way of a gesture of his gratitude, he made them both a coffee. "You could do with some decent mugs for your hot drinks. I'll gift you some of mine next time I am in."

"I would add," he continued as he handed out the refreshments, "he was none too pleased to have one of his chief suspects, AKA Hazel, have an alibi for one of the burglaries. Although he did tell me his ears pricked up when Suzie Baby mentioned her suspect, and I must say, Suzie Baby, I am inclined to agree with you. She fits the part for the cleaning lady's estimated height and build. Plus, I have learnt from the man himself that she has a criminal record. Very astute Suzie Baby, very astute."

"Hear that, Martin, I'm an astute detective. I bet you're jealous to have such a sharp-eyed gumshoe on your team."

Martin looked and sounded unimpressed. "If we are talking about the female side of that weird partnership: Janice, I doubt she would have the intelligence to know what was valuable in a flat. Also, let us not forget it was Terry who picked her out of all his subscribers and she was spying on Hazel and Nigel for him; it makes no sense."

"He has a point, Colin."

"I thought the same at first," Colin acknowledged, flicking the hair from his blonde wig out of his eyes. "Why strike up a conversation and become friends with the very people you have under surveillance."

"As I said, she does not have a great deal of intelligence."

"Maybe, but I can now see that it would have been possible. When she was at the hotel, I noticed that Janice had a small tattoo on her wrist, the spider web common in prisons. That might have led to Hazel starting a conversation with Janice if she and Nigel were looking for someone to break into the flats and take most of the risk."

"But the thing is Colin; I have a new theory," Susan admitted, which encouraged Colin to smile and Martin to rub his earlobes. Susan's theories often descended into chaotic ramblings, ending in her screaming at those around her who were pointing out the obvious errors in her thoughts. Patiently, as friends do, Martin and Colin listened. "Since yesterday, I have been thinking about this whole case in a new light."

"There is no case," Martin interrupted.

Susan looked at him, raised her eyebrows, tutted, then continued ignoring him as she often did. "Ever since Nigel gave us back the memory stick with the memo on, I wondered just why he did that. Now I think I know. He's scared; with us still poking around in his and Hazel's business, we are going to uncover something in the end."

"Suzie Baby, if Nigel had as much intelligence as he wished he had, he would know that Martin has had enough poking around to last him a lifetime."

Undeterred, Susan continued, "Nigel is afraid we will uncover what they are up to, doing all these burglaries and stuff. As far as I'm concerned, he has admitted his guilt."

"If only convictions were that easy, Suzie Baby. Don't forget, you managed to prove Hazel's innocence. I would have thought his gesture of handing you the USB stick thingy was a thank you for saving his mistress."

"No, don't forget I have been thinking about the case," Susan countered in a determined voice. "For the minute, take the cleaning lady out of the equation. Maybe she has nothing to do with the robberies. It could be her appearance is distracting us all."

"She is on CCTV, Susan, on a couple of occasions when there was a burglary in the block of flats in which she was seen going in and out. Plus, I hate to remind you, but you did put Janice right in front of the Detective Inspector as your chosen suspect. No doubt he is following the cleaning lady theory, which I think holds water."

"A woman has the right to change her mind, plus this theory is far more plausible. Alright, Janice seemed to fit the cleaning lady, but it's just too much of a coincidence that she and Hazel met up via Terry. A better theory is that there is no cleaning lady, and in answer to your question Martin, it could be someone in the flats was hiring a prostitute at the time and did not want to admit it to the police."

"Sounds very kinky, Suzie Baby, a hooker dressed as a cleaner. I suppose there's no accounting for taste. All the same, a hooker just at the same time as the robberies, that is a bigger fluke than Hazel meeting Janice via the ex-husband."

"Look, you two, just give me a chance," Susan protested. "Nigel and Hazel get the info and then Ernie's youngest brother James does it. He is another ex-con who is out of work and I bet is well suited to breaking and entering houses."

There was a respectful pause as both Martin and Colin considered the theory. After all, Nigel and Hazel had no idea the police were investigating them. It would make sense. James was, after all, family of sorts, as one of Hazel's divorced husbands. Granted, he was not in paid employment, but he did seem to have a job of sorts duping free meals from mourners, which in turn could easily provide an alibi if he needed one. There was still the question of the police CCTV of the cleaning lady, who was either involved or a very busy sex worker.

"Well, it is a theory, though not a perfect one," Colin concluded.

Susan continued having taken that comment as a strong encouragement which it was far from. "I also spoke to Terry to ask him just what sort of thing this flash Pinkcast watch can tell them back at the depot, which will be the same information that Nigel will be working with. Well, it will blow your mind. He did a live test for me while I was on the phone, no less, he broke into their server. Apparently, the IT staff at Pinkcast are not very good at their job. Anyway, Terry told me my height, weight, how many hours of deep sleep I had last night, the computer that I use at home, how far I had walked that day, my average heart rate and my current blood pressure. I can tell you it spooked me out. So, Nigel has all that information as well as, very important this, knowing where the watch and presumably the customer is, at home or not! And there is more. He also told me that, looking at Nigel's computer access log, Nigel had looked at three addresses, in particular, the last time he logged on. He gave them to me and I am going to give them to the Higgs-Boson bloke for him to see if anything happens at those addresses."

"Well, Suzie Baby, I must say I am not wholly convinced about your theory, but knowing of three potential burglaries does seem to be a good idea. I'm sure old man Higgs will be pleased; he needs all the help he can get, even yours."

Martin was quiet. The other two put it down to his lack of general enthusiasm about digging deeper into a case, which he would deny was even there. In fact, he was thinking, making up his own theory.

"Still," Martin broke the silence, "I cannot see it. Plus, it is not much to do with us now; it is all in the hands of the police, which is for the best. I just need to drop Grant his secret memo back, and I can finally return to my preferred daily routine, leaving all this detecting behind for..."

Martin was interrupted as Susan blurted out a blasphemy as she watched her coffee cup up-end and displace its hot liquid contents across the keyboard of her laptop.

There was a frenzy of activity as the three of them scrabbled around to grab anything that looked the slightest bit absorbent to mop up the spill. Colin pulled a wad of tissues out of his handbag, Susan grabbed Martin's newspaper, and Martin grabbed the roll of paper towels from beside the kettle and joined in the action.

After much mopping, shaking and wiping, Susan pressed the power button on her laptop, and they all waited in anticipation. As usual, the screen came on, showing a slightly out of focus picture of Susan in a Spanish resort bar with three of her friends, all quaffing large cocktails. Then the small box appeared waiting for her password. She tried entering it several times, but on each occasion, the computer ignored her completely. Colin pointed out that although he was no expert, he presumed that the keyboard was now so high on caffeine that it was not sending the correct letters to the screen, a hypothesis they all agreed on. The solution came from Susan, who decided to take the laptop to Ray, who they knew repaired them for a living. She might get a reasonable rate, 'a mate's rate', as she termed it. Plus, she was working up to holding his snake.

The innuendo of Susan holding a man's snake was not lost on Colin. In fact, he milked it until Susan made it clear that Ray was butt ugly and not her type. At which point Colin reluctantly desisted and suggested that he too might like to see Ray's snake both out of curiosity and never having held a man's snake before.

"Tell you what, you go off with your teenage schoolboy humour and sort out the laptop, fondle his snake or whatever you plan to do. I will, on the other hand, be the adult in this trio and take the memory stick back to Grant to bring everything to a conclusion. I shall then go home and have a relaxing evening with a glass of wine and a movie."

Without a further word, Martin snatched the memory stick from his desk, slung on his jacket and left the office on his way to see Grant at what would, no doubt, be some flash office as large as the man's ego.

CHAPTER SIXTEEN

When he was a child, Martin believed that the Paddington Basin people talked about was a receptacle that Paddington Bear ate his porridge out of. The young Martin could not believe anyone, not even a bear, could live on marmalade sandwiches forever. As he grew up, he became aware of the dreary side of the place called Paddington Basin. That had all changed in recent years when the whole area was redeveloped and turned into blocks of contemporary offices built around the waterway that had opened almost two hundred years earlier.

The last time he had walked through Paddington station and onto the canal-side walkway, it had been no more than a vast building site. Now it was a thriving modern hub of activity. Tech companies, large corporations, all proud of their Paddington address. He walked past the afternoon office workers, scattered around the Sheldon Amphitheatre having a late sandwich lunch, to number Six Sheldon Square, which was one of three similar buildings. It was a far cry from the drab Pinkcast warehouse where he had seen Nigel.

"Good afternoon, sir. Who are you here to see today?" The uniformed receptionist asked in a squeaky voice that reminded him of an American girl he had once dated. The woman speaking to him now looked a lot more attractive than the American whose name he could not recall.

"Grant Fisher of Pinkcast."

She referred to her computer screen. "Wonderful," was all she said, sounding a little too excited, almost as if Martin had just given her an awfully expensive birthday gift. "Just look towards the camera," she pointed to a tiny black box attached to the rear of her computer screen. "Wonderful," she once again commented. She bent down, pulled a small sheet from a printer, folded it in half and slid it into a plastic badge holder, which she then handed to Martin.

"Please read the health and safety instructions on the rear of your identity badge, which gives you important information should we have to evacuate the building. Pinkcast is on the third floor. Please use the elevators on the left; they serve the odd-numbered floors. All offices are well sign-posted when you leave the lift. Have a nice day." Her eyes left Martin and turned to the elderly gentleman standing behind him, who had been patiently waiting for his turn to be photographed, no doubt.

"Shall I read them first?" Martin asked. Why he asked, he had no real idea. Later that day, when he recalled this interaction, he would put it down to practising being sardonic in readiness for meeting Grant.

"Pardon?" She looked a little confused.

"Should I read the health and safety instructions now before I get into the lift or elevator, if you prefer?"

"Whenever it suits you, I suppose."

"Well, it's just that I was thinking if we had to evacuate the building before I got to the lift, then I wouldn't know what to do. So, is it best if I read them now, or would it be better to read them once I am in the lift?"

"Ah." Her lack of decisiveness pointed to the fact that no one had asked her what Martin thought was an obvious question before.

"Son," the elderly gentleman behind joined the conversation, "I've been here many times, never read the damn instructions. My motto is: if everyone else is rushing for the exit, don't hang around for a pee."

"Thank you, sir, wise words indeed. Thank you, miss. You too have a nice day."

The lift lobby on the third floor was a simple rectangular shape. Martin stepped out of the lift to see a door to his left, one to his right and a long corridor travelling on directly ahead of him. The office to his right was bright pink and bore a name in the company's branding image proclaiming Pinkcast Reception.

"Good afternoon, sir, welcome to Pinkcast. How can I help?"

"I'm here to see Grant Fisher."

"You must be Mr Hayden; we are expecting you. Could you stand slightly to the right, please? I need to grab your photograph." She indicated with her hand just where she wanted him to stand.

"It's all right; I was snapped downstairs."

"As you should be, but we also need to photograph you for our security. A little more to the right, please."

"And if I refuse?"

She tilted her head a little to the left, causing her brunette hair, short as it was, to hang across one of her eyes and half-smiled at Martin. "I'd have to ask you to leave. It is our policy that anyone on this floor has their photograph recorded. I have mine here." She lifted her identity badge towards him, from which he learnt she had been blonde at one time. "A little more to the left, please."

"Tell me, why does your policy need to have my photograph?"

"If the building burns down and we need to get out, we can make sure you are safe and well. Full instructions as to the location of the assembly points are on the back of the badge."

"But if I'm outside, I can tell you I'm safe."

"Ah, but if you don't make it out alive, we can identify your body. I do hope that's not the case."

"I'd be burnt, as would my face and my identity badge."

There was a brief yet intense moment as she pondered that thought before ignoring the logic and stating with a little more force than earlier, "It's our policy; you have to have an identification badge before you can enter our offices."

Martin stepped to the left, crossed his eyes, which represented a feeble act of rebellion on his behalf, and allowed his picture to be taken.

Grant Fisher looked very different in the flesh to the way he had during their recent video call. Of course, the same could be said of Martin as he no longer resembled Mr Potato Head, a self-inflicted image he had produced through ignorance. Grant looked as though he had self-inflicted a lot of Botox to his cheeks and eyebrows. His face had all the appearance of an ageing rock star who had spent thousands holding on to his youth only to fail miserably in other people's eyes. No doubt, with his failing eyesight, he still thought he looked pretty good.

"Martin, old boy, great to see you, take a seat. Thanks, Carol."

Carol was the petite young lady who sat outside Grant's majestic office dealing with callers and, no doubt, Grant's ego. Carol was single; Martin had found that out simply by asking her. She had started the conversation by describing him as, "Martin Hayden, Mr Fisher has told me a lot about you; it's a pleasure to see such a famous detective."

There followed a very cosy, friendly conversation during which Martin made it clear he was single, not doing anything later and wondered why such an attractive woman was not married. All she coyly said was, 'I'm still looking for the right person.' Martin was going to point out that he might be that right person and how would they know unless he took her to dinner, when Grant bounded out, slapped him on the shoulder and dragged him into his office.

The office was grand and filled to the brim with Grant's ego. Apart from the three oil paintings of him, there was a glass-panelled sideboard which, as well as a drinks tray of various single malt whiskeys, had a line-up of photographs of Grant with various celebrities. Martin recognised two of them, one being Prince Charles and the other being Hugh Grant.

"Too early for a little snifter?" Grant asked, picking up an expensive-looking decanter.

"Never too early, but I am driving," Martin lied, having decided that the tube would be a lot easier than trying to find a parking space.

"You've done well," Martin conceded. "What got you into watches?"

Grant poured himself a good drink of some sort of malt whiskey and settled into his oversized leather swivel chair behind his equally large desk. A psychiatrist might suggest that the trappings of wealth were no more than some sort of substitute for a lack of masculine prowess. Martin knew for a fact that that was the actual reason, having seen him in the shower after a muddy wintry cross-country run.

"Not just any sort of watch, Martin, a lifestyle watch. I could see the health market taking off, so I got in on the ground floor. Took a trip over to China, had a word with some manufacturers about what I wanted in a watch, and one guy came up with the perfect prototype. Three years later, Pinkcast is now one of the foremost lifestyle watches in the UK market. Keep this to yourself for now, but we are about to burst onto the American market. Pinkcast will soon be a worldwide brand. The perfect timepiece for your wrist and the guardian angel of your health."

"Impressive, our old dorm master would be pleased. He always said you had all the makings of an entrepreneur."

"Old Kennet, yeah, one of the good guys. Always said you were a waste of time, but an international detective agency, not a bad call, old boy. Cheers!" Grant raised his glass and took a large gulp of the amber liquid. "You managed to lever the memo out of that nerd, Terry?"

Martin took the USB stick out of his pocket and placed it in front of Grant.

"It was not too difficult in the end; you could say it handed itself in."

"Top man, Martin, I knew I could rely on you."

Grant put down his cut-glass tumbler and inserted the USB stick into the side of his laptop, tapped a few keys, and a broad smile broke across his face. "Marvellous, and a relief to me, I can tell you."

"How do you know it's there? Is it not password protected?

"Not from my password, anything relating to Pinkcast I have access to."

"What? Everything? I thought it was protected by Nigel's password."

"That might well be the case, Martin, but I am the Chief Executive Officer and majority shareholder of Pinkcast. There is nothing in this company that I am not allowed access to. That is the first rule of my business, it's all my business and anyone here should have nothing to hide from me, especially that little shit Nigel. I'm telling you, Martin, between you and me, I would like to see him out on his arse. I'm only keeping him until the American deal is finalised, then he is out. Silly bugger, screwing around with the staff. I would guess this whole Terry industrial spy thing began with her tempting him with her big tits. You know what women are like, Martin."

Martin was confused. There would have been a time when the mention of big tits would have distracted him, but today it was the words, 'anything related to Pinkcast I have access to'. Martin had not worked for any company, either big or small, except his father's, which he did not count as work. But the top dog of the company who was able to access everything just did not sound right.

"Everything you say, even, for example, Nigel's calendar."

"Yep. That was how I first found out he was messing around with the staff."

Again, Martin would have pictured Nigel fooling around with Hazel in the bedroom, but not today. Today he wondered about having a global password. He wondered just what Grant might be able to do with such a key to all the data held by Pinkcast. He would later consider himself to be acting like a true detective.

"And just what sort of data do you hold about your customers once they have bought your watch?"

Grant closed his laptop, pushing the computer to one side. "I can assure you we fully comply with all relevant data protection legislation. We would be foolish to ignore those laws."

"I am sure you do, but for example, the watch you gave Susan, how much data do you hold on her? I am only asking out of passing interest."

"Well, in general terms, as I cannot discuss an individual, we, of course, hold name and contact details, which is only right in case of a problem with the watch or we need to contact the owner. We also have direct cellular communication with the watch for such reasons as updating software and monitoring the efficacy of the application within the watch."

"What about tracing their movements? Is that recorded and held within your organisation?"

"Martin, old boy, I'm not too happy about discussing these things. Our computers, of course, hold enormous amounts of information, little of which is of any interest to us. Some misguided people think that the big brother state is out to get them. The cold facts are that mobile phones, thousands of CCTV cameras, and even simple store loyalty cards all collect data on our lives and habits. It's the way of the modern world. Hence there are strict data protection rules. Most companies just want to increase sales. Few, I would imagine, really care where their customers go for a walk on a sunny Sunday afternoon."

"I am sure you are above reproach. But in theory, you could find out where Susan is right now."

"It would take a while, I guess and remember it would only show where her watch was located, nothing else." Grant sounded as if he was pleading his case in a witness box.

"Maybe, but then you would also have statistics about her health, weight, height, all that sort of thing that your watch records to ensure the wearer is leading a healthy lifestyle."

"I'm not sure exactly where this conversation is going."

It was clear to Martin that Grant was becoming more defensive and guarded with his words. Knowing him from school days, Martin guessed Grant was hiding something, and he was getting close to a secret.

"I am just interested; I am not a great one for technology. I also think a little knowledge is always helpful for us detectives."

"In theory, I guess you're right; such personal details will be within our databanks somewhere. I am not sure what sort of value there would be in knowing how overweight our client base is. Thanks again for getting the memo back. I have to ask you to leave now, as I am expecting a call from my potential investors in the States."

They both stood and shook hands. Martin wondered about Grant, someone he knew at one time always exaggerated things and he guessed adulthood would not have changed him that much. For some reason, he could not quite explain; Martin knew the memo held the key to a number of questions, together with the answers that Grant did not want to give.

As Martin left the office, he once again looked at Carol as she efficiently tapped away at her keyboard. She looked sweet.

"Any chance this detective will have the opportunity to question you over dinner one night? Help you find the right person?" Martin winced a little internally; that sounded a little too clichéd, even for him.

She stopped tapping, looked up at him and smiled kindly. "A generous offer for which I thank you. It's just I prefer female detectives if you get my drift."

Martin gentlemanly apologised. He resigned himself to his original plan of a quiet night in with a glass or two of wine. He wished her well before he found his way to the lift and exited the building. Thankfully there had been no need to evacuate as he had forgotten to read the instructions.

CHAPTER SEVENTEEN

The first thing Martin noticed as he walked through the door of his home was the tantalising fragrance. An appetising aroma of light spices, a melange of herbs and the smell of chicken gently cooking alerted his tastebuds. The mouth-watering ambience was a total surprise to him. He was more than aware that tonight his mother expected him home, which meant she would be cooking for two—nothing unusual in that arrangement. The pleasant cooking odours wafting through the house was the surprising part. His mother had always kept her cooking simple, plain and overall dull, as she had never really taken to any of the culinary arts.

"Smells good, Mother. What are you preparing?" he asked as he walked into the kitchen to find a taller, thinner, younger woman than his mother, stirring a pan on the cooker. "Becky! What are you doing?"

"Martin, why do you ask such stupid questions? What do you think I am doing?"

"Cooking."

"I see now why you became a detective, incisive observation and a keen knowledge of activities that are carried out in the kitchen."

"What I mean is why are you cooking? Is my mother all right?"

"She's fine. She's upstairs calling one of your uncles, I think. We were talking about recipes and cooking, and she liked the sound of my special slant on a chicken and bacon casserole. Spoiler alert, it's the oregano that makes it special. So here I am. Pass that jug with the chicken stock in it, please." Becky held her hand out, waiting for Martin to hand her the jug, which he managed to do without incident.

He took the opportunity of standing next to her to carry on with the interrogation about the exact circumstances that had led to her cooking in what he considered to be his kitchen.

He then pointed out that she was getting paid to be the family accountant, not the cook. As she continued adding the herbs to the frying pan, Becky reminded him that there was no written job description; therefore, she had no defined list of tasks she should carry out. Their last conversation was that she should spend some time helping his mother's convalescence and she had decided cooking was a part of that. Also, Becky pointed out that she was staying for dinner, which he would see would turn out to be a business dinner connected with her role as the family accountant, so all was well.

As much as he tried to persuade her, Becky refused to discuss business any further until they were all sitting around the table eating and only then could the conversation start. Martin walked out of the kitchen and found himself a bottle of red wine and a glass. He sat down in the living room and started drinking; he had an ominous feeling about tonight. So far, the planned quiet evening was not going as expected.

On the plus side, Martin could not deny Becky's chicken and bacon casserole was delicious. Her cooking prowess, Becky put down to cooking for her grandpappy when she had lived with him. It was not, she quickly pointed out, the cause of his death. The other conversations were polite and banal as Mother, Becky, and Martin finished their meals with Mother declaring that Becky was an exceptionally talented cook. Martin might not be quite so gushing and was seriously concerned that Mother might be grooming Becky to take over the family cooking as well. Mother might have done just that had she not had another idea floating around her mind, which she was now ready to share with her son.

"Martin, we need to speak about an idea that Becky has suggested for us to secure more savings against our income tax bill."

Martin did not like the sound of that. Saving money should have been something he would embrace. After all, what was wrong with saving money. It was just that he was a little apprehensive as Becky was involved.

His mother continued, "It appears that if we make Hayden Investigations a limited company, then almost all the costs connected with it will be tax-deductible. Your salary, rent, running that car of yours, tube fares, even Susan's salary, they are all costs. I cannot imagine why our previous accountants did not mention such a shrewd strategy."

Martin did not have to imagine why; he recalled an in-depth conversation with the old accountant, Mr McFarlane. It went along the lines that Martin's business should be a limited company, a common tax vehicle, nothing out of the ordinary. Martin, knowing a little about companies, pointed out that becoming such an entity would mean he needed to publish accounts each year, which Mother would no doubt have a view of and those accounts would show zero income. This, Martin was in no doubt, would cause more than a bit of friction with his mother as to just exactly what he was doing with his time at the 'office'. Old man McFarlane had very Victorian values and was a staunch believer that women should stay in the house cooking and cleaning and have nothing to do with men's business. He liked the way Martin was misleading his mother over his work and was happy to keep the idea of forming a limited company well under wraps. This arrangement Martin had stupidly forgotten about when he engaged Becky to do the accounts.

"Those sorts of things can get complicated. You need to have things like directors and registered offices, all that sort of stuff, and I am sure we will not save very much, will we, Becky?" Martin emphasised the last part of his sentence to try and indicate to Becky that he thought it was not such a good idea. If he imagined he might have some telepathic connection to Susan, there was no such link with Becky.

"There are a lot of savings to be made," Becky eagerly pointed out. Then added, as if she was driving a stake through his heart, "it's common for the family solicitors to hold the registered address, avoid nasty bailiffs turning up here if things go wrong. As for directors, well, I was thinking you and Susan would make perfect directors."

"Susan!" Mother did not sound the least bit happy. There was a glimmer of hope, after all, Martin thought. He waded in with another salvo against the idea.

"Sorry, Becky, I too would not think Susan is best suited to the many complex responsibilities of being a company director."

"I disagree." Becky pointed out firmly, at some length, that Susan's employment record would contribute to her being a valuable director of any company. She was reminding Martin that he had employed Susan on the strength of her impressive experience in the workplace. Becky did not want to admit the truth of her knowledge of Susan's employment history. Instead, she based her campaign on the curriculum vitae that Colin had earlier composed, based loosely on facts, to convince Martin that Susan was the person he should employ. Becky was sure this was going to be a sound basis. Using her newly acquired position of a family accountant to the Hayden family, she began by reciting all the experience that Susan had gained working at the world-renowned auditors of PricewaterhouseCoopers. Becky as any friend would do, embellished further the original quotes that Colin had created, adding that Susan had been seconded during that time to work at Coutts bank as an advisor.

"Coutts bank," Martin's mother repeated. "Well, they do not allow just anyone to work there."

Becky felt that was a useful embellishment. She then added something only a close friend would know about her coy pal, which was that Susan had spent a year abroad working with disadvantaged children in Spain.

Martin's eyebrows rose at that point. He knew in fact that Susan had spent a year in Spain serving in a bar, working for drinks and the opportunity to meet men of all shapes and sizes. Tempted as he was to point out the blatant lie Becky was putting forward as fact, he did not want to put Susan down in front of his mother. He simply nodded politely as

Mother responded favourably to an account of Susan which made her look to be a cross between George Soros and Doctor Barnard.

Finally, Becky warmly added that having known Susan for several years, she would be the first to recommend Susan, a person who was shy about her talents and experiences.

Martin's mother seemed impressed as well as surprised. To her, Susan had always been an ordinary little girl who should be serving in a supermarket and not working with her son. "That girl does hide her light under a bushel, Martin. I think then, given what Becky has told us, that Susan to become a director of Martin Hayden Investigations Limited is a good idea. Becky, please be a darling and make it happen so we can have Martin and Susan as directors of Hayden Investigations."

"Mother, I think we should discuss this important decision further. There are many things to think about before we dive into such a commitment."

Becky leaned over the table and cupped her hand over Martin's, giving him one of her broad smiles. "You're such a worry pants at times, Martin. It will be fine; people create companies at the drop of a hat, and only when they get really big do things get a little more complex. I guess you have a long way to go before we get there." Her sarcasm was not lost on Martin.

"Good, that's settled then. I think it is rather exciting. My son being a company director sounds so much better than a private eye which makes you sound like some sort of shady American character." Mother turned to Becky, telling her,

"Of course I know dear Martin is nothing like a shady person. He is my pumpkin pie."

Martin hoped that Becky was as good at creative accounting as she was at dropping him in at the deep end.

***

It was a nerve-racking experience for Susan, but she did it, and now she was proud of herself. There she was holding a snake for the very first time; she was not sure just how she had managed to summon the courage, but she was glad she had. The snake felt almost comforting as it slid around her arm and hand. Of course, her heart was beating almost as fast as when she was running to catch a plane to Majorca after she had heard her name being called over the tannoy. She thought Colin was pleased with her effort, even if he did call the snake an elongated worm. Thankfully he did not use that description until they were on their way back, having left the laptop with Ray overnight with a plan for Colin to collect it in the morning.

Susan next called Detective Inspector Higgs-Boson about the three addresses that Terry had given her. He sounded more than interested and although he would not commit, he did say that he would find a way of covering those addresses over the next couple of days.

To compensate for all the excitement of the day and the nervous energy she had used, Susan hit the shops and did a tour of the Southside Shopping Centre in Wandsworth. Now in the comfort of her bedroom, she was trying on the clothes she had purchased from River Island and Next, as well as a pair of comfy trainers from The Office.

Standing in just her bra and jeans, Susan looked at the new clothes strewn on the bed. She was lucky. Not so long ago, she had been jobless and about to be thrown out of her flat. She had been fortunate in meeting Colin as he was the one who pointed her towards the advertisement in the paper for her present position, a position she would never have dreamed of applying for without his encouragement. It was a role that she was enjoying so much and getting well paid to do. Sometimes she wondered what she had done to have so much luck. A knock at the door interrupted her thoughts.

She was not expecting anyone, but then it was only a knock at the door and it was most likely going to be one of her neighbours coming to borrow something. She slipped on her dressing gown, dashed barefoot to the door and opened it to find Terry standing there. He had a strange look in his eyes.

"Can I come in?" his voice was soft. Was he trying not to be heard by the neighbours? How had he been able to get past the door entry phone system? Many questions were developing in Susan's head, all contributing to the fear that she was starting to feel.

"How did you get in?"

"It's very easy to sneak in the door. You can sometimes see a resident enter a number on the keypad. This time I slipped in as someone went out. No one asks any questions; we all assume everyone is innocent. Oh, sorry, that sounds a little creepy."

Susan would agree. She had half a mind just to close the door, but being scared and showing you are frightened were two different things to Susan.

"So why are you here?"

"I have some more information about Nigel that I need to share with you, and it's important." His eyes travelled up and down her dressing gown. "I can come back later if you want."

She looked at him once more. She figured that she could either take him down, or scream loud enough to get help if it came to it.

"Come in, go through to the lounge," she pointed down the hallway. "I'll just get decent."

Now fully dressed, Susan sat opposite Terry so she would be closer to the door.

"Before you start to tell me just why you are here and what information you have, how did you know where I live?"

"Sorry, I should have mentioned it to you on the phone earlier. Pinkcast has your address amongst the data they have on you and I wanted to tell you what else I found face to face."

"About me?"

"No, it's best I explain. I don't want to keep you too long. It looked as if you were getting ready for an early night."

Susan told him she was trying on new clothes. She did not want anyone to think that she was planning to be in bed before nine at night; those sorts of rumours would ruin her reputation. She then bluntly asked him to get on with it.

"Well, as you know, I pulled down some data off the Pinkcast server today about you. At the same time, I downloaded Nigel's data log. It shows the sorts of things he has been doing on the computer, emails he sends, letters he writes, as well as what files he has accessed. Well, when I told you about the three addresses he seemed to be staying in for a while, the log was where I obtained that information. It also timestamps when you do things, I didn't tell you the times because that was not needed."

"Do you have a point?" Susan did not like the way he seemed to be telling her very little while using as many words as possible.

"Sorry. Well, he started accessing the data files which contained the three addresses. The time was 16.42. Now that number stuck out in my mind for the simple reason it was the year of the battle of Edgehill, a famous battle as it was the first in the English Civil War. Am I boring you?"

"Yes."

"Okay, I'll get to the point. Later I was looking to see what Hazel had been up to, as you know I..."

"Yes, I know."

"Well, at that exact time, 16.42, Hazel was with Nigel. I have audio to prove it. Here," he held up his mobile phone, pressed the keyboard and the voices of Hazel and Nigel played out clearly as if they were in the room with them. Susan listened to the two of them talking about their next weekend away. Nigel stated he could not stay more than an hour or so as his wife was expecting him home as on any typical night. They then kissed.

"You can turn it off now; that is more than enough for my innocent ears. I never knew you were able to record their conversations; I thought you could only tell the places that Hazel visited."

"Oh no, the software I put in the phone allows me to control all aspects of it, including the microphone. It is quite standard stuff for investigators. I would have thought you would have known about it."

"We don't discuss our techniques," Susan countered. "Again, what's the point of your visit, apart from boasting that you can record your ex-wife with her lover?"

"My point is Nigel could not have been accessing his work computer and downloading files as he was at Hazel's. There must be someone else retrieving his files."

"Besides you?" Susan pointed out.

"Yes, besides me. The strange thing is that when I break-in, I leave a partial trail back that goes nowhere. You must have heard about the tracing of IP addresses to find hackers. This one is different; Nigel's password was used. That's odd for a hacker unless they are close to, in this case, Nigel. But there's something else. About ten minutes after Nigel left, Hazel answered the door. This is what happened." Once more, he pressed the keyboard, and Hazel could be heard speaking.

'What are you doing here? You were meant to call when... what...?'

"There was then silence and a moment later, the signal stopped. Either the phone was turned off or damaged to prevent it from working. I think someone had told her what I was doing. Whoever came to her door, they came to warn her. They did not want to call her as they knew I could trace all her calls."

"You do realise she might have been attacked and is now lying dead on the floor of her flat. Have you tried to check on her some other way?"

"I'm not that uncaring, I called her landline number, and she answered. I, of course, put the phone down when I knew she was okay. The upshot of this is that something strange is going on. I'm not sure what it is, but I think there might be some sort of criminal activity afoot."

***

He wanted to tell her off like any father, or older brother would have. As Martin listened to Susan recount the events of the previous evening, he felt the anger rising in him. Nothing happened, but that was not the point he would claim. She should not have let Terry into her flat, be alone with him without really knowing what he wanted or intended. She should have left him outside her door and told him to speak to her at the office in the morning, or at the very least, instruct him to speak to her over the phone. Martin was protective of Susan for the simple reason he not only liked her but cared for her and did not want to see her hurt in any way. He also knew as he began to calm down that he was not going to go off the deep end and chastise her, as that could hurt her just as much. He was only relieved that Terry had left without any incident once he had shared what he wanted to with her.

The information that Terry had disclosed changed the thinking of both Martin and Susan. Susan was now convinced that Nigel had nothing to do with all this. Her focus instead had shifted onto Hazel and trying to imagine just who had knocked at her door and warned her about the tracking device in her mobile.

"It has to be Terry's mate Ashley. Remember how he was so surprised that Terry was tracking her. Brothers are there to protect their sisters; he must have gone around there and told her."

Martin could understand brothers protecting sisters. He felt a degree of sympathy for Ashley, and of course, he would want to tell his sister that her ex-husband was stalking her.

"But," Martin reasoned with Susan, "that does not make him complicit in any crime, does it? He is just being a good, caring brother."

"I think you're wrong," Susan was not as forgiving as Martin. "Ashley has all the abilities to break into a computer, even more so if Hazel gave him Nigel's password."

"Come on, Susan, people do not just share passwords."

"Do you want me to tell you your credit card pin number or the password to your laptop?"

"That's different. We work together and we know each other."

"Hazel and Nigel are shagging, are we?"

"Don't confuse me with questions like that. All I am saying is that it is unlikely that Nigel would share his password with Hazel when she could then pass it on to Ashley."

"You have to admit that when you then add Ernie's other brother into the picture, there's a trio set up perfectly for a criminal enterprise like robbing houses. Ashley gets the information, Hazel passes it on and James robs the flat."

"All circumstantial, Susan. I have now learnt that Grant Fisher has a master password that opens anything within Pinkcast, including Nigel's documents. Plus, I would imagine all the personal data required to commit these crimes. He must be a suspect as well. He might be the CEO of the company, but he is one weird person and I would not put it past him to orchestrate such a crime just because he can."

"That is the trouble; it is all circumstantial, nothing concrete to go on."

The door opened and Colin stepped into the office with the repaired laptop, which he waved above his blonde wig, proclaiming that it was all fixed and all done for nothing. He knew where he was going for his computer repairs in the future.

The debate began once Martin had generously offered to make coffee. Colin and Susan were trading wild ideas and complicated theories. Just about every word they spoke sent them off on a tangent and of the suspicions that they threw into the debating ring, few were making sense.

Slowly but surely, everyone remotely connected to Terry's family became a suspect capable of committing multiple crimes. Throughout what at times became heated, Martin maintained that they should just let the police get on with investigating the burglaries, which was their job after all. In the end, it was Colin who sought to clarify or make sense of the madness.

"The thing is, darlings, you are pub police. You know the crime, you know lots of possible suspects, but lack the oomph to go out and gather hard evidence. You prefer to stay in the warm, cosy pub with a drink. Hard evidence gives you the facts. I know I'm going to sound like Martin, but I think we should leave this to the police. I'm sure through their observations, they will have a clearer picture of what is happening. We should focus on those things that affect us, like being in the same room as two company directors."

"I know, I'm excited. I haven't told Martin yet, but I suspect he already knows. Susan Morris, company director, sounds cool!"

"Hold on, you two. I only heard about the plan last night, yet it seems to be public knowledge already. I understood and expected that Becky would more than likely call Susan late last night to tell her the news. But Colin, how did you find out so soon? You haven't spoken to Susan this morning, have you?"

"No. Becky called me the other day to confirm what was in Suzie Baby's CV, seeing as I helped her create it. Becky wanted to be sure she got her facts right so that she could convince your mother that Susan would make an amicable and able director of Hayden Investigations Limited. Clearly, it worked."

"Do I have control over nothing in my life?" Martin sounded exasperated.

"We're men, Martin; we think we're in control only because women allow us to think we are."

"Also, Martin, it's going to be our company, and we're going to be partners." Susan threw her arms around Martin, hugging him enthusiastically.

A sombre voice spoke from the doorway, "Am I interrupting anything?"

Detective Inspector Higgs-Boson looked taller for some reason. Smartly dressed as ever, he appeared to be looking around for somewhere to either stand or sit, neither of which were going to be easy options.

"Have you ever considered renting a larger office? You might find it easier to conduct your business."

Colin offered him his seat, which Higgs-Boson graciously refused, saying he did not plan to stay long and that he was fine standing. He then addressed Susan in his subdued voice, "Yesterday, Susan, you gave me three addresses which you believed could be potential victims of the recent spate of burglaries connected to Pinkcast watches. I was considering how best to observe those addresses, given my limited resources. Fortunately for me, not so for the residents, two of those addresses were robbed yesterday evening. That just leaves one address I need to keep an eye on. I have one of my officers outside that address as we speak. Yesterday, when you gave me those addresses, you told me that Terry gave them to you, is that correct?"

"Yes," Susan sounded a little hesitant as she felt the eyes of everyone in the room on her as if she was performing on a stage. "He told me he had obtained the details from a computer log showing what Nigel had accessed. But last night, he told me that it could not have been Nigel as he had been away from the office at the time."

"Well, I'm here to tell you that this morning we have arrested Terry on suspicion of conspiracy to commit robbery. My dilemma is that I have to wonder just how much you are involved in all this."

"Hold on," Martin stood up alongside Susan, "she has nothing to do with all this. We are looking into activities at Pinkcast, which have nothing to do with robberies. Our investigations are just overlapping. If Susan were involved, why on earth would she give you the addresses that were about to be robbed?"

The Detective Inspector remained silent; he was obviously thinking, weighing up his options. Susan seriously thought she was about to be arrested and could feel her legs weaken. It was Colin who broke into the tension.

"If you are going to nick her, then you don't have a lot of solid evidence. Apart from giving you information, which no doubt you did not act on quickly enough to prevent a crime, she was acting on the instructions of the police to carry out observations that a police officer should have performed. Suzie Baby also pointed out a new potential suspect, who you had not considered. I would imply she is not the stereotypical villain. Unless you have a cast-iron case against Suzie Baby, I would suggest that arresting her would bring you a great deal of embarrassment."

"We'll see. I will be interviewing Terry a little later and I am looking forward to hearing what he has to say." Higgs-Boson turned and walked out of the room.

He did not see Susan collapse into a chair or hear her noisy sigh of relief. She began to wonder what Terry might say under interview conditions. She was innocent; she knew that and so did the two others in the room. She had read about miscarriages of justice, the police getting it wrong, looking at evidence that appeared to show one thing but turned out to be something else. Would they start asking her for alibis for the times of the robberies? But there again, a clever brief could say, after the police gave her the times and dates of the robberies, she could concoct an alibi for each one with ease. Susan felt panic starting to rise in her chest. Luckily for her, she had two strong men beside her. Sadly, only one had any idea what to do.

Colin opened his handbag and dug around inside the jumbled contents. "Martin, come here."

Obediently, Martin stepped forward. Colin opened a lipstick, moved it across Martin's top lip. Martin flinched back at the action. Then Colin quickly wiped the offending red lipstick off his lip.

"What was that about? You trying to convert me?" Martin added his hand to wipe as much as he could from his top lip. "Has it gone?" he asked Susan, who nodded confirmation.

"Where's your car, Suzie Baby?"

She told him and Colin dragged both her and Martin out of the office to her parked car. They tumbled Martin into the back seat while Susan took the front passenger seat, and Colin started the car and began to drive away.

"Where are we going, and what exactly are we doing?" Martin asked from the back seat as Colin progressed through the traffic, not sticking wholly to the highway code. He was in a hurry.

"He has a point Colin, where are you driving us to?" Susan asked. The last half an hour had been confusing for her.

Colin continued to focus on driving as he asked, "Suzie Baby, at home, where do you keep your make-up?"

She frowned, not sure she had heard the question correctly. Nevertheless, she answered, "In my bathroom."

"I thought as much, so do I."

"Oh, why didn't I think of that? No purple lipstick. It's so obvious now! Clever Colin, you've cracked it!" she exclaimed.

Martin called from the back, "Could someone please tell me what the hell is going on?"

***

There was silence as Colin drove with a determined purpose towards his destination, of which Martin had no idea, until a few moments before the car came to a standstill a short distance from Ray Hill's house.

Martin was just about to comment that he now knew where he was but still had no idea why they were there, when together all three of them looked towards the front door, just in time to see a blonde woman step inside Ray's house and the door close behind her.

As he straightened his skirt and made himself ready to exit the car, Colin commented to Susan, "There is either your cleaning lady, or an overused sex worker."

Tagging along, Martin followed the other two trying to get an answer to his questions, amongst which were: "Why are we here?" "Who was she?" "Do either of you know what we are doing?" None of his enquiries were answered.

Colin banged heavily on the door. "Ray, open up. This will be a good time to talk." There was no response, so Colin knocked even heavier on the door before turning to Susan and asking her to call Detective Inspector Higgs-Boson to tell him they have the cleaning lady the police are seeking. Once more, he banged on the door.

Martin became aware of several net curtains being pulled to one side as neighbours wondered why there was so much noise in this normally quiet cul-de-sac.

A muffled voice came from the other side of the door, "It's not a good time. Come back sometime later."

"You don't get an hour in this game, Ray. Just open the door," Colin once again instructed, his voice deepening as he became more aggravated at Ray's lack of co-operation.

"Maybe she's a sex worker, and he wants his money's worth first before we go in. By the way, why are we going in?" Martin asked, again his question was ignored.

Once more, Colin banged on the door, partly to make more of a scene with the neighbours. If Higgs-Boson was slow at joining them, at least the neighbours would spur the local bobbies into action.

"Ray, it's over. We know what you are up to with Hazel and Ashley. It's all over now. The police are making their way here as we speak. You might just as well let us in, so at least we can start to make arrangements so that someone gets to look after your snake once you are taken away."

There was the click of a lock. The door opened slowly. There in the doorway stood a dejected-looking Ray Hill holding a wig in his left hand, his face made up, deep red lipstick, light blue eye shadow, his eyelashes coated with mascara. He wore a black t-shirt with the words 'snake whisperer' printed on it. The skirt he was wearing was a reasonable length if you wanted people to think you were a cleaner.

"You are doing us transvestites no favours at all dressed like that," Colin sharply commented.

CHAPTER EIGHTEEN

Edward de la Roi was not his real name; it was the preferred name that he used whilst serving guests at the Ritz Hotel in Piccadilly. He was born in Braintree and legally called Brian Murphy, which always confused him as a child as he would insist on spelling his address as Briantree.

Today Edward was in the Palm Court serving afternoon tea to a diverse range of people. Tourists, locals, older people and young wannabes all believed the idea of having tea at the Ritz was something special. The customers had spent, what in some cases was a small fortune, for the opportunity to drink tea from posh china cups and eat small sandwiches and even more miniature cakes, in order to say they have had tea at the Ritz.

Over the years he had worked there, he had seen many strange sights in the Palm Court. He recalled clearly a group of six elderly women dressed in nineteen twenties costumes, who halfway through their tea got up and started to dance the Charleston, much to the shock of the management and enjoyment of the other clients.

Today Edward served a trio of people, whom without doubt he was going to include in his long-planned memoirs, which he had provisionally entitled: 'Tea with the Posh and the Tosh'. The group included a youngish man who had breeding and style and, without doubt, fitted into the refined surroundings of the Ritz. With him was the exact opposite, a young woman whose accent was sharp and common; she seemed to be dazzled by the opulence and far too loud in her comments. The third part of the mismatched trio was a transvestite, not that Edward was prejudiced against such people, far from it. He had himself once dabbled in dressing up in female clothes to please an ex-boyfriend. However, this transvestite was ageing and a little too extravagant for the Ritz. He was not so much overdressed, more tasteless. As Edward served them sandwiches, he snatched part of a conversation about bathroom cabinets and toilets, not the sort of dialogue he thought appropriate for the London Ritz.

"What I still do not understand," Martin started to ask as he picked up a version of a simple egg sandwich, described as 'Egg Mayonnaise with Chopped Shallots and Watercress on Brioche Roll', "is how did you know that Ray was dressing up as the cleaning woman?"

"I thought you'd never ask about my immaculate detective skills," Colin bragged. "That day Suzie Baby and I took the coffee-soaked laptop for repair, Ray answered the door a little flustered, as if we had caught him doing something he should not have been doing - well, a man living alone often finds himself in that position. I noticed, though, as did Suzie Baby, a smear of red beside his lips, obviously lipstick. Well, he was either trying out a new look, or dressing his snake up and getting personal; who was I to judge. Then Suzie Baby mentioned the same thing on the way back. You do not want to hear our conversation after that, save to say it was riotous.

"Next day, when I popped in during the morning to collect the laptop, well Martin, when you get to my age, you can't go more than a few yards from a lavatory, such is the weakness of an old man's bladder. Anyway, I had to use his loo, which was cleaner than I thought it might be for a man living alone." Susan nodded in agreement, having herself visited that same toilet a few days earlier. Colin continued, "Well, I was surprised to find in his bathroom cabinet a selection of women's makeup: lipstick, blusher, eye mascara, as well as a sensible foundation used by us transvestites across the world to hide our stubble. Well, I thought…"

"Hold on, Colin," interrupted Martin, "you went to have a pee and after, or before, you rummaged around the poor man's bathroom cabinet?"

"Why not? I always do, don't you?"

"No," Martin said emphatically.

"Suzie Baby, back me up on this one; you went to his loo. You did what, apart from the obvious?"

Susan crammed what she considered was a teeny ham sandwich into her mouth. The Ritz described it as 'Ham with Grain Mustard Mayonnaise on Brioche Bread'. The explanation did not change her opinion of it.

"Of course, I looked in his bathroom cabinet, saw the same stuff, but just assumed that it had something to do with Hazel. I know he said that she never stayed, but she might have popped around for some nooky during the day. Sex is not just for Christmas." She laughed loudly, catching the attention of Edward de la Roi.

"Whoa! Whoa! Whoa!" Martin wanted some sort of clarity to this conversation. "Both of you made use of Ray's toilet, then afterwards you have a good rummage around his bathroom cabinet? His private bathroom cabinet, I should point out."

"Martin, sweetie, everyone does that. You use someone's toilet, then preferably after you wash your hands, you have a little peek into the bathroom cabinet. It tells you a lot about the person, I can tell you." Colin stopped talking to sip his tea, 'Russian Caravan, a classic blend of Oolong Bao Zhong and Darjeeling Second Flush'. Although he preferred PG Tips, he was making the most of this treat that Susan had promised him ever since he had first met her.

"Susan, you have been to my house and you have used the facilities; tell me you did not look in my bathroom cabinet whilst alone in the toilet," Martin enquired, convinced he already knew what her answer would be.

Susan glanced at Colin with a guilty look before looking down at her plate and picking up another ham sandwich, which she held poised just in front of her mouth.

"It's what I do, Martin. I'm sorry, I just find it interesting peeking inside and getting to know more about the person. I know from your cabinet that you are clearly obsessive about how you smell. You have four types of deodorant, two types of mouthwash, a very swish looking electric toothbrush and, what did surprise me, five different types of toothpaste. Plus, I saw a packet of Wind-eze tablets. I never knew that you suffered from wind, Martin. If you ever need to fart in front of me, don't be embarrassed; we're friends."

"Susan, I do not want to discuss my flatulent habits in the Ritz. It is not the done thing. Colin, let's get back to Ray and his bathroom cabinet. What did it tell you?"

"He was either a tranny, like moi, or he made-up for a reason. He was Hazel's boyfriend, yet no sign of her purple lipstick. Let's not forget, he had been in prison. Suzie Baby told us about the two burglaries out of her list of three. When we popped in with our broken laptop, he must have only just got back home after the crimes he had committed. We had nearly caught him dressed as the cleaning lady. At the time, I noticed, there was a bag in his living room under the workbench with an odd selection of stuff very similar to what was often stolen. He seemed to be a likely candidate for the burglar."

"So that was it," Martin asked, "a lucky hunch?"

"A reasonable hunch, I would say."

They stopped talking as Edward de la Roi approached them to serve more tea. Edward hoped his appearance would prevent the common woman from laughing loudly.

Once Edward had left, the three continued to recall and talk about the events after the police arrived at Ray's house. They had arrested him with the loot that he had only hours before stolen. It was never made clear just how the officer who was meant to be watching the flat had missed the cleaning lady arrive and depart. A nearby McDonald's Drive-thru was primarily deemed to be the culprit. The police then moved on to Hazel; she too was arrested, as was Ashley.

Soon after, Colin spent a few hours with Detective Inspector Higgs-Boson at an ice cream bar, learning what had happened. It seemed the fair thing to do as far as Higgs-Boson was concerned, as Hayden Investigations had helped him with the case.

The three of them, Hazel, Ray and Ashley, added their version of the story, and it soon became apparent that Ray might have had a conviction for too much cannabis. The police years ago had suspected him of breaking and entering a number of houses, but they had not had the evidence at that time to take him to court.

He became close to Hazel while she was working at Pinkcast. Using some of the knowledge he had picked up in prison, he could see the value of accessing a list of people who had enough disposable income to buy a Pinkcast watch. Their homes could prove to have rich pickings.

Hazel was already having an affair with Nigel when Ray suggested that she could get some information for him, which she was happy to do. Being Nigel's lover and working with him, it was not hard for her to get his password so that she could collect the addresses of potential victims. It worked well for a while until Hazel got herself sacked from the company.

As brother and sister, Hazel and Ashley were very close, and there were few secrets between them. When Ashley heard that the breaking and entering was not going well, he suggested a different approach.

As well as the password, Hazel obtained Nigel's remote log in details for those times when he worked from home. After that, all Hazel had to do was occupy Nigel at her place, while Ashley remotely logged on as Nigel and took the details he wanted.

It was not long before Ashley refined the process further. He looked to see where the occupants might be to pick the ones who would be away from their homes for long hours. This helped Ray no end. It allowed him to walk in, highly confident that the place he was about to break into was empty, as well as knowing the sort of computer equipment that might be in the property—all in all, an excellent little operation.

However, what they did not foresee was Terry deciding to track his wife and breaking into the Pinkcast computer in pursuit of that objective. Nor did they realise that Nigel, in his desperation to get back the documents that Terry had stolen, brought his boss, Grant, into the fight to retrieve the supposed industrial secrets. Things after that began to unravel for the trio.

"In any investigation," Colin began, "there's a breakthrough moment, and you can look back and say, that was the decisive turn of events that brought the whole scam down like a pack of cards. And Martin, do you know what that moment was?"

"I guess you are going to tell me?"

"Yes I am, Suzie Baby's arse. Sweet as it is, it was that part of her anatomy which knocked the coffee onto the keyboard and started a chain of events, part of which was looking into bathroom cabinets, leading to the solving of the case. Higgs-Boson was pleased with our participation."

"I'm glad I could help. Have you heard any more about Terry?"

"They have charged him with offences under the Computer Misuse Act 1990: 'unauthorised access to computer material'. Well, they had little choice. I hope the court is not too hard on him. He needs help with his mental state more than being found guilty of a crime."

"Poor old Terry, he should have stuck to fighting the alien invasion instead of taking up a side-line of stalking his ex-wife," Martin said, as he tried to recall the name of the familiar tune the pianist was playing. Unfortunately, he could not and he knew it would bug him for the rest of the day. "The other thing I would love to know is what exactly was in that so-called secret memo that Grant and Nigel were guarding so carefully?"

"Didn't you tell him, Suzie Baby?" Colin spoke between mouthfuls of miniature chocolate eclairs.

"I wasn't sure if I should, being Grant is a friend and all that."

"I keep telling you both, he is not my friend. Come on, Susan, spill the beans. What have you found out? Did you look in Grant's bathroom cabinet?"

"No, I took a copy of the file while we had it, just in case. You know it's the sort of thing good detectives do. Colin got Nigel's password out of Higgs-Boson, so it was easy to open it in the end. I was, just like you, interested in what was inside.

"Apparently, a Pinkcast watch is not at the forefront of Information Technogym accessories. In fact, it's well at the back. The document details how inaccurate the thing is. You could be having a heart attack, and it will still give you a pleasant reading for your blood pressure. Your weight gradually moves down as it magnifies the amount of exercise you do, and the solar battery lasts about half an hour, no good if you are paddling down the Amazon. In fact, the watch is rubbish, which is damming enough, but Grant's company is teetering on the edge of bankruptcy. He needs his American investors if he is ever going to turn the thing around, and I guess he has a new watch designed.

"If the report gets out, the Americans will run for the hills and Grant's beloved Pinkcast will be consigned to the history books, joining such ill-fated technology as Google glasses and curved TV's."

Martin laughed, not too loudly, he was in the Palm Court after all, and hilarious laughter was frowned upon, that much he knew. He wondered what he should do with this newly acquired information, make it public and sink Grant's company or just keep quiet, letting the greedy American investors lose shed loads of money. It was a tough choice; Martin knew he would have to think about that one.

"Susan, I have something for you." Martin handed her a very official-looking form, which she at first squinted at, then drew her new glasses from her handbag, put them on and glanced at the wording on the document.

"Makes you look intelligent," Colin commented, to which Susan simply poked her tongue out at him in a childish manner.

"It's a form you need to fill out to become a company director of Hayden Investigations. I have one also. Plus, another raft of forms that we will both have to sign. You have your friend Becky to thank for all this extra work. Plus, you'll have your name on our website, which, as you say, any modern company has to have and company email accounts as well."

"Do you want me to sign it now?"

"Suzie Baby, if you're going to be a company director, you'll have to read the whole bloody thing or do what everyone does, just sign it and be dammed."

Martin smiled as he mentally ticked off the list of things he had to talk to Susan about. Sign the forms, tell her about the website, get company email accounts, and compliment her on her new glasses. He wanted to ask her about just one other item: he needed someone to join him for his friend's wedding weekend. He was planning to ask her to join him. It was just he needed to phrase his invitation very carefully; he did not want her to get the wrong idea.

The End

Acknowledgements

I truly believe that when certain people receive an email from me with the subject line: 'New Book', they do one or both of two things. One, transfer it to spam; two, hide behind the settee, in the vain hope the email will magically disappear.

Luckily for me, I have some associates who are not so squeamish and refrain from such drastic action and instead respond enthusiastically to my request. They give up their valuable time to read my latest book and point out improvements.

Hence, in recognition of their bravery and commitment, I want to publicly thank these stalwart bibliophiles who endure and help me.

So, I say to the following: Jean, Angela, Irene, Claire, Anthony, Gavan, Pete and Brian, 'Thank you and yes, there are more emails on their way!'

With a special thanks to my long-suffering wife who continues to edit my books, trying to make sense of my abstract thoughts and help put my scribbled words into some sort of order.

Author Notes

Sometimes you just need to step out of the box. To be honest, I may well have got a little carried away this time, adding aliens or at least flying saucers into the world of Martin and Susan. As one reader described Martin and Susan's exploits; *A totally different type of detective story being mostly implausible but nonetheless a fun read.*

Not that this book is impossible to believe. There are reports of unknown flying objects in the sky going way back in history. The talk of aliens having landed on earth, even guiding ancient civilisations, is not new. Add to that, the ever increasing fact that a lot of us now have smartwatches with the technology that tracks our every move is forever increasing.

A story not impossible, but implausible, I'll accept. Either way, if you enjoyed reading and smiled once in a while, then I'll be happy.

While writing this book, I began to think how times have changed over the many decades that I have lived and how we can never really know what is ahead of us. Back when I was at school, having three channels on the black and white TV was cutting edge equipment. Now we have hundreds at our disposal through technology far removed from the TV signal being beamed towards the aerial on the roof. Often we oldies talk about the good old days and how things are not as good today; I disagree. With the rise of such platforms as YouTube and TikTok, everyone has the chance to fulfil their dreams.

The Tokyo 2020 Olympics (which happened in 2021, I won't remind you why) saw one such athlete, who had lost all her official funding, turn to the internet. Crowdfunding, everyday people handing over what they could afford, saw her win gold—a triumph shared by all those who supported her.

Young people have been born into this tornado of technology, accepting it as being the norm. This technology gives them opportunities I could only dream about as a teenager.

Yet once I have passed away, and all the current teenagers become pensioners, I wonder how far technology will have progressed, well beyond my limited imagination. Maybe we will have contacted beings from other planets. Then this book will no longer be implausible, yet with any luck still be funny.

    Until the next time
    Adrian

ALSO BY ADRIAN SPALDING

The Reluctant Detective

The Reluctant Detective Goes South

Sleeping Malice

The Night You Murder

Cloudy Sunshine
(a collection of short stories exclusive to my mailing list)

Join my mailing list

www.adrianspalding.co.uk

The Reluctant Detective Under Pressure
Copyright © 2021 by Adrian Spalding. All Rights Reserved.

All rights reserved. No part of this book may be reproduced in any form or by any electronic or mechanical means, including information storage and retrieval systems, without permission in writing from the author. The only exception is by a reviewer, who may quote short excerpts in a review.

This book is a work of fiction. Names, characters, places, and incidents either are products of the author's imagination or are used fictitiously. Any resemblance to actual persons, living or dead, events, or locales is entirely coincidental.

Cover designed by Allison Rose
allisonthewriter.wordpress.com

Printed in Great Britain
by Amazon